T0161833

By the Author

Edge of Awareness

The Courage to Try

Imperfect Truth

Love Came Calling

Through Love's Eyes

Through Love's Eyes

by

C.A. Popovich

2020

THROUGH LOVE'S EYES

ISBN 13: 978-1-63555-629-2

This Trade Paperback Original Is Published By
Bold Strokes Books, Inc.
P.O. Box 249
Valley Falls, NY 12185

First Edition: March 2020

Credits
Editors: Victoria Villasenor and Cindy Cresap
Production Design: Susan Ramundo
Cover Design By Tammy Seidick

Acknowledgments

I'd like to gratefully acknowledge all the hardworking folks at Bold Strokes Books who give my books a home and help me strive to be my best.

A special thanks to my friend Ellen who helped me mold a pile of words into something readable.

And thank you editors Victoria and Cindy for your patience with my bumbling.

Thank you to all the readers of lesbian romance. Your support means everything.

Dedication

To the casualties of being a teenager.

Chapter One

Brittany Yardin stood before the bathroom mirror and double-checked her makeup. She'd learned years ago how to combine and blend various shades to match her complexion and obscure the scar covering the right side of her face. She took extra time to apply the special concealer she used when she pulled her hair back into a braid. She removed her glasses before she tipped her head back to drip eye drops into her right eye, then lowered her head and blinked at herself in the mirror. The vision in her right eye would never return to normal, but she'd been able to obtain a driver's license, and she focused on her attitude of gratitude. She shuddered at the memory of her young self, standing on the wobbly chair and reaching, then the tumbling pot of boiling water that altered the course of her life. Three months in a burn unit put her behind in school, and her return offered fodder for the mean girl group.

She settled her glasses back on her nose and straightened her tie. She ensured her braid lay flat against her spine and took a deep breath to dispel her growing anxiety. She settled her top hat on her head and headed to the task she'd mostly been able to avoid. Driving a carriage. She'd much rather be spending time caring for the horses, away from the stares and sideways glances, and her coworkers were happy to let her shovel manure in exchange for them chauffeuring guests in the beautifully restored Grand Hotel omnibus. Her boss, Ben, was aware of her discomfort in crowds and tried his best to assign the driving to other workers, but the unusual number of visitors to Mackinac Island this early in May had every available worker busy.

She took another settling breath, headed to the waiting carriage, and climbed onto the seat. At least if she had to subject herself to the scrutiny of a carriage full of guests, she'd be driving the premier coach on the island. She waved to the worker who'd harnessed the two Percherons, sat up straight in her seat, swallowed the lump of anxiety in her throat, and gripped the reins. She urged the horses forward and they strained in their collars as they tugged the omnibus up the paved hill toward the dock where she'd wait for the ferryboat. She breathed in the scent of the horses mingled with whiffs of fudge emanating from the many fudge shops lining Main Street. The clip-clop of hooves hitting the paved streets and the view of the Mackinac Bridge spanning the straits of Mackinac grounded her as she mentally rehearsed her spiel about the island and the Grand Hotel. She approached slowly and watched the crowd as they milled around the giant dock. A few shifted foot to foot, looking impatient for their luggage to be unloaded from the ferry, and others seemed content to gaze at the view of the island and surrounding water while they waited. She turned her face away from the many onlookers and directed the horses to the ferry luggage unloading area. It took a while, and she enjoyed the view of the water and the banter of the ship's loaders as they moved the rainbow of luggage onto the dock trolleys, separating out the ones for her to take back to the hotel. When the final suitcase was loaded onto the carriage, she sighed with relief when nobody boarded to ride back to the hotel. She paused for a family of four to pet the horses before she continued back to the hotel stables. She'd made it through the morning without having to interact with too many people, and that was fine with her.

"Hey, Brittany. How's everything down at the dock?" George, one of Brittany's coworkers, reached for the harness of one of the horses as they stopped at the hotel's luggage unloading area.

She kept a firm hold on the reins. "Crowded." She answered from the carriage seat. "But no riders this morning. I guess they're all going shopping before checking in."

They waited for the baggage porter to unload the carriage before heading to the stables.

"Sorry I couldn't take the run this morning," George said as he unhitched one of the horses.

"No problem. I know Ben has you doing inventory, and it is part of my job." Brittany pulled off the harness from the other horse and carried it to the tack room. "It's probably good for me to get used to it." She took a moment to allow the feeling of triumph over her fear to soak in. Her therapist would be proud that she pushed herself out of her comfort zone. She decided she would be, too. "I'm going to take care of the horses and take off early today."

"That's fine. I'll give you a call if we need you. See you tomorrow and good job today." George grinned and waved as he walked away.

Brittany grabbed a few brushes and headed to the large stalls where the two Percherons stood chewing hay. She brushed the smooth hair on their backs and necks and combed out their flowing manes as she talked to them. She marveled at the peace being near them gave her. No judgments, no pointing and teasing. She finished their grooming and checked their grain and water supply before letting Ben know she was leaving for the day. Part-time work definitely had its advantages.

She took the long route home to her two-bedroom apartment so she could stop at her favorite spot by the water. It was her private place to meditate and quiet the memories of the name-calling voices in her head, which were still hard to drown out, even after all this time. She allowed herself a few minutes to reflect on the torture of her high school experience. She'd come a long way with therapy in the twenty-three years since the accident. Positive self-talk and meditation helped her get through the tough days, and she refused to surrender any more of her life to that pain. Still, some days it was easier to do than others, and today the past held fast. She shook her head to clear away the disturbing memories, unlocked the door to her apartment, and headed straight for the bathroom. She hated wearing makeup all day even though wearing it had become automatic and she wouldn't go out in public without it. She splashed water on her face and squirted face cleanser on a washcloth to gently blot at her scarred cheek and rinsed away the makeup. The initial second- and third-degree burns and subsequent skin grafts had caused significant scarring to the right side of her face and eyelid. The doctors told her the scars might be sensitive for the rest of her life, and they were right. She'd become used to the sight of the pink pigmentless skin over the years, and the painful memories of the accident had faded. The emotional pain of the adolescent teasing, however, had taken much longer to heal, and at the time, she had no idea it would follow her into adulthood as she dealt with stares, whispers, and avoidance of eye contact. Some days were harder than others. Today, though, she considered a win.

Chapter Two

Erika didn't think she'd ever tire of traveling, of bright lights, and of the constant pressure to be perfect. Perfectly manicured, perfectly coifed, perfectly perfect. She was Erika James, one of the top fashion models in the country, and she refused to believe the only thing good about it anymore was her bank account and the one she'd set up for her parents. With her fortieth birthday looming, she feared her time in the spotlight was near its end, so she took every job available and worked twice as hard and long as any other model. She'd been groomed to be a supermodel since birth, so at eighteen, small town Amy Jansons had become Erika James. It was how she identified herself. She'd found a way to be the best and had stayed on top even though there were already several young beauties taking over the covers of *Vogue* and *Elle* magazines, which she'd graced for years. But she'd been with the same agent throughout her career and trusted him to continue the search for new opportunities.

She paced her spacious living room in her tenth floor New York condominium. The upcoming photo spread in a new magazine targeting millennials had her curious. Her agent had pushed hard for her to be featured in the magazine she'd never heard of, but she wasn't ready to star as the mom in the centerfold ad. Maybe he figured she'd be an inspiration to the younger readers as someone to emulate as they aged. Had she become the aging beauty? She grinned as she tossed a pair of shorts and a cropped top into her suitcase. Her age didn't matter. She still maintained a perfect model figure, and she knew quite a few younger models envied her flawless complexion. She'd only had a week off and now she was packed and ready to fly to Michigan for a series of photo shoots. The short time off wasn't what bothered her. The destination did. Guilt still roiled in her gut whenever she allowed the disturbing memories of her teenage years to surface. It had been twenty-three years ago. She'd been a kid. She repeated the words to herself several times until the shame dissipated. She checked her reflection in her full-length mirror and called the porter to deliver her suitcase to the waiting limo.

Erika slid the ferryboat ticket stub into the back pocket of her designer jeans and followed her agent to the section of the vessel designated for their group. She chose a seat next to the window where she could watch the water and enjoy the view of the Mackinac Bridge as they passed near it. She listened to the voice over the loudspeaker telling the story of the bridge and the two Great Lakes it traversed, glad the group had agreed to take the ferry instead of flying to the island. At least if she had to return to this state, she could enjoy the beauty of the waters surrounding Mackinac Island. They'd be spending the next two weeks traipsing from one end of it to the other, stopping at places chosen by the magazine for photo shoots. She looked forward to staying at the historic and elegant Grand Hotel, but she still hoped the two weeks went by quickly, as if her continued absence from the state could erase the memory of the cruel behavior of her past.

She stepped onto the dock as their group disembarked and gazed at the expanse of water as the hotel employee directed them away from the throngs of people. She watched a couple trying to control two excited children as they raced ahead, pointing and laughing. Sadness washed over her at memories of her childhood and her parents' rigid expectations of her. They never would have allowed her to run in public. Or display such playfulness. Had she ever been allowed to have fun and be a kid? She forced herself back to the present and continued with her group toward the Grand Hotel carriage. The driver, a small man with a neatly trimmed beard and warm smile, tipped his hat and climbed off the driver's seat to help them board. "Good morning, folks. Welcome to Mackinac Island. Your luggage and equipment will be loaded on board in a few moments. Will you be traveling straight to the hotel, or did you want to explore a bit before checking in?" He looked to each one of them as he spoke.

Erika's agent replied for them. "We'll head to the hotel first and get settled. We don't meet with the magazine crew until this afternoon, and I know I'd like to freshen up before we go to work."

"I agree wholeheartedly, Peter," Erika said. She envisioned herself soaking in a tub of hot water with scented bubble bath in her private room. She added a glass of red wine and a beautiful view out her window to the fantasy. She hoped there'd be enough time before preparing to pose for the camera, something she was finding more tedious as the years went by. Maybe if this was getting so difficult she should consider retirement. But it was the only life she knew. She couldn't even imagine a new career. What else was there? Being a magazine fashion model was who she was. She had no idea how to be anything, or anyone, else. It was probably just the fact that she was back in her home state with the memories of her nasty behavior as a member of the mean girls in high school. She'd never had the opportunity to say she was sorry and probably never would.

Erika and her group stepped into the carriage for the short ride to the hotel. She watched the people stroll down the main street and enter the various shops along the way noting the difference in atmosphere from her home in bustling Manhattan. Most of these folks were probably enjoying a vacation. She was there for work, and that was fine with her. She was doing what she'd been groomed to do her whole life, something she'd grown to love. At least, she loved the traveling and the attention and the designer outfits. And the difficult parts paid well. She did, however, plan to take time to enjoy the beautiful surroundings. Their carriage turned uphill and the view of the Grand Hotel elicited oohs and aahs from the group.

When they arrived, the carriage driver climbed down from his seat to help them exit the coach, and workers appeared out of nowhere to tend to the horses. An attractive blonde caught her attention, and she detected a flash of recognition in her pale blue eyes before she quickly turned away. Erika was used to being recognizable since her picture had been in most magazines across the country for years. The woman looked as if she had a facial deformity of some kind, but she disappeared before Erika could get a better look. She shook off the unexpected twinge of attraction and curiosity and headed into the hotel.

Erika entered her room, relieved to see her suitcase set neatly by a wall. She hoped everything she'd read about the service at the Grand Hotel being as good as any around the world would turn out to be true. She admired the décor of the suite, although the purple couch was a bit gaudy for her taste. The spacious bathroom had a shower, dashing her fantasy of a hot soak, but the view from the parlor took her breath away. She read the plaque on the wall dedicating the room to Dan Musser, a former chairman of the hotel. She chose a bottle of wine from the well-stocked wet bar, poured herself a glass, and settled into one of the parlor chairs to enjoy the spectacular view of the Mackinac Straits. At $1,650.00 a night, it was no wonder she'd never been here as a child. Her parents spent all their disposable income on her dance and modeling lessons. There wasn't much left for travel or fun vacations to the lake. They'd driven her to succeed and to take advantage of her beauty to become a model. They'd sent her to acting school, no doubt picturing her as the next well-known movie actress, but they'd settled on modeling when they were told she had "no talent for acting" by the administrator. She chuckled at the memory. She'd been accepted by the first modeling agency to which she'd sent her portfolio, much to her parents' relief.

Erika swept away the childhood memories and finished her wine. She did a few yoga poses before she took one more look at the view and headed to the shower. She stripped and tossed her travel clothes on the floor. She'd be primped and prepped soon, undoubtedly dressed in the latest Versace or Armani. She lost track of who the shoots were for, and had largely stopped caring. She got dressed, posed, and went back to her own clothes. Routine, and little more. She stepped into the oversized shower and allowed the hot water to wash away the stress of travel. She allowed herself a few minutes to reflect on the memory of the pale, blue-eyed blonde with the solid looking body beneath the jeans and Grand Hotel T-shirt. Maybe the time spent here wouldn't be so bad after all.

Chapter Three

Brittany rushed back to the stables as soon as George had the horses secured and prepared for the next carriage ride. Of the thousands of visitors flocking to the island, the last person she expected to see was Erika James. She'd followed her career in magazines for years, so she'd recognized her right away. There was no mistaking those gorgeous gold-flecked, caramel colored eyes, smooth blemish free skin, thick auburn hair, and perfect smile. She must be here for some sort of magazine spread featuring Mackinac Island and the Grand Hotel. Of course, it's the only place Erika James would have stayed. Being a world-renowned model, there were probably no cheap motels for her anymore. Brittany needed to find out how long she'd be on the island so she could figure out how to stay far away from her.

She finished cleaning the stalls and stowed the tack away before heading to check on George. She found him polishing the wheels of one of the smaller carriages. "Hey, George. I'm going to take a lunch break. You need help with anything?" She hoped he'd say no. She just wanted to get away and squash the infuriating feelings that seeing Erika had stirred up.

"I'm good here, but the boss was asking for you. I'm not sure, but I think he's got an assignment for you."

"I'll stop by his office on my way out." Brittany's nerves stood on end. Why couldn't he just send her a text? She tapped on his door when she arrived at his office.

"Brittany. Come in, please. Thanks for stopping by."

"No problem, Ben. George mentioned some assignment?" She stood still, waiting for his reply.

He shuffled papers and swiped at his tablet before speaking. "We've got a few unexpected guests this month who need special attention." He signaled toward a chair opposite his desk and concentrated on his computer.

Brittany reluctantly sat and waited for him to finish, her curiosity piqued. She'd appreciated his directness and honesty from the first day she'd joined the crew. Today, he avoided her gaze. "Is there a problem?" she asked.

"No. No problem, Brittany. I know you're uncomfortable interacting with people, but I'm working on a carriage schedule and we're short two drivers this month. Helen's on maternity leave, and Joe has jury duty and is stuck on an insurance fraud case. I'm going to need to assign you to one of the carriages." He tapped on his tablet once more and turned his full attention to her. "Some new magazine has scheduled several photo shoots across the island and inside the hotel for the next two weeks. And since we don't have cars on the island, obviously, that means they need to use a carriage. I'd like you to oversee the crew's transportation while they're on the island. I've allocated you one of the smaller carriages and two carriage horses, and I hope you'll be willing to work more flexible hours, according to what they might need."

He paused and Brittany took the opportunity to interrupt. "Do you mean all I'll be doing for the next two weeks is chauffeuring them around?"

"Basically, yes. You can work in the stalls as much as you'd like, of course. You're a hard worker, and I'm grateful to have you here. It's just for two weeks. Their model's name is Erika James. You start later this afternoon. She wants a tour of the island to get her bearings. George is readying your horses and carriage now."

Brittany stiffened but remained quiet. She didn't want to quit this job, but she couldn't imagine spending every day for two weeks with Erika James. She knew Ben did whatever he could to accommodate her need to avoid people, and this was an unplanned event. It wasn't his fault; he couldn't know the quandary it put her in. "Okay. I'm going to take my lunch now, but I'll get with George when I return." She left his office without another word. *It's only two weeks.*

❖

Brittany finished applying her makeup and positioned her glasses and top hat. She straightened her tie and her spine and climbed onto the seat of the carriage. "Wish me luck." She grinned at George as she lifted the reins and the two carriage horses began the gentle roll up the hill toward the hotel. The short trip didn't give her enough time to settle her nerves, but she was sure there wasn't a trip long enough to do that anyway as she pulled up to the hotel waiting area. The commotion at the exit caught her attention. Erika, a tall dark-haired man, and a buxom redhead carrying a large camera stood in the carriage waiting area.

"I'm telling you, I don't need you here yet. I'm just going to take a short ride to check out the island. We aren't scheduled for any photos until four."

Erika looked perturbed and, if her body language was any indication, frustrated.

Brittany stepped off the carriage and secured the horses. "May I help with anything?" She smiled and directed her attention to Erika.

"Thank you." Erika's face registered relief. "My agent and photographer were just seeing me off." She stepped onto the running board of the carriage, and Brittany scrambled to assist her. "I'll see you two later." Erika settled into her seat and turned away.

Brittany climbed back onto her seat and waved as they moved past the couple, who went back into the hotel not looking entirely happy. It wasn't part of her job to settle arguments within groups, but she couldn't deny her pleasure that her mere presence had helped to settle Erika's angst. It was ironic, though, given their history. She held the reins securely before turning toward her passenger. "My name is Brittany, and I'll be driving your carriage for the duration of your stay, Ms. James. Is there anything in particular you'd like to see this afternoon, or shall I just give you our standard, albeit shortened, tour of the island?"

Erika sat on the cushioned bench with her head resting on the back of the seat and her eyes closed. Slight frown lines creased her delicate brow, and the minor movement in her jaw indicated she was clenching her teeth. Her blemish free skin glowed beneath the light makeup she wore. Age had enhanced her beauty, and Brittany could imagine tracing her fingertips along that soft skin. She did a quick calculation. Erika, or Amy as she'd known her, had been one grade above her before the accident; two when she'd finally left the burn unit and returned to school. She'd have to be nearly forty now. Still gorgeous. She was about to repeat her question when Erika stirred and her eyes fluttered open, captivating her.

"Sorry. I had to regroup for a minute. Please just take me wherever you usually go to show off this beautiful island. I guess the shortened standard tour. I'll need to be back by three o'clock, though." Erika pulled out her cell phone and tapped it several times with her finger before shaking it and stuffing it back into her pocket.

"You'll find the cell service on the island is spotty. I can show you the best areas for reception as we go, but it also depends on your carrier." Brittany turned to urge the two horses along the street toward town.

"Thanks. It'll probably be nice to be unplugged for a while." Erika closed her eyes again.

Erika hadn't indicated she recognized her, and Brittany suppressed a confusing surge of disappointment. What did she expect? That she'd hug her and exclaim how much she'd missed their childhood connection and apologize for her cruelty that drove them apart? She questioned whether she even remembered they'd once been best friends. She'd probably completely erased the memory of the kiss Brittany had never been able to forget. Brittany concentrated on driving the carriage and relaying information as they traveled. There would be nothing standard about the next two weeks.

Chapter Four

Erika pasted on her practiced smile as the carriage crept through town and a few people turned to follow their progress. She guessed it was the horses drawing their attention but hoped it was because they recognized her. Her parents had pushed her into a modeling career, but she'd grown to like the attention, and she was proud of her status as one of the best models on the circuit. Still the best even at thirty-eight. There had been no public advertising for these photo shoots, and it was unlikely anyone other than those involved would know she was on the island. Still, she liked to think her presence might be of interest to someone.

It never failed to delight her to sign autographs and talk to fans about the latest fashions she wore while in Paris or Italy. Sometimes on the runways of New York, she'd have lines of folks who followed her career and loved to chat about the latest magazine in which she'd been featured. She doubted anything remotely similar would happen on this tourist island. Most people came here for the shopping, the fudge, the restaurants, and the jewel of the island, the Grand Hotel. She watched the people riding bicycles alongside the horses. She'd read that motorized vehicles had been banned on the island since the 1890s. No exhaust fumes, no horns, nobody waving frantically, yelling for a taxi. She'd only been on the island for a couple of hours, and she could already feel herself unwinding. Maybe the time spent here would be a nice break.

She turned her attention to the attractive blond driver and the way she gently controlled the two bays as they paraded along the route. She perused her from the top of the black top hat, down along the lines of her shoulders and over the vest, which nicely hugged her breasts. There was no missing she was female despite the typically male outfit. Her braid hung down her back and moved back and forth as she turned her head to speak and point out significant landmarks. She noted the way Brittany ducked her head and kept her face turned away slightly. Her thick glasses obscured her eyes, and she definitely had some sort of scarring on her face that someone had done an excellent job of hiding with makeup. There was something familiar about her, something that made Erika study her, but she'd never have forgotten a beauty like this one. The woman probably had more than her share of people staring at her, and Erika didn't want to be rude, so she looked away and relaxed into her seat to concentrate on paying attention to the tour. She'd wanted to go alone on this excursion to check out the area because she hated going into a shoot cold. There were always variables beyond her control, such as the weather and what outfits the magazine picked for her, but at least she'd be familiar with the terrain.

Erika listened intently to Brittany's mellow voice tell her about Arch Rock and how it was formed.

"This island is beautiful. I'm sorry I've never been here before." Awed, Erika examined the cedar trees and rock formations as they passed.

"This area, about eighty percent of the island, was designated a national park in 1875, and a state park in 1895. Visitors come from all over the world." Brittany steered the horses toward the road as she spoke. "I had a group from China last year who never stopped talking, taking pictures, and pointing the whole tour. I'm not sure if they understood a word I said, but they appeared to be having a ball."

The slight sway of the carriage, the warm spring day, and the fact she'd been up most of the night packing and confirming her schedule, had Erika nodding off before the end of the trip. She was startled awake by a warm hand on her arm.

"I'm sorry to wake you, Ms. James, but we're back at the hotel." Brittany stepped away after speaking, turning slightly sideways.

"Thank you." Erika sat up and stretched.

"You're welcome. I hope you enjoyed the ride and the short tour of the island. I'll take care of the horses and be back to pick you and your crew up by four." Brittany held her arm as she exited the carriage and then walked quickly toward the horses, not giving her an opportunity to speak.

Erika watched Brittany efficiently release the horses from their harnesses as another worker arrived to help. She moved with grace and strength and whispered to the animals as she led them to the stable. She forced herself to look away when she realized she was paying way too much attention to her ass as she strode away. She turned toward the hotel before her thoughts strayed any further toward what it would feel like in her hands.

Erika smiled and waved a greeting as she passed the various groups in the expansive lobby of the hotel, grateful no one stopped her to chat or request an autograph. All she wanted to do was get back to her suite and relax for a few minutes before the makeup session, hair styling, and dressing began. The short nap in the carriage had only accentuated how tired she really was. She opened her door and knew her desire for relaxation wasn't to be.

"There you are." Kathy, her makeup artist, spoke from the parlor where she had a chair positioned facing the window. "The lighting is perfect in here." She stood next to the chair and gestured for Erika to sit. "The crew will be here in an hour." She waved her hand in a hurry up motion.

Erika sighed and closed the door behind her. "Give me a minute, okay?" She retreated to the bathroom and splashed water on her face. She couldn't figure out what had her feeling distracted. She was a professional. She did what she had to do to be ready for the cameras and always look her best. But her thoughts kept veering off to her short carriage ride with the attractive driver. Their conversation had been light and easy, so unlike talking to fans or fellow models which sometimes turned into a competition for the last word. She'd been seen as her real self instead of the image on a magazine cover, and it felt nice. There was something vaguely familiar about her, but she couldn't figure it out. She'd never been to Mackinac Island, and this woman looked as if she was settled into her job and exceptional at it. She probably grew up on the island, although she couldn't imagine what anyone would do during the winter here, or how she could make a living driving a horse carriage. She turned her attention to Kathy to prepare for the afternoon event.

Within an hour, Erika checked her reflection in the mirror, satisfied the flowing Louis Vuitton outfit fit perfectly and her styled hair and makeup matched the casual theme of the shoot. The crew had let her know that they were heading to Arch Rock for various poses and angles as the afternoon sunlight shone through and the lighting changed. "I guess I'm as ready as I'll ever be." She slipped on a pair of sandals and headed out the door.

Chapter Five

Casual elegance were the first words that came to Brittany when Erika sauntered out of the hotel and climbed into the carriage. She could imagine her strolling down a runway, swaying her lovely hips and showcasing her beautiful hair and eyes. The outfit she wore fit her perfectly and probably cost more than Brittany made in a year. The dark brown skirt and soft beige blouse looked like they'd been made for her. And her sandals complemented the outfit as she moved with cat-like grace.

"Everyone ready?" Brittany turned to make sure her passengers were aboard and seated before she encouraged the horses forward.

"Let's do this."

Brittany recognized Erika's agent from earlier and had introduced herself to him as well as the woman carrying the camera. "Okay, here we go. I'll be taking the shorter route to Arch Rock than the one we took earlier." She directed her remark to Erika, who gave her a quick smile.

She steered the two horses slowly through town and past Fort Mackinac without her usual detailed explanation of the area and buildings. The passengers were busy discussing what she presumed were the details of the photo session. They looked intense and uninterested in hearing about the significance of their surroundings. She realized they were only there for a job. To get good photos, not to listen to her. She would just do her job but hoped they'd loosen up, or it would be a long two weeks for her.

She parked the carriage and hopped off to secure the horses while the photographer, followed by the crew, climbed out of the carriage, juggled her camera, and looked around to get the best angle and light. No one told Brittany she couldn't watch, so she leaned against the carriage and watched the shoot begin.

Erika stood on the edge of the trail leading to Arch Rock but far enough away to use it as a backdrop for the picture. Brittany was mesmerized by the subtle shifts in Erika's stance and slight tip of her head or shift in her gaze, and the often subtle movement of her fingers and hands. She could imagine each click of the camera capturing a different shot. She presumed the final photos would be chosen from a group of hundreds, and she was glad she wasn't the one to have to choose. Erika was phenomenal and beyond beautiful. She shifted in her seat and concentrated on the space between the carriage horse's ears to distract herself. Erika was a gorgeous fashion model. Now, anyway. Before…it was different. She allowed her memories to flow while suppressing the discomfort they carried.

Her final skin graft had finally healed enough that doctors had allowed her to leave the burn unit. She'd begged her parents to let her return to school so she could graduate only one year behind her class. But then the group of girls was there... Amy Jansons was a model in training. Her perfect skin, white teeth, and budding womanly figure must have qualified her for the group, but to be fully accepted she probably had to prove herself. Her loyalty.

Against the background of Erika laughing in response to the photographer's joke, Brittany struggled with the recollection.

The tiled floor was hard and cold. She tried to stand and was pushed back down by the leader of the group, the Queen Bee as they called her. Amy stood behind her, watching. Was she second in command? Why didn't she try to stop the taunting? The pointing and name-calling? She looked up into the honey colored eyes, pleading for support, and found fleeting compassion and fear. Fear of being left out, perhaps. Then she heard what she hadn't forgotten in twenty-three years. The cruel chuckle and callous remark. "Leave the freak alone. She's not worth our time."

There was no reason to believe Erika had changed. It was one thing to understand her motives, but quite another to get past the hurt it had caused. If only Amy could have stayed Amy. Her best friend with whom she'd shared secrets and coloring books. And a kiss. She'd transformed into one of the mean girls and lost herself. Brittany shivered with a visceral reaction to her memories and strengthened her resolve to keep her distance from Erika James.

"I think we're done here." Erika's agent hopped into the carriage, ignoring both Erika and her photographer.

Brittany bristled at his lack of regard for the two women but concentrated on her job and held the reins of the napping horses. "We'll be on our way as soon as you're ready." She tried to smile as she made sure her passengers were seated, but anger at her recent memories refused to allow it. She'd be respectful and efficient. That's all that was required. She remained quiet the whole trip back to the hotel.

"Thank you for the ride today, Brittany." Erika spoke over her shoulder as she moved past her toward the hotel entrance.

"You're welcome, Ms. James." She quickly led the horses away from the hotel to the stables.

"Welcome back. How'd your first photo shoot with the rich and famous go?" George guided one of the carriage horses into its stall as he spoke.

She shook off the residual pain of the disturbing memories and concentrated on the lessons her therapist had taught her to ground herself. *Keep breathing and stay in the present.* She was in the stables with George and the horses. She was safe. "It was interesting, for sure. Ms. James is an excellent model, and the photographer is a hard worker. She must've taken hundreds of pictures in the short time we were there." She cleared her throat, relieved her voice sounded strong.

"So, your assignment for the next two weeks might not be so bad?"

Brittany gently stroked the neck of one of the horses to calm herself while she considered her reply. "I'm not sure. They pretty much ignored me the whole time."

"Good. I was hoping it wouldn't be uncomfortable for you. Let's clean up and go home for the day." George grabbed a broom and moved away.

❖

Brittany decided to cut across the Grand Hotel porch on her way home. She glanced into the windows as she passed the few couples seated in the lounge chairs enjoying the peaceful view. Groups of hotel guests sat at tables inside having a meal or drinks. She spotted Erika seated at one of the tables engaged in what looked like a heated conversation with her agent. Erika had changed into a pair of skinny jeans and a T-shirt. She looked beautiful, but the lines on her forehead and the tightness in her jaw gave away her tension. She had her arm draped over the back of her chair, maybe in an attempt to feign calm, but Brittany could tell something was wrong. She shook off the desire to run inside, confused as to why she'd consider rescuing Erika. She'd done nothing to rescue her from the mean girls' torment years ago. She took several deep breaths to push aside the terrible memories. Erika was an adult. She'd have to deal with whatever was going on.

She turned away from the scene inside and continued to the path to her apartment realizing she wanted to do for Erika exactly what Erika had refused to do for her twenty-three years ago. Protect her. Well, it wasn't happening. She took a few minutes to admire the sunset before she unlocked her door and went inside, her shoulders releasing as she entered her safe space. She made herself a cup of tea and settled into one of her Amish rockers. She took a sip and leaned her head back while memories came back of when they'd been children together. When they were close. It was a lifetime ago. No reason to hang on to childhood crushes or the heartache they brought. She was an adult now with a job and a comfortable life. She made herself a cup of soup and a grilled cheese sandwich before she returned to her living room and turned on her TV. She was happy, and no ghost from her past was going to mess with that, no matter how attractive that ghost might be.

Chapter Six

"I'm not doing it, Peter. I told you years ago when we first started working together I wouldn't take my clothes off even for *Playboy*. They don't even do nudes anymore. I won't do it." Erika clenched her fists in her lap but held Peter's stare. She tried to ignore the attention they were attracting and lowered her voice.

"Need I remind you of your upcoming birthday, my dear?" He leaned back in his chair and crossed one foot over the opposite knee as he steepled his fingers. "Two of your scheduled magazine covers canceled. I'm trying to convince *Vogue* to use you for this fall's issue, but they're looking at younger models. I'm sorry, Erika. I've done my best. You're a beautiful woman. You might as well use it to your advantage while you still can."

"Peter." Erika paused to take a deep breath before continuing. "We've been together for years, and I trust you're looking out for my best interests. But I can't believe you'd ask me to do this when you know how I feel about it. I want to be known as a fashion model wearing the latest designs. It just feels desperate and degrading." Her hands shook in her lap, and she struggled to breathe. She sipped more water, scrambling for answers. Her self-worth was tied to her work. What would her parents say if she took her clothes off for the camera? She shivered, feeling faint.

Peter stood and helped support her as she walked back to her room. "Are you going to be okay?" he asked as he sat across from her in the chairs by the window.

She sighed heavily. “I suppose I knew this day was coming, but I’m not ready to give up yet. I have name and face recognition in the industry. Can we just keep trying?” She hated pleading, but she didn’t know what else to do.

“All right, Erika. I didn’t mean to sound like a jerk earlier. I’ll make a few calls, and we’ll talk again tomorrow. We’ll be taking pictures at the fort in the morning. You get some rest.” He squeezed her hand and softly closed the door behind him.

Erika poured a glass of wine from her wet bar and settled back into her seat by the window. She watched the moonlight sparkle on the water in the distance as if displaying a path through the surrounding darkness. She contemplated Peter’s words. But she refused to consider doing nude shots for her last years as a top model. She admitted the constant traveling and pressure to be “on” seemed a little less exciting than it had years ago, but she knew she was good at her job and still had a lot to offer. Fully clothed. She sighed and swallowed some wine before changing into her nightshirt and spending a few minutes in meditation before going to bed. She’d find a way to stay on top. She had to.

Erika took twenty minutes to do some yoga after she woke from a restless sleep. Kathy was due to prepare her for the first shoot soon, so she took a sip of dark roast coffee and carried her cup into the bathroom. She adjusted the water temperature in the shower and stepped under the spray, hoping it would rinse away the gloom that had overtaken her after her conversation with Peter. She closed her eyes and allowed the water to cascade over her head and shoulders. She squirted body wash onto her hands and gently kneaded her breasts. They were nice breasts. Still full and firm and just the right size for a model. She was proud of them, and she knew they could still hold their own against those of the younger women. Her nipples hardened, and she slid slippery fingers down her taut belly and into her soft curls. Her intention had been to wash and quickly rinse, but she hadn’t been this aroused by her own touch in a long time. Any touch, she realized. She closed her eyes, surprised when Brittany's pale blue eyes twinkled behind her closed lids. She continued her exploration, squeezing her clit between her thumbs and stroking her inner thighs with her fingers. Her breath caught, and she leaned back against the shower wall as her orgasm surged through her.

She stepped out of the shower and took a few settling breaths to push aside the bewildering residual pleasure at her Brittany fantasy. She took a few minutes to collect herself before she dried off and put on her undergarments and robe to wait for Kathy. She sipped her coffee and wondered about her sensual response, one that was so unlike her. She attributed it to the relaxed atmosphere of the location and her lack of sexual activity for what seemed like forever.

Erika watched from the hotel exit as Brittany directed the carriage toward her. She smiled and waved, but Brittany turned away toward the direction she turned the horses and stopped. She noticed the carriage was larger than the one they'd used the day before. She watched as the magazine crew loaded a few props onto the back of the carriage and two men with cameras took the back seat. She settled her sunglasses on her face and slid into the seat directly behind Brittany. "Good morning, Brittany."

"Good morning, Ms. James. Looks like you've got a large group this morning."

"It's going to be a longer shoot today so Kathy is along to touch up my hair and makeup if necessary and help with clothing changes. Joe and Phil are from the magazine to observe and change venues if necessary," Erika said.

Peter shielded his eyes from the sun and looked up at Erika. "You don't need me today, so I'm going to try to make some phone calls. I'll see you later tonight."

Peter walked away, and Erika hoped his mentioned phone calls would turn into real work for her, because she wouldn't change her mind about the nudie magazine. She faced forward and caught Brittany's pale blue eyes. They reminded her of a hazy summer day.

She smiled and a fleeting flash of recognition took her breath away. *It's impossible.*

"If you're all ready, we'll get going." Brittany turned toward the horses and gently shook the reins.

"Do you live on the island?" Erika hoped Brittany would turn toward her again, but she stayed facing forward.

"Yes. I've lived here for most of my adult life." Brittany clucked at the horses urging them up the hill.

"This is a lovely place. How long have you worked for the Grand Hotel?" She wanted more personal information, but Brittany's demeanor was a little more closed off than it had been the day before, and Erika hoped she could change that.

"The whole time I've lived here. I love the horses."

Erika settled into her seat and gave up trying to extract any more information. Clearly, Brittany wasn't in a talkative mood, and Erika felt her face heat at the memory of her sensual shower this morning, where Brittany had been the main player. Perhaps it was better to keep some distance. They arrived at the fort, and she had work to do. She prepared to pose for the camera, ready to lose herself in the fantasy of her life once again.

CHAPTER SEVEN

The photo shoot at the fort took much longer than the first one Brittany had witnessed, so she secured the horses in the shade, stretched out on the front bench seat, and closed her eyes. She dozed for about ten minutes before being startled awake by loud laughter as Erika's group filed out of the fort and began loading their equipment into the carriage. She shook off her drowsiness and rushed to help them board. "Did everything go well today?" She directed her question to the group, but no one but Erika paid attention to her.

"Yes." Erika chuckled. "It was fun. I found the fort fascinating. I learned that the British built it during the revolutionary war and relinquished it to us around 1798. I love the history on this island."

Most people were impressed with Fort Mackinac, so Brittany wasn't surprised by Erika's enthusiasm. "I'm glad you had time to enjoy it." She watched until the crew finished loading their equipment before she climbed aboard to settle on her seat. "Is everyone ready to head back to the hotel?"

She started when Erika grabbed her arm. "Could we take a little tour after we drop everyone off?"

"Sure, as soon as the equipment is unloaded," Brittany replied automatically, then squirmed in her seat. Professionally, her response was the right one. Personally, it was the last thing she wanted to do. She concentrated on her therapist's voice in her head. The memories and disturbing feelings were a form of post-traumatic stress disorder.

She had a right to her anger, but she didn't want it to rule her life. If she couldn't let it go, it would define who she was forever. Erika's reemergence in her life was an opportunity to test her resolve to heal and forgive. "How 'bout I pick you up in an hour? After lunch." Everyone but Erika ignored her as they filed out of the carriage and into the hotel. Erika smiled and lightly touched her arm before going in, and Brittany hoped she didn't notice that she'd flinched slightly at her touch.

She made her way to the stable feeling out of sorts and frustrated. "Hey, George. I'm going to take Erika on a tour after lunch. I'll take care of hitching the horses back up." Brittany secured the horses and watered them before she retreated to the restroom. Her short nap while waiting for the magazine group had refreshed her, but she still finished a cup of coffee while applying sunscreen on her face. The burned skin was sensitive to the sun, and based on the heat of the morning, she expected the afternoon sun to be intense. "I'll be back in a few minutes. Can I pick you up anything from the Gate House?" Brittany spoke over her shoulder as she stopped at the barn door and waited for his answer.

"No, thanks. I brown bagged my lunch today." George waved and turned toward the tack room.

Brittany took her time walking to the small casual restaurant a short distance from the hotel where she picked up a sandwich and lemonade. She continued to a secluded spot behind the stables and settled on a fallen log. She'd just finished her sandwich and was sipping her drink when she startled at rustling behind her.

"Hey, Brittany. I didn't mean to startle you. Mind if I join you?" Erika grinned as she stepped over the log and sat.

Brittany blinked away her surprise, unsure what was odder, Erika sitting on a log next to her, or looking comfortable doing it. She'd changed into the skinny jeans she'd been wearing the night before and a soft looking polo shirt with an unfamiliar designer's logo. She tore her gaze away from Erika's breasts filling out the expensive shirt before speaking. "What are you doing here? I mean, were you looking for me? I'd have been back to get you as soon as I finished my lemonade." Brittany shifted on her seat and considered walking away, but Erika was a guest at the hotel, and she was an employee. She took another sip of her drink and waited for Erika to answer.

Erika stretched her legs out in front of her and then folded forward, holding the position for a long moment. She was about to speak again when Erika sat up and spoke. "Sorry. I'm missing my usual workout routine, and I felt like taking a walk. Finding you on this log was a nice surprise. This is a lovely spot." She scanned the area around them.

"It's one of my favorites, but it won't be so quiet next month. The Gate House is a popular place for lunch, and the crowds spill out all over the place." She slid a few inches away from Erika as she spoke. Erika didn't avert her eyes like most people did when they spoke to her. Her gaze caressed and unnerved her. She'd either recognized her, or she looked past her disfigurement. She doubted the latter was the case, but if she had recognized her, it could be an awkward upcoming week. Surely, though, if she'd recognized her she would have said something? Unless she was waiting for the right moment to bring it up. The constant questions and doubts were making her crazy. "Are you ready to take the tour?" She stood and turned toward the hotel. She'd do her job and let the personal aspects take care of themselves.

Brittany steered the horses toward the Surrey Hills Museum and Butterfly Conservatory before turning toward the Fort Mackinac Avenue of Flags. She focused on the history of the area and asked if Erika wanted to go inside. Erika looked relaxed seated behind her and to the left. She'd lean forward occasionally to listen and smile but chose to remain in the carriage. Too bad. Brittany could have used the breathing space. She kept her voice neutral and tried to make sure none of the hurt from the past made its way into her tone. Erika was just another passenger taking a tour. That was it. Nothing more. She repeated it to herself like a mantra.

Erika spoke first when they came to a stop in front of the hotel. "Thank you for the tour, Brittany. You sure know this island, and I can tell you love it."

Brittany turned to face Erika, but words stuck in her throat when their eyes met. She spoke past the lump of emotion. "I do love it here." She turned away to focus on securing the horses and helping Erika out of the carriage, but she surprised her by hopping out easily and gracefully. "You're in good shape."

Erika sighed, looking sad. "I have to be. I have twenty-two-year-olds for competition." She tipped her head to one side and grinned. "Thanks for noticing." She turned and headed into the hotel with a little wave over her shoulder.

Brittany parked the carriage and settled the horses in their stalls for the night before she waved good night to George and headed home. It had been an emotionally draining afternoon, and she resolved to push aside all thoughts of Erika. At least for one night.

CHAPTER EIGHT

It is her," Erika whispered to herself and flopped backward onto the bed. She couldn't believe that in all her worldly travels, she'd only now come across the girl she hoped never to have to face again. *Brittany. Of course.* Memories of her cowering and whimpering in the hallway, covering her scarred face with her hands, tears trickling between her fingers, engulfed Erika. She sat up and shook her head to dispel the images. Brittany'd grown into an attractive woman, and it hadn't taken long listening to her voice and watching her smile for the scars on her face to become unnoticeable.

Erika stood and stretched before pouring a glass of wine and settling into a parlor chair. She should tell Brittany she recognized her, but guilt tore at her gut and squeezed the air from her lungs. What would she say to her? How could she explain the despicable behavior of an insecure fifteen-year-old needing to fit in and gain acceptance from her peers? To belong to the group? Brittany had to have recognized her, and she couldn't understand why she hadn't confronted her. She tipped her head back and groaned. Why would she? She probably hoped to never see her again. Having to cart her around the island every day must be awful for her. Tomorrow. She'd talk to her tomorrow and try to come up with words of apology. She rinsed her glass and went to the dining room for dinner.

The room was crowded, and she noticed quite a few people look her way as she settled at a corner table. She smiled at them in the hopes of seeming approachable in case they wanted to speak to her or get an autograph. She took it as a sign she was still recognized, even on this tourist island. She ordered a salad and a bowl of soup and sipped a glass of iced tea as she waited. The thought crossed her mind that many here knew Erika James, but only one besides Peter knew Amy Jansons. Alone, she finished her soup and picked at her salad as unwelcomed memories and feelings surfaced. Erika James eradicated Amy Jansons years ago after the halls of high school. She became a fashion model recognized and defined by her beauty. It was all people had noticed when they'd looked at her for years, and there was no sense in expecting them to look deeper now. The young and innocent Amy no longer existed, and mourning her loss was pointless. Erika returned to her room to get ready for bed. Hopefully, this shoot would finish quickly and she could move on, back to the life she'd carefully cultivated. Even if it was a little lonely sometimes.

Erika chose the same corner table for breakfast she'd occupied the night before. A couple from Ohio stopped to ask for her autograph and chat before leaving. She enjoyed the attention from fans, though requests for autographs had become fewer over the years, and she never turned any down. All too soon, she could be just another face in the crowd, and the thought made her tremble inside.

"Hey. Good morning, beautiful." Peter leaned over and kissed her on the cheek before sitting across from her. "You look fantastic. The photos from the shoot at the fort are perfect. The magazine is thrilled, so far." He thanked the server when she placed a cup of coffee on the table for him.

"Hi, Pete. It was fun. I learned a lot about it and the island. So, did you get any leads on more work?" She moved her silverware back and forth on the table to calm her nerves.

Peter was quiet as he cradled his cup with both hands and raised his head to meet her eyes. "*Vogue*'s going with a nineteen-year-old newbie this year. Smooth bronze skin, charcoal brown eyes, and perfect smile." Peter let go of his coffee cup, took her hands in his, and squeezed gently. "I'm telling you this, not to upset you, but to keep you grounded in reality. *Naturalé Mag* is still hoping for you. I think you should consider it."

"I told you I'm not interested in a nudie magazine. What about *Elle* or *Bazaar*?" She hated sounding so desperate, but panic was creeping in.

"Sorry. Their words were, 'We're going in a different direction this year.'" He let go of her hands and sat back in his chair.

"I see." She stared into her cup hoping answers would appear, like reading tea leaves. "Do I have work after we're done here?" Her stomach dropped when he didn't answer right away.

"I'm working on it. I'm doing my best, Erika, but it's getting more difficult. The big publications want young and fresh. I'm checking on the smaller, lesser known ones, too. New magazines might be an option, but they can't afford the top models. I'll keep looking. You'll be in and around the hotel today, and I'll get back to you either tonight or tomorrow." He took a quick bite of croissant and then stood. "The *Naturalé* shoot would keep you working, at least. I'll be in touch." He left a fifty-dollar bill on the table and headed for the exit.

Erika checked her watch and left for a short stroll along the porch before she was due to meet Kathy to prep for the day's event. She ignored the butterflies in her stomach and hoped words would come to her if she ran into Brittany, but she was nowhere to be found as Erika wandered across the porch and toward the stables. She figured the magazine bosses had let whoever was in charge know the carriage wasn't needed today, as it was parked next to another inside the barn but away from the horses' stalls. A surreal feeling washed over her as she breathed in the scent of the horses. Standing in a barn was far removed from her city life in Manhattan and globetrotting, but wasn't unfamiliar to the child she once was. She'd begged her parents for a horse throughout her childhood only to be told it would be irresponsible. She couldn't take a chance of falling off a horse and messing up her skin or body in any way. She'd finally given up and concentrated on her modeling classes instead.

She headed back to the hotel. What did Brittany do on her time off? Did she have someone special in her life? Her disappointment at not finding Brittany surprised her. She wasn't looking forward to their conversation, but she knew it was necessary. She spent a few minutes people watching before heading back to her room to prepare for the day. She settled into the chair Kathy had set for her and pushed away concerns about her future.

"You're distracted this morning, Ms. James." Kathy gently lifted her chin as she tipped her head side to side to examine her makeup.

"Just thinking about the shoot," she lied. "We'll be doing more walking than usual."

She checked herself in the mirror and saw a maturing, though still model perfect figure and a designer outfit that fit her perfectly. She stood to her full height and followed Kathy out the door. Maybe doing the nude photos would show the other magazines what good shape she was in, and she could compete with the younger models. Maybe.

Chapter Nine

Brittany had never seen the burn wards so full. She joined the rest of the monthly volunteers at a round table in the nurses' office. "Hey, Joanne, I've never seen so many kids."

"We received a huge donation from one of our donors last month, so we were able to add fifty beds to our clinic. I wish there weren't so many who needed to be here, though." Joanne looked sad but determined. "We've all been working overtime. Thanks for coming again this month. The younger patients especially appreciate your visits."

"It's the least I can do to give back a little. I remember the fear and loneliness when I was here. I was in pain and frightened, and the adults who visited and shared their stories helped me believe I'd be okay." Brittany wanted to make the most of her short time at the burn clinic so she didn't elaborate. She couldn't know how much emotional healing her visits gave the young patients, but her time spent with them provided her with as much healing as her therapist.

Joanne squeezed her hand before she stood and led the group to don sterile gowns and masks.

Brittany spent the afternoon encouraging as many youngsters as she could. Too many lay enclosed in plastic, protected from infection. She protected herself from her rising memory-induced panic with deep breaths and focused on the patients. It had lessened in severity over the years, but she forced back tears when she recognized the dread on the children's faces. She focused on projecting positive energy and hope. She assured Joanne she'd return when she had time off again and left the clinic.

Brittany took her time walking to her car to settle her emotions. She'd never stop visiting and supporting the clinic that had saved her life. The doctors, the nurses, and her parents had all played a huge role in her recovery, and her heart filled with gratitude. She took a breath and expelled it before unlocking her car door and settling behind the wheel.

She removed her glasses to wipe the escaping tears and rested her head on the car seat. She closed her eyes to block out the agonizing memories of her own traumatic experience and concentrated on the healing she'd achieved. Her visits unsettled her but also brought her gratitude. She had the ability to offer comfort to the suffering youths, although she knew words of empathy and compassion only touched the surface of their pain. Her presence as an adult survivor showed them the possibilities of healing, and that was what would stay with them. She replaced her glasses and took a few minutes to collect herself before concentrating on her drive.

She guided her vehicle toward the ferry and thought of Erika. She'd enjoyed taking her on the short tour yesterday, but toward the end, she sensed Erika wanted to talk about something. She'd looked as if she wanted to speak but had turned away. Perhaps Erika had recognized her after all. She'd probably say something before she left the island, but if not, she questioned if it would make any difference. She parked her car in the long-term parking lot and boarded the ferry back to the island.

Being off the island for the day reminded her she was due for a visit to her parents. Mackinac Island was her home now. She had a few friends, and work to support herself, but she missed her parents' love and encouragement. She relaxed to the feel of the rolling waves and let her mind wander as she watched the wake and the view of the bridge as they passed it. Erika, a world-traveling model, had lived two blocks away in the small town where they'd grown up. They'd been close once, sharing their lives and secrets, but lived in completely different worlds now. She shook off her musings, followed the small crowd off the ferry, and began the walk to her apartment. She got halfway there and changed direction toward the stables. She missed the horses when she was away, and since the return of Erika in her life, she needed to be where she was accepted and valued.

"Hey, Brittany. What're you doing here? Don't you have the day off?" George set down the harness he was holding as he faced her.

"I do. I've been at the burn unit in Community General all day. I wanted to stop and see how you were doing."

"Ah. Your volunteer day, huh?"

"Yeah. It was sad and healing at the same time." Brittany sat on a bench, grateful for George's friendship.

"Everything's been quiet around here. Your famous model and her group were here for about an hour taking pictures with the horses and sitting on the carriages. I just sat back and watched. Erika James is a real beauty, for sure." George settled next to her on the bench. "Are you getting along with the group okay?"

"Oh yeah. It's been fine. They do their thing, and I just concentrate on my job." Brittany stood and stifled a yawn. "I think I'll head home. I'm pretty tired. I'll see you tomorrow morning." She waved as she left the barn.

Brittany took the path past the hotel porch on her way home. If her suspicions were correct, and Erika had recognized her yesterday, she wanted to get the uncomfortable reunion over. She checked the area outside and peeked into the lobby but didn't see Erika anywhere, so she continued home. She'd spent over twenty years filled with anger and resentment. Maybe having Erika here was a chance to deal with it and heal. They didn't have to be friends, although she had a hard time suppressing memories of when they had been, things had gone way beyond that, but it would be good to clear the air.

Part of her was grateful she hadn't seen Erika. Her off-island visit had drained her, and all she wanted to do was relax with a cup of tea before going to bed.

❖

Brittany waited for the magazine group in her usual spot the next morning. She wiped her palms on her jeans and shifted in her seat. She told herself there was no reason to be nervous, but her stomach knotted as she watched Erika approach with the carriage.

"Good morning, Brittany." Erika climbed into the carriage, and the photographer slid onto the seat next to her while the rest of the crew hopped on the back.

"Good morning. Did you have a good time at the hotel yesterday?"

"Yeah!" The photographer resettled her camera on her lap. "I had no idea the hotel had such a great history." She grinned ear to ear.

Brittany smiled. Other people's enthusiasm was always nice to see. "Did you enjoy the day, Erika?" She turned to face her.

"Yes. It was interesting, but I sort of missed the carriage ride and your description of things."

Brittany squirmed, unused to anyone holding her gaze so directly but gave in for a moment to the feeling of someone looking past her scars. "Thank you. I'm glad to hear I'm interesting." She turned to the others who had joined them. "Are we ready to head out for today's adventure?"

"All set back here," one of the three magazine representatives said.

She guided the horses toward their destination of the day and automatically started providing information. "Mission Point is one of the most scenic sights on the island. The Mission Point Resort is a bit north of here and has a gorgeous view of the straits." She stopped speaking, and the space was filled with chatter about clothing and fabric and light, and she zoned out, instead enjoying the beautiful morning. Before long, Brittany steered the horses to the edge of the road and secured the carriage while the group unloaded equipment.

"This spot is breathtaking." Erika stood at an opening in the brush along the shore. She looked mesmerized.

So are you. Brittany hoped she hadn't spoken aloud as she stepped next to her, the unexpected thought unwanted and quickly pushed away. "Yes, it is. The groups I bring here spend a lot of time taking pictures. I hope your photo shoot goes well." She walked back to the carriage to wait for them to finish and to shake off the confusing feelings being close to Erika sparked.

Chapter Ten

"Again?" Erika slogged out of the water and nearly tripped over the rocks strewn along the shore. The photographer had positioned her against the outcropped rock with one foot in the water and the other braced on a branch of a scrub bush. She'd stumbled and slipped on the wet rocks, almost falling headfirst into the chilly water before she caught her balance and climbed out. She silently sent a prayer of thanks to her personal trainer for her physical conditioning. "Okay. Where do you want me this time?" She dried off her legs and feet below her designer Capri pant legs while the photographer waited for her.

"There." She pointed to a spot on the shore farther from the water. "I like the way the light will sparkle on the water behind you."

Erika posed for several more shots before they stopped for the day. It had been a good day, and the smile on the photographer's face indicated she agreed. She pushed aside her anxiety and mentally rehearsed the conversation she hoped to have with Brittany soon. She removed her soggy sandals and padded barefoot back to the carriage.

"Welcome back." Brittany spoke from her perch on the front seat.

"Thanks. This is a beautiful spot, but I'm pooped." Erika shivered and wished she'd brought a sweater. She tipped her head side to side trying to stretch out the tension and pushed her intention to talk to Brittany until the next day. She needed hot chocolate and a hot shower. She shivered again.

"Here." Brittany hopped off the wagon and opened the door to a storage area under it. She gave her a blanket and one to her photographer, who sat hugging herself. "You two look like you could use these."

"Thanks." The intense spark of desire took her unawares when Brittany passed her the blanket and their fingers brushed.

"If you're all ready, we'll head back to the hotel." Brittany smiled as she twisted to address the group.

Erika held her gaze and caught her slight hesitation as she turned to face forward and urged the horses to begin the trip back. She wrapped herself tighter in the blanket to force away the mental image of sharing the space with Brittany. She reminded herself that they were no longer Brit and Amy. Friends sharing a kiss. She'd destroyed any chance of friendship between them twenty-three years ago. Thoughts of anything more would be ludicrous.

The trip back to the hotel dragged on much longer than the morning trip to Mission Point. Erika reluctantly handed the blanket over to Brittany when they exited the carriage. She turned to face her and steeled herself. "I'm going to take a hot shower and put on some dry clothes, but would you meet me in the dining area for a cup of hot chocolate later? I'd like to chat."

She squirmed under Brittany's scrutiny until she looked away and answered. "Sure. I'll get the horses settled for the night and meet you there."

Erika watched her walk away and vowed to maintain her courage. She was positive Brittany knew who she was. Now it was time to own up to her past. Once in her room, she removed and tossed her soggy shoes into a corner and stripped quickly before getting into the hot shower.

She took a few minutes to decide before she chose a pair of black Capris and a soft cotton polo shirt. Casual, but stylish. She checked herself in the mirror twice, unsure why she wanted to look her best for Brittany, and grabbed a sweater on her way out the door.

The crowded dining area surprised her until she realized it was Friday and the weekend was coming up. She'd noticed quite a few more people in the halls of the hotel for the past couple of days but hadn't taken any time to think about it. Her uneasy stomach and sweaty palms reminded her of the impending conversation. She sat at one of the few empty tables and switched her intended hot chocolate to a glass of wine. She took a sip and set the glass down when Brittany entered the room and searched for her. Their eyes met, and she suppressed the urge to run in the opposite direction. She smiled and waved. "Hey there." Brittany slid into the seat across from her and glanced at her wine glass. "That doesn't look like hot chocolate."

"I decided I needed some liquid courage tonight. May I buy you a glass?"

"No, thank you. I think hot chocolate sounds good." Brittany pulled her jacket tighter around her. "I'm a little chilled tonight. May evenings can still be nippy this far north."

Erika took a drink of wine to postpone the inevitable while silence stretched between them. She began to speak when Brittany interrupted by placing her hand over hers.

"It's okay, Amy. You look scared to death. Want to take a walk? I know a nice quiet spot with a log as a front row seat to the full moon." Brittany ordered two cups of hot chocolate to go while Erika finished her wine in one gulp and stood to put on her sweater.

Erika silently rehearsed what she wanted to say as they carried their cups out the door. She hadn't missed her use of her real name. It confirmed Brittany knew who she was, and hearing her name spoken after so long was startling. But what she wanted to know was how much anguish and anger Brittany carried. Once they were seated on the same log they'd shared before, her mind went blank. *How do I begin?*

"Are you warm enough?" Brittany asked.

"Yes. Thank you." Erika paused. "I need to talk to you, Brittany, and I think you know what I want to talk about." She shifted on the log to face her. "I guess I want to start by apologizing." She held her breath, anticipating a harsh response.

There was a moment of tense silence. "I appreciate your apology, but even after so much time, I can't understand why you did it." A tear rolled down Brittany's scarred cheek, and she tipped her head down. "We were friends."

Erika wanted to touch her, hold her, take away her pain, but she settled on scooting close enough so their thighs touched. Brittany didn't move away. "I'm not sure I have the words, Brit. But I'd like to try."

Brittany raised her head and met her eyes. "Can we do this inside where it's warm? I hadn't realized how cold it is, and honestly, I'm not sure I want to have this conversation where other people can hear it."

"Sounds like a good idea. I have a couple of parlor chairs in my room. We can sit and talk there." Erika stood and held out her hand. "Come on."

They walked quickly to the hotel. Erika dropped into one of the chairs eager to get the confrontation over. She had no idea how she was going to begin, and words didn't seem like enough. What could she say? She never thought she'd see Brit again, much less have to explain her outrageous behavior.

Chapter Eleven

Brittany sank into the comfortable parlor chair and watched Erika James, the beautiful self-assured model, transform into the fifteen-year-old self-conscious Amy Jansons. Her perfect posture probably hid some of the discomfort, but Brittany could tell her words were being pushed through uncomfortable memories. She refrained from reaching out to offer reassurance. Brittany needed to hear this.

"Did you recognize me right away?" Erika leaned forward with her hands clasped, her forearms on her knees.

Brittany nodded. "The day you arrived."

"I wasn't positive until the day we sat out on the log." Erika stood and poured a glass of wine. "Would you like some?"

"I'll have water if you have one." Brittany reached for the bottle and their fingers touched. The same warmth spread through her hand as she had when they'd contacted earlier under the blanket. "Thanks." She leaned back in the chair to give herself some distance.

Erika took a sip of wine and walked to the window. "I want to try to explain my actions in high school. It's something I've never forgotten and always regretted."

Erika looked miles away as she spoke, and Brittany wondered if she could see that time period as clearly as Brittany could.

"I struggled with self-worth in high school, as I think most kids do at that age." She took a sip of wine. "My parents decided I was going to be a famous model when I was four. They taught me my worth was tied to my looks. Each year before school started, my mother would sit me down with the latest fashion magazines and show me how I was to stand, sit, walk, smile, and what kind of clothes to wear. She cautioned me about falling into complacency and looking sloppy. I didn't even know what complacency meant. They convinced me I had to live up to the world's standard of beauty in order to be good enough. Just being me wasn't enough. I even changed my name so I could be the person everyone else wanted me to be, so I could leave the old one behind. I left Amy behind a long time ago. I think the times at your house might have been the last times I was her." Erika sighed and sat in the chair across from her.

Brittany couldn't keep from interrupting. "I remember. You used to come over crying, telling me you were no good. But you were, and you are."

Erika gave her a sad smile. "I remember, too. You said the same thing then. I don't believe my parents did any of this to suppress my self-esteem. I believe they recognized my potential to make a good living because of my looks. All my modeling instructors encouraged me to pursue a modeling career, so my parents encouraged it, too. I really believe they wanted to help me. They loved me and wanted the best for me."

Brittany rolled the water bottle between her hands. "Do you remember the day you came over and told me you were running away from home? We sat on the floor in my room and drew pictures of horses."

A happy smile spread across Erika's face. "I remember. You asked where I'd go, what I'd eat. You convinced me not to go. You were my best friend." She looked sad again as she continued. "You always told me I was special because I was me. You didn't deserve to be treated like we…I…treated you."

"No, I didn't." Brittany paused. "But it was over twenty years ago." She looked at her watch and stood. She felt like she'd been thrown back into the school hallway, splayed on the floor fending off the taunts. She needed some air and open space. "It's getting late. Could we meet for breakfast tomorrow and continue talking? I think you're not scheduled for photos until after noon."

Erika stood and stretched. "Yeah. Let's do that." She set her wine glass down and walked her to the door.

"Good night, Erika."

"Sleep well, Brit. See you tomorrow."

Erika was the only one who ever called her Brit, and she liked the way it sounded as it rolled off her full lips. But Erika was no longer Amy. They had a way to go before trust could be restored, and a part of her hoped it could be. There was some old saying about holding on to anger and how it poisoned you instead of doing anything to the person you were angry with. She wanted to let go of that old thorn so the wound could truly heal. She took her time walking home to allow the words Erika had spoken to sink in, and she gazed at the water as she passed. She did, however, want to hear more from Erika the next day.

Brittany leaned against the wall and breathed in the cool May night air before unlocking the door to her apartment. She never would have imagined she'd see Amy again, much less listen to her apologize for her participation in the terror. She left after high school to pursue her career as a fashion model and never came back to their small town. Did she ever return to visit her parents? Were they proud of her? It sounded as if she fit the mold they'd expected. She shivered, unsure if it was from the cold night or the bitter memories. So many memories and so many unknowns. She hoped Erika would be on the island long enough to help give her some closure. She wasn't sure how close to forgiveness she could get, but she looked forward to whatever more Erika had to say for herself.

She made herself a cup of chamomile tea and sipped it while she watched the late evening news. The weather reporter assured her tomorrow would be warm and sunny. She hoped her time spent with Amy...no, Erika, wouldn't be awkward. She had to respect what she called herself now; she wasn't the person Brittany remembered. She turned off the TV and went to bed hoping for dreams of past happy days and drawing pictures of horses.

❖

Brittany woke to the morning sun radiating through her bedroom window. She sat up to check the time. Her usual routine would have her at the stables by seven, but her assignment of chauffeur for Erika James meant she only had to be there when they needed her. She hadn't bothered to set her alarm, but now she wished she and Erika had set a time for their breakfast meeting. She'd been in such a hurry to leave she hadn't thought of it. She lay back on her bed and tried to think about what more Erika would have to say for herself. She made a cup of instant coffee and turned on the morning news. Nothing new had happened overnight, so she shut off the TV and sat in silence for a few minutes, until Erika overtook her thoughts once more. Her feelings began to interrupt her serenity, so she rose to take a shower.

Brittany took a few extra minutes to apply her makeup. She told herself it was because they'd be in the dining room with many other people, but the truth was she wanted Erika to continue to look past her scars, to see her as she was. And, maybe, to see something attractive in her. She stilled to analyze her feelings as her therapist had taught her. The pain of the past had already been dulled and nudged away by time, but would Erika's return be a setback? She mentally shook herself, determined to stay open to listening to her story. She finished dressing, put on her glasses, and headed out the door.

In the dining room, Erika looked poised and gorgeous sitting at the same table they'd occupied the night before, but Brittany could still see the dark circles under her eyes that she'd done a decent job of covering with makeup. "Good morning." She pulled out the chair across from her.

"Morning. Last night I realized we hadn't set a time to meet, so I hope this is good." She detected a slight tremor as Erika wrapped her hands around her coffee cup.

A few people looked their way, probably checking out the beauty seated across from her. "This is perfect." For the first time in years, she realized she hadn't considered they were looking at her. The freak. She sucked in a breath and ducked her head. Erika drew attention because of her beauty. Brittany drew attention as well. Like a curiosity in Ripley's Believe it or Not.

"Actually…" Erika stood to accept a carryout bag from the waiter. "I'd like us to go back to my room. Easier to talk there."

Brittany didn't care if Erika noticed her relief. "Sounds good."

Chapter Twelve

Erika removed their breakfasts from the bags and set the food on the small table between the parlor chairs. "I got us omelets, whole wheat toast, and fruit cups. Help yourself to a cup of coffee." She handed Brit a set of silverware wrapped in a linen napkin.

"Thanks for getting all this." Brit put a pod in the coffee maker and turned to lean back against the counter. "And thank you for rescuing me from the crowds."

Erika smiled and held her gaze. "No thanks necessary. I wanted a quieter, more private, place to talk." She swallowed a bite of omelet, hoping to still her quivering hand. She'd chastised herself for her behavior while a member of the clique in high school, but she'd never tried to analyze it fully. She took the cup of coffee Brit offered and forced herself to do it now. Brit deserved it. "Let's eat while it's still hot. I need to try to explain my awful behavior so many years ago." She sipped her coffee and then dove in.

"Jill was the popular girl in school. She was the one we all wanted to be like. She was pretty, a cheerleader, popular with the boys, and instinctively took over the leader position. I didn't see her sadistic side until she and a few girls created a group. They started hanging out together in the cafeteria. Then, with Jill in the lead, they began to roam the hallways and harass girls at their lockers. It was a nasty form of entertainment for them." Erika shook her head and took a couple of bites of her breakfast before continuing. "I watched them grow stronger, membership to their little group coveted by lots of girls. Anyone who wasn't accepted by their group feared their wrath. I was scared to death of them yet craved their approval. My greatest fear was not belonging, and I never would have if it weren't for my looks. I was pretty, so they accepted me."

She swallowed some coffee to quell the tightness in her chest. "I went along with their mean antics and suppressed my disdain. I was so happy to be included, I never gave any thought to our victims. When you returned to school after your accident, you became the perfect prey to bolster their sense of worth.

"Jill discovered I was in modeling school just before you returned. I think she perceived me as a threat, and I was certain she was going to kick me out of the group. It was a double-edged sword, I suppose. She feared I'd push her out and take over as leader of her group, or if she got rid of me, I'd start my own and people would want to hang out with me instead. She had no idea that I couldn't survive without her approval." Erika looked at her half-eaten omelet. Her appetite had fled, replaced by what felt like a rock in her belly. She raised her eyes to meet Brit's, begging for understanding. Or absolution? "That's why I participated horrendously in your abuse. I'm so sorry, Brit. It was so wrong, and so awful. I don't know what else I can say."

Brit looked thoughtful as she poked her fork at her eggs. "I remember Jill. I remember her being called the Queen Bee. I thought it was because she was the leader of the group that swarmed like bees through the hallways, stinging anything in their path. I can't say I understand the mentality, but I guess I kind of get it. I needed to fit in and be accepted by my peers, too. I needed friends and the sense of security belonging brings, and I was devastated by your involvement with the clique. We were friends, and I cared deeply for you. I never expected to be betrayed by you."

Brit stood and made them each another cup of coffee. "When I think about it, I suppose you were a victim as well, in a way. You lived with the fear of losing your position in the popular girls' gang if you didn't go along with their bidding. You had to be the person your parents wanted you to be, and having a group of friends probably made them happy." Brit handed her a full cup of coffee and settled in the chair next to her.

"You know what I hate the most?" Erika took Brit's hand in hers. "If it had been anyone besides you they'd chosen, I don't think I would've been so upset. Hell, there were others aside from you, and I didn't feel nearly as bad about them. I hate to admit I could've been a Jill. But, you know, I think she must've been in constant fear of losing whatever identity she had tied to that role, too." She released Brit's hand and let out a bitter laugh. "I suppose we were all casualties of being a teenager."

"Yeah. But we're adults now, and I should probably go get your carriage ready for this afternoon." Brit stood and set her empty coffee cup on the counter. "Thank you for your honesty. I appreciate it."

Erika watched Brit open the door and leave. She tipped her head back and closed her eyes to settle her stirred up emotions before beginning to prepare for the afternoon photos. She'd made her apologies, but why didn't it feel like enough?

❖

Brittany stood outside Erika's room and took a deep, settling breath before heading home. Her intention to go to work early had melted under the heat of the emotions Erika's words had created. She needed time to process them and search herself for forgiveness. She needed to figure out if she was blocking it or if she truly could never forgive. How much would it hurt for the rest of her life if she couldn't? She had to find a way, or she'd carry the pain forever. A part of her had hoped her memory of the event was wrong and it had been someone other than Erika standing in the hallway taunting her. She checked the time, made herself a cup of tea, and settled in her rocker.

The Amy she'd known as a kid had grown into Erika. A world-renowned model. She was rich and famous with a life utterly removed from the small town in which they'd grown up. She closed her eyes and drifted back to a summer afternoon, sitting in her room next to

Amy drawing pictures and working on a puzzle. Their fingers had touched as they both reached for the same piece and the heat racing up her arm was an unfamiliar, yet pleasant, feeling. The kiss that followed was even more unfamiliar and even more pleasant. Did Erika remember the kiss? Had it meant anything to her? Brittany stood and rinsed her cup. It didn't matter if she did. Those days were long gone, and she needed to focus on the present.

Chapter Thirteen

"Hi, George. How're things at the stables?" Brittany found her carriage parked in its usual spot.

"Hey, Brittany. Things are good here. Nothing new." He leaned on the side of the carriage. "You doing okay? You look tired."

"I'm okay. I just didn't sleep well." Brittany checked the wheels on the carriage and grabbed one of the harnesses. "I'll see you later." She hitched the horses to the carriage and climbed onto the driver's seat.

She contemplated what to say to Erika as she waited for the group to arrive. She believed her regret was sincere, and maybe they could start over, although she couldn't believe she'd have anything in common with a world famous fashion model. She hoped Erika would help her figure it out.

"Ready to go?" Brittany watched Erika and her crew load their equipment and settle in the carriage.

"I think we're all set." Erika sat in the seat she'd hoped she would. Directly behind her and close enough for them to talk.

After she coaxed the horses into a slow walk to the destination of the day, she turned to Erika and smiled. "You look great." Brittany knew little about fashion or fashion designers, but the flowing skirt and low-cut blouse fit Erika perfectly and accented her flawless figure.

"Thanks. This is the first time I've worn this designer, and I love it." Erika brushed her hand down a sleeve. She leaned forward and lowered her voice so only Brittany could hear. "Are you all right? I've been thinking about you since you left this morning."

Brittany took a moment to consider her response. "I'm all right. I just need some time to process what you told me. I've been in therapy off and on since the accident, so I've got a pretty good handle on my PTSD. I'm comfortable living here, I work and I'm mostly happy, but I was certain I'd never see you again, so it was a shock when you showed up."

"Nobody knows how fate works. Why me? Why this magazine? Why here and now? All I know is I'm glad it happened. I'm glad I had an opportunity to try to make amends." Erika was interrupted by her photographer demanding her attention.

Brittany guided the carriage to the side of the road and watched the group work. They'd become quite proficient at climbing in and out of the carriage with their gear and setting up the scene they wanted. Erika looked relaxed, elegant, and at ease in her element. One Brittany couldn't imagine, or desire. Their connection as kids in a small town, on the floor of her bedroom drawing pictures seemed a lifetime ago. She'd grown and changed since those years, just as Erika had. Pushing aside the memory of their one and only kiss, however, she found impossible.

Brittany parked the carriage securely and fed and watered the horses before she grabbed a brush and headed to one of the Percheron's stalls. "Hey, Buddy." She called softly so as not to startle him before she touched his back. "May I brush you a bit tonight?" She wrapped her arms around his massive neck. He turned his head to rest it over her shoulder as if he recognized her need for comfort. She pushed her cheek against his warm neck, and tears welled as she realized it'd been years since she'd sought comfort from his gentle presence. "One of the girls who tormented me in high school is here. I don't understand. She was my friend. We grew up in the same neighborhood. She apologized, and I believe she's genuinely sorry, but I still feel so angry and hurt. I don't know if I can forgive, but I know I want to." Buddy nickered but didn't pull away. "Okay, boy." She let go, stepped to his side, and combed his flowing mane and brushed his coat until it glistened. The methodical work helped calm her stormy thoughts, and she finished feeling better than when she started. "Thanks for the company, old friend. Sleep tight." She returned the brush to the tack room and headed home.

"Mind if I walk with you?"

She turned toward Erika, surprised. "Of course. I'm on my way home. You're welcome to come with me and have a cup of tea." She tried to remember if she'd left any clothes lying on the floor.

"I'd like that," Erika replied quietly and stayed close as they walked.

"No meeting with your agent tonight?" Brittany slowed her pace, enjoying the feel of Erika so near. The feeling confused her. Why did she want to have anything to do with her?

"No. We're meeting in the morning before we head to the Surrey Hills Museum and Butterfly Conservatory. I think it's going to be a fun shoot. I love butterflies."

"Yeah, it's a great place. I love going there."

"You could come in with us while we're there." Erika looked excited.

"I wish I could, but I'm responsible for the carriage and horses. I'm not allowed to leave them unattended. You have a good time, and you can tell me all about it when you're done. Here we are." She unlocked the door and stepped aside for Erika to enter.

Once inside, Brittany fumbled with her teapot. She'd never had anyone over to her apartment. She took a settling breath and counted to ten like her therapist had suggested for stressful situations. She set the pot on the burner and retrieved two cups. She was putting the teabags into the cups when Erika walked up behind her. "Can I help with anything? Sorry. I didn't mean to startle you." She put her hand on her forearm.

Brittany stared at her hand on her arm. She raised her eyes and fell into her golden stare. "Is green tea okay? I might have something else. I'll have to look. Or I have coffee..." She stopped her rambling, unsure of what to do. She looked down at her arm and back up again.

"It's okay, Brit," Erika whispered, squeezed her arm, and leaned toward her. "May I kiss you?"

Brittany panicked but couldn't move. Every muscle in her body froze. She was sure her heart stopped, and she'd fall over before Erika could catch her. She realized she held her breath and decided she'd probably pass out before she needed to answer. She squeezed one word past the lump in her throat. "Okay…"

Erika cupped her face between warm hands and pressed her lips gently against hers. Memories flooded back of a small dark room amidst crayons and puzzle pieces and her first kiss ever. This was her second. Why did it have to be with the one woman she could never have anything real with?

Chapter Fourteen

Erika tried to look relaxed as she waited for Peter to arrive. She drank her coffee, barely tasting it. What was she thinking? She'd been flooded with childhood memories of her and Brit, in her room, drawing pictures, sharing an innocent kiss. She'd never forgotten the kiss, and last night she couldn't stop herself from repeating it. But Erika kissing Brit was different from two kids sharing a close friendship. She'd been so focused on wanting to kiss her she hadn't even asked Brit if she was dating anyone. Did she even give her a chance to say no when she'd asked for the kiss? Her fuzzy, lust filled memory told her she had. She'd been too busy with her career to date seriously, and she had to be ever mindful of who she hooked up with to keep it from the tabloids. But there had been no one she'd kissed who'd made her tingle like Brit did.

Erika's ruminations were interrupted by Peter's arrival. "Hi, beautiful." He gave her a peck on the cheek and sat across from her. "You look a little pensive this morning. You okay?"

"Yeah, I'm fine. How'd all your phone calls go yesterday?"

Peter ordered a cup of coffee and pulled a notepad out of his pocket before answering. "Once I finally found an area where my cell phone worked, I managed to get a few leads, but I'm afraid I wasn't able to get any firm commitments. Good news is the magazine we're working with here wants you for a series they're doing titled 'Parks across America.'" You'll be their featured model. The next series of shoots is in Central Park. Right at home for you." He grinned and sipped his coffee.

"It sounds good. How many shoots did they commit to?" Erika enjoyed a moment of relief. Maybe there'd be no more pressure to do the nude scenes.

"They didn't commit to anything. They just said they loved what they had so far here on the island and wanted more of you."

"So, nothing definite?" Erika watched Peter's response closely.

"No. But I've seen the photos they've taken so far, and they're great. I think you're a shoo-in."

"Okay. So, no more *Naturalé*." She let out a relieved sigh and grinned until the uncertainty in his eyes punched her in the gut. "That is what it means, doesn't it, Pete?"

"Maybe. I'll keep trying to pin them down to a contract. At least it would keep you busy for the rest of this year." He finished his coffee and stood. "I'll let you know if I get more info."

Erika watched him leave the room, then turned back to her breakfast. She pushed aside her misgivings and turned her thoughts back to Brit.

❖

Erika stood at the door waiting for Brit to show up with the carriage. Part of her worried she'd send someone else because she didn't want to see her. After their shared kiss, they'd sat and chatted over their tea, sharing silly anecdotes about their work. It was relaxed, but they didn't mention the kiss, and the unspoken words hung heavy in the air between them. When she left, Brit had kept her distance, and it was clear another kiss wasn't going to happen. She began to pace, certain she'd offended her. She'd shown up on the island and marched into Brit's life uninvited. Within four days, she'd disclosed who she was, tried to explain her teenage behavior, and kissed her. Kissed her as if she had a right to. She shivered in anticipation and willed her breathing to return to normal while she waited.

She straightened and smiled when the horses plodded toward her. Brit looked relaxed and confident as she guided the carriage to the loading area, and some of Erika's tension eased. She waited for her photographer to join her before boarding the coach. "Good morning." She spoke as she stepped aboard.

"Good morning," Brit said. "I think you'll enjoy the Avenue of Flags today. I imagine the photos will be awesome."

Erica relaxed into her seat. Brit was acting as she always did. She must be okay with the kiss. "I'm looking forward to it." She concentrated on the photo shoot and the possibility of having dinner with Brit afterward. The ride was quiet, and she enjoyed the serenity of her surroundings as they made their way to the location. She stepped off the carriage and followed the photographer and the crew, and when she looked over her shoulder, Brit gave her a quick smile before turning to the horses.

The day was long, but the shoot was good. Erika made a point of sitting close enough to Brit so the crew couldn't hear their conversation on the way back to the hotel. "Would you have dinner with me tonight?" she asked.

"Sure. I think that would be nice."

"Is the dining room at the hotel all right?" An unfamiliar uncertainty washed over her as she waited for Brit's answer. She'd asked women out before, and in truth, she'd never been turned down. Of course, none of them were more than a night or two and it was a given that would be the case. Women enjoyed her company, but in their world, there was always someone new on the horizon. She wasn't sure where her relationship with Brit was headed, but she knew she wanted to spend more time with her. They'd shared a childhood connection, but now she hoped to share an adult one.

"It's fine. Okay if we sit against the wall, toward the corner?"

"Wherever you're comfortable."

They arrived back at the hotel and set a time to meet before Brit left.

Erika arrived first and secured their table. It wasn't long before she spotted Brit and waved. She strode to the small two-seat table, and the waitress appeared within minutes to take their order.

"I'm glad you agreed to have dinner with me." She smiled. "I wanted to talk about last night." She hesitated. "I hope I wasn't out of line kissing you, but I couldn't resist." She sat back in the chair waiting for Brit's reaction.

Brit took a sip of water and avoided eye contact. "I would've stopped you if I was uncomfortable." She took another drink of water, keeping her eyes averted.

"I was going to apologize if I offended you. I'm glad you're okay with it, because it was a super nice kiss." She flashed a smile.

"No need for apologies. It was a nice kiss. Even better than the first one." Brit looked directly at her, but her emotions were shuttered.

"Yes. I remember our first one, too." She stroked her hand. "I was worried you were seeing someone, and I didn't even bother to ask first."

The server interrupted their conversation and put their meals down. Erika watched Brit's face, and now the emotions in her eyes were clear. She looked confused and uncomfortable.

Brit shifted in her seat. She looked nervous. "I'm not seeing anyone. Romantically, I mean. I see my therapist when I need to. I'm happy on my own." She took a bite of her food, looking down at her plate.

Erika decided to let Brit lead the conversation. She picked up her fork to eat her dinner and hoped Brit would speak or it was going to be a long evening.

She waited a few minutes before speaking again. "I'm glad the weather's turned out so well for these shoots. Is it usual for this time of year on the island?" An inane question, but she was at a loss as to how to reach Brit.

"We usually get some rain this month, but mostly at night. It's been dryer than normal." Brit bent her head and took a bite of food.

Erika returned to her meal, wishing Brit would open up.

Dinner ended on an uncomfortable note, and Erika was determined to put Brit at ease. She just wasn't sure how. She wished she hadn't given in to her impulse to kiss her. She probably hadn't given her enough time after their heavy conversation to process her feelings before jumping on her. She had to make things right. It'd been hard enough to apologize for her behavior in high school, now she had to do it again.

"Thanks for the dinner invitation, Erika."

"Let's walk out back and check out the sunset." Erika took Brit's hand and tugged her out the door. "Are you sure you're okay with the kiss?"

"I'm sure." Brit stopped walking and turned to face her. "I've never kissed anyone else, so I'm not sure what I'm supposed to do or how to feel." She looked down at her feet.

Erika gently placed her hand on Brit's cheek. It made sense. Brit had spent months in a burn unit as a kid, then had the courage to come back to school, only to be harassed. Then, as an adult, moved to Mackinac Island and chose to work where it was safe. With horses. She'd probably never allowed herself to be vulnerable with anyone. "You don't have to do anything, Brit. You're perfect the way you are, and whatever you feel is okay."

Brit placed her hand over hers and turned her head to kiss her palm. "I feel seen with you. It's a new feeling for me, and a little scary."

Brit's instinctive response and her honesty and vulnerability took Erika by surprise, and she vowed to work to earn her trust.

CHAPTER FIFTEEN

Brittany woke to birdsongs drifting through her open window. The months of May and June were her favorite. The birds were nesting, and the lilacs were blooming. Memories of the winter's deep-freeze gave way to thoughts of warm summer nights. She stretched and smiled at Erika's words. Erika had said she was perfect. Her parents used to tell her the same thing, and she ought never to let anyone tell her different. But those were her parents. Erika was a friend. One who'd kissed her twice. Now she wished she'd tried dating, although there'd only been one woman she'd trusted and allowed close enough to consider.

Barb was a conservation officer who lived on Drummond Island and was occasionally stationed on Mackinac Island, and she'd turned out to be a dear friend. Brittany had never been driven to kiss her like she did Erika. She contemplated the idea of friendship compared to something more, but her mind muddled. She'd read about friendships and love relationships, but real-life ones seemed far more complicated. She swung out of bed and went to the shower to prepare for her day.

She made herself a cup of tea and put two eggs in a pot to boil. Erika probably had room service at the hotel and ordered whatever she wanted. She couldn't imagine the lifestyle Erika maintained. She wondered if she'd settled into it easily because Erika's family hadn't been rich. Reflections on Erika's family reminded her she needed to check on her own parents. She planned to review the magazine group's schedule for the week and plan a day off the island.

She left a few minutes early so she could talk to Ben before going to the stables.

"Brittany. I'm glad you stopped in. How's everything going with the magazine?" Ben looked up from his laptop.

"It's good. I came by to see if you had their schedule for this week. I'd like to plan a day off the island to see my parents." She leaned against the wall.

"I do have it. In fact, they've extended their stay for three days. I've printed out a copy of their itinerary for you." He handed her a sheet of paper.

"Thanks." She scanned the information and found a day toward the end of the week. "It looks like maybe Thursday will work. I'll let you know." She turned to leave but stopped at the sound of his voice behind her.

"Do what you need to, Brittany. I appreciate your flexibility with this group. I'll get George to cover for you if you need it."

"Thank you, Ben." She smiled while she ambled to the stables, mentally planning her trip. It was only a two-hour drive, but the ride took all her concentration, and she was exhausted by the time she arrived.

"Good morning," Erika called.

"Good morning. Am I late? I thought we didn't need to leave until nine." The unfamiliar stirring as she watched Erika get closer took her by surprise. She turned toward the carriage to wipe down one of the bench seats.

"You're not late. I just wanted to see you." She leaned on one of the wheels. "Will you have dinner with me again after the shoot today?"

"I'd love to." Brittany relaxed and quit trying to look busy.

"Cool. I'll see you in a little while." Erika leaned to brush her lips over Brittany's cheek before she headed back toward the hotel.

Brittany attempted to define her feelings as she watched Erika walk away. She had liked kissing her, but kissing her as an adult flooded her with new emotional and physical responses. She struggled with reconciling her feelings of closeness to Erika with the memories of her as her tormentor. She changed her plans from a visit to her parents to an appointment with her therapist.

❖

"I'm glad your photos went well today." Brittany spoke from her seat, holding the horse's reins.

"Me, too. It sure went smoother than the last time we were close to the water." Erika climbed onto the carriage and squeezed her shoulder. "We probably won't need the blankets this trip."

The afternoon had warmed nicely and Brittany enjoyed the view of the sunlight sparkling off the water. "Would you all like me to take a longer route along the water's edge back to the hotel?"

The group chimed in their agreement, all except Peter. Brittany noticed his sour expression and made a mental note to ask Erika about it at dinner. She explained the significance of the area and gave a short history of Mission Point before guiding the horses back to the hotel.

"Enjoy your evening. I'll see you tomorrow," Brittany said as she waved to the group and waited until they unloaded their equipment. She and George unhitched the horses and settled them in for the night before she rushed home to clean up and change for dinner.

She rinsed her face and blotted her scarred skin before applying fresh sunscreen. She regarded her reflection in the mirror. What did Erika see when she looked at her? She'd kissed her, so did it mean she saw her as young Brittany, before she was *scar face*, or did she see beyond the hypertrophic burn scarring, despite the massage and gel sheet therapy? She sighed, wishing she'd never had to learn, firsthand, the meaning of those words. She finished dressing, selecting a pair of dress pants and lightweight polo shirt she usually reserved for meetings with the CPA she worked for, before she checked her reflection one more time and headed out.

She took a path along the water to the hotel side entrance. This late in the evening, more formal attire was required in the dining area so she went directly to Erika's room. She only had to knock once before Erika was standing in the doorway looking beautiful. “We didn’t specify a place or time, so here I am.” Brittany raised her hands palms up in a *hope it’s okay* gesture.

Erika pulled her into the room, wrapped her arms around her neck, and kissed her. It was a demanding kiss and Brittany didn’t resist. She ended the kiss and backed away a step. “It’s great.”

Brittany shifted foot to foot, unsure of what to do with her hands, so she let her arms hang by her side. Erika seemed to have gotten over any uncertainty about making her desires known, but Brittany had no idea what she wanted. For the moment, she’d just see where it went. She tugged at the bottom of her shirt. “I’m afraid this is the fanciest outfit I have, so I’m not sure about dinner in the dining room.”

“No worries. I ordered room service.”

Brittany smiled and began to relax. This would be fine. They’d shared breakfast here once, and she’d survived it. Dinner would be just as easy. “It’s fine.” She settled into one of the parlor chairs to wait for whatever came next.

Chapter Sixteen

"Shall we sit on the lovely purple couch to eat?" Erika set a plate of food and silverware on the end tables on either side of the couch. "I've got coffee, tea, and water, or we can peruse the wet bar. I think there's some soft drinks in there behind the wine and booze."

"Water's fine with me." Brit sat on one end of the couch and reached for the plate of pork tenderloin. "This looks fantastic. I didn't realize how hungry I was."

"Go ahead and start. I'm going to make myself a cup of tea." Erika set her empty cup in the coffee machine and waited for the hot water. She used the time to collect her thoughts. At least she'd asked the last time she'd kissed Brit. Gentle, innocent Brit deserved more respect. She just hadn't been able to help herself when Brit had opened the door looking so lovely. She carried her cup to her end of the couch. "I'm hungry, too. And I want to apologize for presuming I could kiss you like I did."

They ate in silence for a few minutes before Brit spoke. "I appreciate your apology, but it's not necessary. I like kissing you, and I like that you want to kiss me. I admit I'm still a little…bemused? I don't know if that's the word. But whatever it is, I'm going with it." She grinned and shrugged.

Erika set down her fork and took a sip of tea. "As long as you don't feel like I'm taking advantage of you. I've spent most of my adult life getting whatever I wanted, and I usually make decisions based on what I want, without asking anyone else. I like you, Brit, and I don't want you to be uncomfortable."

"I tell you what. If I ever feel taken advantage of or uncomfortable, you'll be the first to know." Brit took her hand and squeezed gently before releasing it. "I was going to ask you earlier, but I didn't get the chance. Peter looked upset today. Is everything all right with him?"

Erika sighed, unsure how much she wanted to disclose. "He's okay, but he's having a hard time finding work for me." She considered telling Brit about *Naturalé Mag* but hesitated. "I'm not sure what I'll be doing after we're done here on the island."

"I'm surprised. You're beautiful, and from what I've seen, pretty darn good at what you do." Brit took a drink of water. "Is it because you're not twenty anymore?"

"Yeah." Erika sighed. "I'm thirty-eight this year, and younger models are pushing me out of the spotlight. It's the nature of the business, but I don't think I'm ready to give it up yet."

Brit surprised her and moved to sit close. "You'll be fine, even if you don't model for the rest of your life."

"Peter has one magazine interested in me, but I don't want to work for them." She snuggled closer to Brit, enjoying her warmth and softness.

"Ben told me you'll be here an extra three days. That's a good sign, isn't it?"

"I think so. This magazine wants to feature me for a series at a number of parks throughout the country, too. So, if Peter gets a contract, I would have some work on the horizon." She focused on the positive news to quell the churning fear in her gut.

"Would you like to tour the stables when we're done eating?"

Erika pushed aside her misgivings about future work and finished her tea in one gulp. "I'm ready."

Erika followed Brit as she led the way. She was excited to be able to see the horses up close and maybe touch them.

"Hey, George," Brit called to him when they entered the barn.

"Good evening, Ms. James. It's good to see you again." George extended his hand in greeting.

Erika took his hand, glad to meet one of Brit's friends. "I'm excited to see all the horses. May I pet them?"

"You stick with Brittany. She knows the ones you'll lose your fingers to, and those that'll nuzzle you to death." George grinned and waved as he turned and walked away.

"Let's visit Buddy first." Brit took her hand and led her toward the larger horses. "He's a sweetie. A real gentle giant."

Erika missed the feel of Brit's hand in hers when she released it to push open a gate. She breathed in the scent of horses and listened to their munching on hay. She'd seen large draft horses before, but this huge Percheron was bigger than she could have imagined. His golden coat shone, and his light mane cascaded over his neck. It was obvious he was well groomed. "He is a beauty." She stood outside his stall, certain she'd be squished if she got too close. She watched him shift his weight on his back legs and noted his rump was taller than her shoulder even when she straightened to reach her full five eight height. She watched his lips quiver and flap as he pushed his nose toward Brit when she offered him a carrot.

"I visit him when I need a big hug." Brit rubbed under his chin, and he stretched his neck and tipped his head as if to give her better access.

"I see why you like him." Erika stepped closer and hesitantly reached to pet his head. He was warm and didn't pull away when she moved her hand to his smooth cheek. She stepped back and watched as Brit whispered in his ear when he lowered his head as if listening intently. It was lovely the way Brittany seemed to have a connection with the giant animal. Erika couldn't think of anyone or anything she shared that kind of connection with.

They strolled through the stables and several horses nickered, probably hoping for a carrot or sweet treat. She watched Brit interact with the horses and their reaction to her. Buddy was the gentle giant, but Brit's tenderness surpassed any human she knew. "You're good with them," she whispered in Brit's ear.

Brit turned her head and swiftly skimmed her lips across hers. "There. Now I've kissed you." She chuckled softly, grabbed her hand again, and pulled her toward the back door and outside into an open field.

"What are we doing out here?" Erika asked.

"Watch." Brit pointed toward the darkening sky, stepped behind her, and wrapped her arms around her waist.

The cloud obscuring the full moon drifted away and bathed them in luminous moonlight, and Erika melted into her embrace. "Beautiful. Thank you." She'd been with plenty of women over the years, but the sensation of safety and caring in Brit's arms took her breath away.

Chapter Seventeen

Brittany turned over and hugged her pillow as memories of her evening with Erika rolled over her like a warm blanket. The pain of the past hadn't disappeared, but Erika's apology and explanation had helped dull it somewhat. She rose to get ready for work. She smiled knowing she'd see Erika soon, but winced when she realized their time on the island was close to ending. She vowed to make the most of the time they had left but not to forget she was leaving. She went to take a shower.

She ate her breakfast while watching the morning news. She turned up the volume when a local story came on about a famous model spotted on Mackinac Island. She supposed it had to happen. Someone had recognized Erika James and put the word out. She hoped it didn't mean she'd be mobbed by fans. She hurried to dress and headed out the door.

She rushed to the carriage and waited for Erika and her crew. "Good morning." Brittany smiled as she spoke, inexplicably happy to see her

"Good morning." Erika wore a wide brimmed hat with the brim hiding half of her face.

"It looks like you saw the news this morning," Brittany said.

Erika sat back in the seat but continued to face her. "I didn't but Peter did and told me about it. So far, I've only met one couple in the hotel who stopped me for a picture."

"Are you worried?" Brittany checked the surrounding area. Nobody lurked about.

Erika shook her head. "I just don't want the paparazzi descending on this tranquil place."

"Maybe they won't find you. It was only the local news. They probably don't care about our little population. And with the poor cell phone service here, it would be difficult to spread the word about where you are on the island."

Erika looked thoughtful for a moment. "Yes, it would."

Brittany waited for her passengers to settle in the carriage before she urged the horses to the road.

Their destinations for the day were three different spots along the coast and then a stop at one of the fudge shops in town. She watched Erika pose near the water and was struck by her poise and grace. She waited while the crew hopped on and off the carriage. She kept an eye on them in case they needed help, but they had their routine down. Erika climbed onto the seat directly behind her. It was the seat she'd come to think of as hers. "You looked great out there."

"Thanks. I'm looking forward to the fudge shop." Erika removed her hat and turned her face to the afternoon sun.

Brittany waited until the crew was out of earshot and turned toward her. "Will you have dinner with me tonight?" She wanted to spend some time alone with Erika to find out how much longer she would be on the island.

"I'd love to."

Brittany was encouraged by her instant positive reply. "Make it about six at my place. You remember how to get there?"

"I do. It's a date." Erika looked around, and there were a few people watching, so she sat back and gave Brit a sweet smile.

Brittany reviewed her options as much to clear her head as to decide on what to cook for dinner. She'd seen Erika eat meat and eggs but not fish. She hoped she liked it because she had some fresh perch in her refrigerator she'd gotten from George, and if it were as good as the last batch he'd given her, it would be perfect. She steered the horses toward town and began her information introduction regarding their destination. "Ryba's fudge shop has been a staple here on Mackinac Island since nineteen sixty. They're a family owned business, which began about nineteen thirty-six on Detroit's east side, and they've been a part of the Detroit Auto Show since the nineteen fifties. The original owner died in nineteen ninety-six, but the family still owns and operates the company." She grinned and turned toward the group. "On a personal note. It's my favorite."

❖

Brittany set plates, silverware, napkins, and glasses on her small kitchen table. She stepped back and regarded the room. Erika was used to fine china and linen. She traveled the world, ate in fancy French restaurants, and drank expensive wine. She realized she hadn't considered wine and searched her cupboards for something she knew wasn't there. She had water, iced tea, and coffee. It would be enough. She turned on her stereo and sat to wait. At six fifteen, she began to worry. She sent a text, hoping it would go through and answered the knock at the door five minutes later.

Erika looked beautiful as she stepped into the room and held up a bag from Ryba's Fudge. "I brought dessert."

"Thank you." Brittany stepped aside for Erika to enter. "Did you get my text?"

"Yes. I was on my way so I didn't respond. I'm sorry I'm late, but is it okay if I explain while we eat? I'm starved."

Brittany served the fish. "This perch is fresh from the Straits of Mackinac." They sat and each took a bite.

"This is wonderful. I love perch. It should be the state fish." Erika spoke with a mouthful but swallowed before continuing. "I had a talk with Peter tonight. That's why I was late." She took a sip of water. "He's the one who alerted the media I was here. He told me it was an attempt to bring attention to me. To keep me 'in the spotlight.'"

Brittany raised her eyebrows. "Is it common to do that? And shouldn't he have asked you first?"

"No, it's not common, but he figured since I'm falling out of the fashion scene, he'd give it a try. He's my agent, so he's responsible for promoting me." She put more fish on her plate then raised her eyes. "I'm scared this might be the end for me, Brit. He also told me the magazine I'm working with now is waffling on a contract offer for that shoot in the national parks." She set her fork down. "I've never been in the position of no work on the horizon before, and I'm just not ready to give it all up. My worth and who I am is tied to my work. Does that make sense to you?"

Brittany paused to consider her answer. She wanted to be honest but sensitive to Erika's feelings. "It does make sense, in a way. You were groomed to be a model your whole life and it became who you were, not just what you did for a living. But you're intelligent, resourceful, and probably financially stable. I'd think you know other retired models who you could talk to about how they handle retirement, don't you?"

"I do, and as soon as I get back to New York and reliable cell service, I'll talk to them. Let's finish dinner so we can break into the fudge." She gently squeezed Brit's hand, let go, and picked up her fork.

Brittany glanced at Erika a few times while they finished eating, happy to see her brighten up. After they finished the meal, she pulled out two pieces of fudge from the bag and handed one to Erika. "Here. Fudge always makes me feel better." She smiled when Erika took a bite and smiled. "Oh, and it's brook trout."

Erika tipped her head. "What is?"

"The state fish of Michigan is brook trout."

Erika laughed but still looked sad. "Peter and I are going to talk to the magazine tomorrow and try to work out a deal."

Brittany stood and reached for Erika's hand to pull her to the couch. "Let's relax. I'll pour us a cup of tea." She grabbed the bag of fudge and set it next to Erika, unsure how she could help her. It wasn't a world she fit into, and it wasn't one she understood. But she could be a friend, and maybe that's all Erika really needed right now.

CHAPTER EIGHTEEN

"So far, I've been approached by two couples for autographs, Peter. Two couples. Only *two* in two days! Did you expect the paparazzi to show up?" Erika's mixed emotions swirled through her. She was happy she hadn't been mobbed, but a part of her took it as a sign her appeal as a model was over. Why wasn't she recognized and surrounded by adoring fans? Why weren't the newspapers lined up to photograph her? A world-renowned fashion model was available. Her heart sank. Maybe it really was over.

"Give it a few more days, Erika. News travels slowly here. Most people are vacationers and care more about seeing the sights than any famous person. And we'll be talking to the magazine people later today. I've got to go find a spot where I can make a phone call. I'll see you later." Peter left before she had a chance to reply.

She locked her room door after Peter left and changed into her swimsuit. She'd discovered the hot tub when she'd taken a short walk after breakfast and intended to make good use of it in her remaining days on the island.

She sighed as she sank into the hot water, grateful to have the tub to herself. The scent of chlorine, the sound of the foaming water, and the feel of the jets massaging her tense muscles finally relaxed her, but she wished they could reach the emotional tension and fear that ran so much deeper. She slipped into meditation and released the disturbing thoughts as they snuck in to spoil her serenity. She spent another ten minutes in the bubbling water before it was time to get ready for the afternoon shoot. At least she still had a few more days in the spotlight before her world possibly crumbled.

She rushed to wash her hair and rinse off before Kathy arrived but took a moment to examine her reflection in the mirror. It wasn't full-length, but she could see herself above her knees. Her fit and toned body, firm breasts, and tight butt reflected back at her. She did a few facial exercises, abandoned her perusal, and put on her Victoria's Secret underwear and robe.

"Good morning, Ms. James." Kathy whizzed past her through the open door with an armload of items. She set them on the table between the chairs and arranged them in an order only she understood before she turned to face her. "Are you ready to begin?"

Erika settled into her usual parlor chair, which Kathy had designated as having *the perfect light.* "I'm ready." She sat quietly as Kathy began her artistry. Her memories took her back to her childhood when she'd sat in a kitchen chair at their Formica table while her mother permed her hair and fussed over her.

Sit up straight. Don't frown, or you'll get wrinkles. Make sure your fingernails are clean and polished. Never go out in public in wrinkled clothes. What would the neighbors say?

She sighed loudly.

Kathy stopped mid-brush. "Are you all right?"

"Yes, sorry, Kathy. All this fussing over me reminded me of my mother when I was a kid." She readjusted her seat in the chair determined to remain still and quiet the voices in her head. She needed to stay focused on her career, not her past.

Erika watched Brit hitch the horses to the carriage. The few days she'd spent on the island with Brit seemed more like a vacation than work. She couldn't remember a time she'd stood in the moonlight with someone or had been invited to a home cooked meal. Her world was fast paced, with fast food and fast hookups. Glitz and glamour defined her. Ruled her life. She caught Brit's eye and smiled. There was no glitz and glamour for her. Just honesty and beauty.

The group arrived, boarded the carriage, and they headed to the destination of the day. She sat in her usual seat directly behind Brit. "Where are we headed today?"

Brit turned toward her to answer. "We'll be going to an area where the year-rounders live. It's a beautiful part of the island."

"What is there to do here in the winter?" Erika could think of a few things but pushed away her X-rated thoughts.

"About twenty horses stay on the island year-round. They mostly pull taxis. I drive them occasionally, work for a CPA, and help some of the local businesses with their taxes. Many people have snowmobiles to get around and cross the water if it's frozen. It's much quieter than in the summer." Brit parked the carriage under a cedar tree. "Here we are."

It sounded idyllic, and Erika couldn't fathom what a winter spent in such quiet routine would be like. She followed the photographer up a hill to a striking view overlooking main street on one side and the water on the other. She turned in circles admiring the view until she was called to the area they wanted for the photo. "This is fantastic. I see why you wanted a photo shoot up here." She spoke to the magazine crew, always aware that being someone people liked to work with could mean a better reputation and more work down the line. The rest of the shoot took all afternoon and she was happy to be done for the day. She hoped Brit would have dinner with her again. She took her seat behind her and leaned close to speak. "Have dinner with me tonight?"

Brit answered without hesitation. "I'd love to. What time?"

She checked her watch. "About six thirty. I'll order room service again from their fantastic menu." She settled back in her seat and used the time it took to get back to the hotel to unwind.

She waved to the crew and Brit as she exited the carriage and headed to her room.

Erika expected to have a message from Peter waiting for her when she returned from the day's shoot, but she didn't find a note. She checked her cell phone for a text, but the screen was blank. It could be he was somewhere without service. She undressed, careful to hang her designer outfit on the rack in the bedroom, and then stepped into the shower. She leaned her forehead against the tiled wall while the warm water poured over her shoulders. What would she do if Peter couldn't find her more work? Who would she be? She remembered Brit's suggestion to contact a fellow model. She reaffirmed her decision to wait until she was back home with good cell reception and her computer. She shook off her distress and stepped out of the shower to dry off and dress.

She dismissed the idea that she was being obsessive and sent a text to Peter before she ordered dinner. She set the food and plates on the end table when they arrived, poured a glass of wine, and relaxed into a parlor chair to peruse a magazine and wait for Brit. Destiny had brought them back together as adults. She didn't know why or where it would take them, but it was a nice distraction from the uncertainty in the rest of her life right now.

Chapter Nineteen

It smells good in here. What's the dinner menu today?" Brittany hung her jacket on the back of a chair and walked directly to the food on the end table.

"Hello to you, too." Erika grinned and stood with her hands on her hips.

She looked adorable and sexy in her tight jeans and T-shirt, and she gave in to her desire to wrap her in her arms. The intensity of her feelings surprised and startled her. She took a step back and searched Erika's eyes for explanation. She couldn't locate words for whatever she was feeling. Maybe she didn't need any. Erika blinked but didn't move. It made her wonder if she'd felt whatever had passed between them, too. She spoke and the spell was broken. "Hello." It sounded like a gurgle.

"The dinner of the day is veal cutlets. I suppose we should eat while it's still warm." Erika squeezed her hands then began loading food onto the plates.

Dinner conversation was sparse as they concentrated on the meal. "They sure have good food here." Brittany sat back in her chair and sipped from a water bottle.

"They do. I've eaten all over the world, and the cuisine here is as good as anywhere I've been." Erika finished the last of the food on her plate and set it on the table.

"No word on more work yet?" Brittany hesitated to ask, but she hoped to hear Erika would be on the island longer.

"Nothing from Peter yet. I sent him a text earlier. I'm cautiously optimistic." Erika shrugged.

"I don't know a thing about what you do other than what I've seen since you've been here, but you're so good at it I wondered if you could just go directly to the magazines yourself?"

"There are freelance models out there, especially since there's the internet, which makes searching for work fairly easy. But I've been with Peter and my agency since I started modeling, and the one big thing I can't change is that I'm thirty-eight. The competition is fierce, and as Peter keeps telling me, 'young and fresh' is what sells. So, I'm not sure what I'm going to do."

Brittany remained quiet, unsure what to say and certain she had nothing to offer. She hoped Erika would decide to stay longer on the island to see if they could rekindle their friendship, but she supposed that wouldn't happen. Where would it leave her was another unanswered question.

"Oh, I checked tomorrow's menu. Baked swordfish. You interested?" Erika rose and moved their empty plates aside.

"Sounds great. Would you be up for a picnic? It's supposed to be a warm evening, and I know a perfect spot by the water where we can spread out a blanket." Brittany held her breath while she waited for an answer.

"It's a date." Erika flashed a smile.

Brittany settled on one end of the couch and took a drink of water. "Tell me about New York City."

"Well." Erika poured herself a glass of wine and relaxed next to her. "There's always something to do. Broadway plays and movies and plenty of shopping." Erika grinned. "I do love shopping." She sipped her wine. "There are skyscrapers and smaller, older buildings, and lots of traffic. Most of it is taxis. Not too many people own cars there. I can't imagine myself trying to navigate through the city. There's a great rail system that people use to get around, too. My apartment, condo really, is on the tenth floor with a spectacular view." Erika shifted so their arms touched.

"It sounds very different from here, that's for sure. The biggest city I've been to is Detroit. They have tall buildings and lots of traffic, too." She considered her quiet, serene life, so different from Erika's globetrotting and busy city existence. A part of her thought it might be fun to visit, but living there sounded overwhelming.

"I've lived there most of my adult life, so I'm used to the hustle and bustle. And it's where the work is." Erika stood and stretched.

Brittany tossed her empty water bottle in the bin. "I better head home. Thanks for dinner, again. I'll see you tomorrow."

Brittany mulled over Erika's words regarding a date as she walked home. Were they dating? She had no frame of reference since she'd never dated anyone before. She'd gone out to dinner with her friend Barb, and a couple of times with Joanne from the burn unit, but she hadn't been compelled to kiss them. The feelings it evoked threw her off balance, but she knew she enjoyed being with Erika. Even so, she'd have to decide soon if it was a good idea to spend so much time together, since she'd be leaving to go back to her big city life.

She unlocked her door and stepped into her apartment. Her motion-sensing nightlight flashed on as she entered, and she smiled at the memory of her parents' housewarming gift. They hadn't wanted her to walk into an empty, dark apartment. It reminded her once again that she needed to plan a visit. She missed her parents and looked forward to seeing them, but the magazine photos were almost finished. Even though they'd extended the schedule for three extra days, it meant her time with Erika was limited, and taking a day away from the island seemed like a way to miss precious time. She pushed away images of standing on the dock to wave good-bye as Erika returned to her home in New York. She got ready for bed, eager for dreams of Erika's sweet kisses.

Brittany woke at her usual time despite not setting her alarm. She set her coffee to brew, then showered and dressed. Erika's group didn't need her until late morning, so she planned to walk toward town where she could get good cell phone reception and call her parents. It wouldn't be the same as a visit, but it would be better than nothing. She took her coffee outside to her small patio and sat to watch the birds for a few minutes. She considered how much she wanted to tell her parents about Erika. They might've seen the newscast about her being on Mackinac Island, and she mentally rehearsed what she'd tell them about their reunion after so many years. She knew her mother would worry. She was aware of the heartache after the high school torment, more so than her father. Her warm hugs and whispered prayers at the time were a huge consolation for her wounded soul.

She went inside and rinsed her coffee cup before heading toward town to make her call. A few early risers walked their dogs or were out for a morning jog, and she found the spot she was looking for. Her mother answered on the second ring.

"Good morning."

"Hi, Mom." Brittany relaxed at the sound of her voice. "How're you and Dad doing?"

"Your dad's arthritis is getting worse, but we're managing. Is everything okay?"

"Yeah, I'm fine and things are good here on the island. I've missed you but wasn't sure when I'd be able to visit, so I called. Have you seen anything on the news about Mackinac Island?"

"We did. Erika James is there posing for a magazine. Have you seen her?"

"I have. In fact, I've been assigned as her carriage driver, so I've been transporting her and her crew to their photo shoots." Brittany didn't feel the need to tell her mom about all the kissing she and Erika had been doing.

"Has it been hard for you, dear? I remember what Amy did to you." Her mother sounded hesitant, as if she was afraid to ask.

Brittany sighed, glad to be able to share her feelings with her mom. "It was at first, but we talked, and she apologized, and I believe she's genuinely sorry."

Her mother was quiet for a long moment. "I'm glad she apologized. Did she…I mean…why do you believe her?"

Brittany appreciated her mother's concern and her attempt to protect her. "We're adults now, Mom, and I can see the young Amy, the Amy I knew as a friend, in her. She was pretty broken at the time, and she did what teenagers do. It wasn't right, but at least she's sorry for it now." Why did it sound like she was making excuses? It was true, wasn't it?

"You know best. Just be careful, dear. I don't want to see you hurt again."

"I promise I'll be careful. Give Dad a hug for me. I'm hoping to make it for a visit soon. I think Erika's magazine shoot will be over shortly." Brittany disconnected the call and smiled. She could always count on her mother's support. Truth was, she realized her mother had cause to worry. Erika was no longer a teenager driven by her need to fit in, but she was a world famous model driven by image and the need to look perfect. She could be sent halfway around the world when she left Mackinac Island, and Brittany might get a few phone calls or texts once in a while. She needed to protect herself and keep her budding feelings for Erika under control. She took a deep breath for resolve and headed home for breakfast before going to work.

❖

Brittany hitched the horses to the carriage and parked to wait for Erika and the crew. Her thoughts strayed to her evening with Erika and the intensity of the feelings it had generated. She greeted the group as they boarded a few minutes later but didn't see Erika. She was about to ask about her when Peter exited the hotel with Erika close behind. He shook his head as he walked away from her, but what bothered her was Erika's obvious agitation. She looked near tears as she approached the carriage. Brittany bristled. Peter had done or said something to upset her, but she held herself back from intervening. It wasn't her place. "Ready to head out?" she asked.

"We're ready." The photographer spoke from the seat next to Erika, who not only didn't say anything, but didn't even look at her.

She steered the horses up a hill toward the destination of the day but kept an eye on Erika as they got closer. Her transformation from upset to smiling and engaged with the camera showed her professionalism. How much effort did it take her to bury her feelings for the sake of work? And at what cost? She told herself she needn't worry about Erika. She'd been a professional her whole life. She could take care of herself. Brittany needed to worry about protecting her own feelings.

Chapter Twenty

The hot water swirled around her, and Erika leaned her head back against the side of the hot tub. She closed her eyes and tried to settle her nerves before she met Brit for dinner. She had decisions to make, and she couldn't let her growing feelings for Brit factor into them. She'd be leaving the island soon, and whatever was happening between them would have to be put on hold. She had to go where the work was. Back to New York. She processed the information Peter had given her as she scissored her legs underwater.

Unless this park thing came through, there were no magazines waiting in line for her or even new designers eager for her to showcase their creations. The only thing waiting for her in New York was her condominium filled with stuff. Stuff she'd collected from traveling the world. She turned over, held the side of the tub, and kicked her feet. She still had time to accept *Naturalé*'s offer, and Peter had pushed her to agree to it. She'd been adamant from the beginning, when she first signed with the agency, that she would absolutely not do nude scenes. She felt it to be sleazy and unprofessional. She was good enough to be a respected model sought after by top fashion designers.

The few models she'd heard about who had taken their clothes off were never taken seriously by top magazines again. He advised her it was her only option, but she couldn't allow herself to believe it. She was nothing if she wasn't modeling. It was all she knew. What was she if people didn't recognize her face, if she just blended into the mass of nobodies? She squelched the fear bubbling in her chest threatening to choke her. She'd figure out something. She had to. She exited the hot tub and wrapped herself in one of the hotel's plush towels before going to her room.

She dressed and checked herself in the mirror several times before going to order their meal. She picked up the swordfish and decided to add bread pudding to her order. She took the food to her room to wait for Brit. She pulled out two bottles of water from the wet bar and a bottle of white wine, just in case. By the time Brit arrived a short time later, she had everything organized. "Hey there. You look beautiful." Brit kissed her softly, grinned, and looked at the food. "That's a lot of food. I brought this." Brit held out a large insulated bag. "We'll pack it in here and set the blanket on top." She held out the bag toward her as if it were a prize.

Erika packed their dinner in the bag and took Brit's hand. "Thank you. Let's go eat." She followed Brit along a path to an open area among the trees with an idyllic view of the water.

"Here it is." Brit spread the blanket on the ground. "We'll be able to see the sunset from here, too, if you want to stay long enough." She sat and reached out her hand.

Erika set the bag on the blanket next to her, took her hand, and sat. A warm breeze floated across the water, rustled her hair, and brought a welcomed sense of peace. "This is a lovely place." She leaned back on her hands, stretched out her legs, and watched the late day sun sparkle on the water.

Brit retrieved the food from the bag, filled a plate, and handed it to her. "Wine or water?" she asked.

"Whatever you're having." She set the plate on her lap and took a forkful of fish. Brit surprised her when she poured two glasses of wine and handed her one. It was the first time she had seen Brit drink alcohol. There were probably many more things she didn't know about her and she hoped she had time to learn more.

"I come to this place whenever I need to unwind. I feel safe here." Brit looked far away for a moment, and then turned toward her. "I'm glad you like it. I've never brought anyone here before." She took a sip of wine and picked up her plate. "You're spoiling me with this food."

Erika smiled. She liked being the one to spoil Brit. Her fears of the future didn't go away when she was with her, but they felt more manageable somehow. She picked up her plate and finished eating, determined to enjoy the tranquility of the moment. "Was everything okay today? You looked upset with Peter earlier." Brit sipped water and shifted to sit next to her. Their legs touched.

Erika refilled her wine glass and rested against Brit's side. She snuggled closer when Brit put her arm around her. "He told me he hasn't been able to find any work for me. All the magazines want younger models." She sipped her wine and watched golden streaks traverse the blue sky as the sun sank toward the horizon. "I've been offered a spread in another magazine, though." She hesitated, unsure if she wanted to disclose she was willing to do a nude spread.

"Yeah? Great. Is it here in Michigan?" Brit pulled her closer.

"No, it's in New York. It's for *Naturalé Mag*. It's the only offer I've got." She tensed and waited for Brit's response.

Brit moved away and turned to face her but held her hands in hers. "You don't have to do it, Erika. You're beautiful and intelligent and in great shape. You can do whatever you want to."

"I'm aging out of my profession, Brit. The cameras want young and beautiful. I'm tired of trying to keep up, but I'm also not willing to let go. Peter's doing his best to find me something, but every time he thinks he's got an offer, they cancel when they find someone younger." She sighed deeply and finished her wine.

"It's your decision, but I hope you'll reconsider. You told me you were a rich fashion model. It sounds like you don't need the money. Why would you compromise yourself? I guess I should shut up. You're the one who knows about this stuff. I only know what I've overheard from some men ogling the nudes in their magazines. It didn't sound very respectful." Brit refilled both their glasses with wine.

"I decided when I first started modeling that I never wanted to pose nude. It just feels wrong and unnecessary. I've done spreads wearing only a bikini showcasing my fit, toned body, but they were in reputable fashion magazines. Not one with salacious intentions. Just the name of the magazine, *Naturalé Mag,* is disturbing. What a reader imagines my body looks like underneath a beautiful designer outfit is up to them, but displaying myself naked just feels desperate. Modeling is all I know. It's all I am. What am I going to do if I'm not modeling?" She finished her wine in two gulps.

"What about the magazine here now? Didn't you tell me they want you for a bunch of parks photos?" Brit looked optimistic as she rubbed her arms.

"Peter told me they canceled it and extended the time here by three days instead. There's nothing out there for me." She stood and began to pace.

"Hey." Brit stood, pulled her into her arms, and turned her toward the water. "Another beautiful event of Nature."

She leaned back into Brit's embrace and watched the sun descend, inch by inch, below the horizon, as if sinking into the water to extinguish itself for the night. The sky flared with flames of orange and yellow light before dimming to a soft glow. "Gorgeous. Thank you." She turned in Brit's arms, framed her face with her hands, and kissed her. There might not be any answers, but for now, she could be content being right here.

CHAPTER TWENTY-ONE

Brittany lay still and listened to the country song playing on her radio. She had two hours until she needed to report to the stables. She turned to her side and lost herself in the music for a few minutes enjoying the melody and lyrics. She liked starting her day with a song she could silently hum throughout the day when she felt stressed. She took a shower before dressing and brewing her coffee. Her worry over Erika's future reminded her their time together would end in a few days.

She hoped she'd turn down the offer for nude photos. Years ago, they only featured nude pictures in magazines, but these days, they'd be all over the internet forever. Maybe it was her own distaste for feeling exposed, vulnerable, which bothered her. She cringed when she thought of Erika uncovered and defenseless, displayed for all voyeurs, forever. She shook off the disturbing feelings and finished breakfast before she headed to ready the carriage for the day.

She began wiping down the carriage as soon as she arrived. "Good morning, George," she said.

"Morning. Where you headed today?" he asked.

"We're going back to Mission Point. They want some shots of whatever's blooming this month." She finished her cleaning and polishing and tossed the used rags into a bin. "I'll see you later."

"Have fun." George waved as he walked away.

Erika and the photographer were waiting outside when Brittany arrived with the carriage. "Good morning. Need any help boarding?"

She asked because it was part of her job, but they'd been climbing in and out of the carriage easily since they arrived without her help.

"No. We're good," the photographer answered.

Brittany watched them settle into the seat and pressed the horses forward. "You may remember the information I gave you about Mission Point before, but today you'll see the sculpted gardens up close. They're quite impressive when everything is in bloom." She concentrated on watching the horses plod along the route. Erika had smiled at her when their eyes met, but she remained silent on the trip.

"There are some nice shops there, too." Brittany realized she was talking to herself when she glanced at Erika, who was leaning back with her eyes closed. The photographer was fiddling with her camera, paying no attention to anything around her, and the rest of the crew gazed back and forth from one side to the other. She continued to steer the horses in silence until they neared their destination. "We'll be arriving at the foot of the eighteen acres of grounds in a few minutes. Do you want me to park along here or go farther?"

The photographer looked up from her camera and bent to inspect the area. "This is good. Thanks." She jumped off the carriage and called to Erika to follow her.

Erika blinked a couple of times and tipped her head side to side. "I guess I'm on." She winked and stepped off the carriage to follow the camera. She looked awake and ready for anything.

Brittany watched Erika work until they moved beyond her field of vision. She allowed her mind to wander to their time watching the sunset over the water. She'd relaxed in her arms, making her feel as if she was special.

❖

Brittany parked the carriage and took care of the horses before heading home to change. Erika had whispered in her ear on their way back, "Pork Tenderloin and caramel cheesecake. Six p.m." She wouldn't have cared if they had crackers and cheese. She just wanted to spend time with her for however long she was available. She hurried along the path trying to think of something to take so she wouldn't show up empty-handed. She chuckled. Erika was a rich supermodel staying at the Grand Hotel. What could she possibly need she couldn't just order? As quickly as the thought materialized, she knew. She took a small detour along the way.

She showered quickly and put on her newest pair of black jeans and a dark blue polo shirt. She'd been told it made her eyes stand out, so she guessed she looked nice in it. She took a light jacket in case they did more moon or sunset watching, and then carefully wrapped Erika's special gift.

Brittany knocked on Erika's door at exactly six o'clock, and Erika answered on the first knock. She held the present behind her, looking forward to the surprise. "Hi there," she said, unable to suppress her grin. Erika looked exquisite in a flowing black cotton blouse and white jeans.

"Come on in." She pulled her into the room, but before she could wrap her arms around her, Brittany handed her the gift.

"Oh my, God. Pussy willows! Thank you, Brit. Where did you get them?" She retrieved a glass from the bar, filled it with water, and put the branches in it.

"I grew them. It's a small hobby of mine. I tend a few plants and trees, and I remember how much we liked them as kids. They were our 'baby rabbit's feet,' remember?"

"I do. What a thoughtful gift." She stroked one of the fuzzy catkins slowly and smiled. "Many good luck charms on one branch." She counted slowly, caressing each bud. "This one's worth six days of good luck. Thank you." Erika looked far away for a second, then turned and kissed her thoroughly. She pushed her against the door and pressed her body against hers. Erika ran her tongue over her upper lip and groaned when she pulled her closer. As quickly as Erika had started the kiss, she ended it. She leaned back but kept her hands on her hips. "Sorry. I couldn't resist."

Brit grinned. "I don't see any reason for you to apologize." She stroked her face lightly. "You ready to eat?" Brit went to the food and filled both plates. She needed to settle herself after the unexpected kiss, and she was hungry. She held the plates out in front of her. "Shall we eat?"

They sat in the parlor chairs to eat. "Thanks again for the great meal. I think I inhaled it tonight. I'm totally spoiled."

"I didn't take my time with mine, either. I'm enjoying having you to share it. I travel the world and meet people everywhere I go, but mostly eat alone, or with Peter. But it's usually a business meeting meal." Sadness passed over Erika's face as she spoke but disappeared quickly. She covered a yawn. "I'm sorry. I can't believe how tired I am today."

Brittany took her hand and squeezed gently, wondering how often she had to suppress her feelings and how much energy it took. "Let's finish our cheesecake." She cut a piece for each of them and settled on the couch. Erika leaned against her, and she watched her eyes flutter closed. She rose and gently positioned Erika's head on an armrest. She kissed her on the forehead before quietly leaving. Brittany took the long route home, needing to clear her head. She'd enjoyed Erika's reaction to her gift of pussy willows. It solidified her belief her Amy, her friend, was still alive inside her. She leaned against a tree to watch the late day sun sparkle off the water. She never tired of the view from anywhere on the island, and Erika acted like she enjoyed their times doing it together. But then, Erika had enjoyed views in France, Italy, New York, and other places in the world she'd never see. How long would it take before boredom settled in? How long before Erika would race to pack and head back to her high-speed life in the city? Brittany pushed off the tree and headed home, wondering why she was contemplating any of it.

Chapter Twenty-two

Erika woke to the soft sound of the closing door. She rolled off the couch and stretched before getting some water and going to examine Brit's gift. She stroked the catkin on one of her pussy willow branches and allowed her thoughts to wander to the past. She never expected she'd see Brit again. Her guilt never left her throughout the years but neither did the memories of their kiss or their childhood friendship. She had to keep it all suppressed in order to function as Erika James, the adult, well put together, supermodel. She never allowed the knowledge of her bad behavior to be publicized, and it seemed a lifetime ago that it was so important to be admitted into the popular girl's clique. She'd left high school and never looked back. Never returned for reunions. Twenty-three years later, was she still striving for acceptance? Now from the fashion world, not a teenage gang. A gang who'd derived self-worth from picking on others. Did she need to forgive herself, too, now that Brit, the victim, was back in her life offering forgiveness, and maybe more? She got the sense Brit had feelings for her, and she admitted to herself her growing feelings for her, but it couldn't go anywhere. She'd be leaving for New York in a few days to try to continue her reign as a top fashion model. She'd make sure Peter found her something. She would find work, and her life would go on as it always had, full of parties and shoots and fashion. Why did the thought of it feel so hollow? Or lonely? She stretched out on the bed and fell asleep fully clothed.

❖

Erika woke before her alarm, glad she wasn't scheduled to wear the outfit she'd slept in. She tried to remember the last time she'd fallen asleep with her clothes on and couldn't, but she knew she didn't like it. Her feelings for Brit, and her uncertainty about her future, had her more unsettled than she wanted to admit. She took a shower and waited for Kathy to arrive. She didn't know where they were headed for the day, but she planned to question Peter about the future and make sure she got answers. She began to pace while she waited. She checked her phone for the time and a message. Kathy had never been late before. She made herself a cup of coffee and waited another fifteen minutes before sending a text to Peter. The signal on her phone indicated it was weak but the text had gone through. She decided to wait another fifteen minutes before going to look for him. She ordered an omelet from room service and made another cup of coffee while she waited. The text came within five minutes.

Sorry for the delay. Magazine feels it has what it needs. Looks like you're off the hook for more photos here. I'll get back to you with a timetable for leaving the island unless you want to make your own way back. P.

Erika knew what it meant when people said they felt numb after getting bad news. She tossed her phone on the bed and plopped into a parlor chair. She managed to accept delivery of her breakfast, but she'd lost her appetite. She started at the soft knock at the door and watched it open slowly.

"Erika?" Brit peeked around the open door and stepped into the room. She knelt on one knee in front of her. "Ben gave me the news this morning. Are you okay?"

Erika tipped her head back and shook it. "I'm not sure. I've had photo shoots end earlier than planned, but never without letting me know ahead of time. I don't know what to do. Why would they cancel a series of shoots without telling the featured model?" She forced back tears until she no longer could, and they spilled over her cheeks like a waterfall.

"I know this sounds weak, but it'll be okay." Brit wrapped her in her arms and held her until she stopped crying.

"I'm all right," Erika sniffled. "I need to blow my nose." She gently kissed Brit's hand before she stood. "Help yourself to the omelet while it's still warm."

She returned from the bathroom more composed. Brit had the omelet cut in half, a fork and cup of coffee on either side of the plate, and all of it set on the table between the parlor chairs. She couldn't help but smile as she took her hand and led her to a seat.

"Let's share." Brit sat in the other seat and handed her a fork.

"Thank you. I'm feeling a little better. I suppose it's not the end of the world. I'm worried that Peter won't be able to find me more work. That stress on top of this sent me over the edge. I can't figure out why the magazine didn't give me a head's up." She took a bite of her half of the omelet.

"So, they just canceled without warning?"

"Yes. Like I said, it's not unusual for a magazine to plan for more time than they need, or less sometimes, but the crew lets everyone know if they'll finish early. I just wish they'd mentioned it to me, or to Peter." She took another bite of food and sipped her coffee.

"Peter didn't even know?" Brit asked between bites.

"I texted him this morning when my hair and makeup artist was late, and I thought maybe she was ill. He replied the magazine was done and didn't need me anymore." She was paraphrasing, but it was how it seemed. She was no longer needed.

"Huh. Maybe he only found out when you did. I'm sorry it happened to you." Brit brushed the back of her fingers on her cheek. "You're a strong woman. You'll get through this."

Erika appreciated Brit's support and knew she was correct. She'd been in the business long enough to know that jobs came and went quickly. She just wished she knew what was coming next. She couldn't allow herself to believe her only option was the nudie magazine.

"I expect Peter to be here shortly, and I'll find out what's going on."

"I need to check in with Ben about my schedule. Will you be all right?" Brit finished her coffee and stood.

"I'll be fine. We'll meet later and compare notes." She smiled, realizing she believed her own words. She would be fine. For now, anyway. She poured herself a cup of coffee and sat to wait for Peter. She was finishing it when he arrived.

"Come in, Peter." Erika held the door open. She closed the door before continuing. "What's the deal? I can't believe the magazine didn't give us any indication it was pulling out early."

Peter stood at the window for a moment before turning to answer. "I didn't know either. This was a new magazine, so I'm thinking they didn't have any experience with big name models. I'll make sure they fulfill the payment part of the contract. You'll get paid for your time."

"Thanks, Peter, but what comes next?" She sat on the couch.

"I plan to head back to New York to try to line something up, but I wasn't lying when I told you there were no offers out there. I'm hoping if I show up in person, I'll find you something, but consider the *Naturalé*, Erika. They're willing to pay big for you."

Erika sighed. "I'll stay here until I hear from you, at least for a while. I know you'll do your best." She stood to see him to the door, hoping his best was good enough. If she went back to New York she might be able to do some networking. At least she could get in touch with a few models she knew. She hadn't planned on staying on the island, but as soon as she said it, she knew it was the right choice. She couldn't face her empty apartment, where the walls would close in on her with no work to go to.

Chapter Twenty-three

Morning," George called from inside the stables as Brittany walked by.

"Good morning. How're things?" Brittany stopped to find out if George knew anything about the magazine crew leaving.

"It's quiet here. I heard about the magazine quitting early. You okay with it?"

"I'm a little disappointed. It was kind of fun once I got used to it." She didn't need to share her fear of Erika leaving soon or their many kisses she'd miss.

"I'll be glad to have you back." George grinned.

"I'm going to check in with Ben now. I'll see you later."

"Come in, Brittany," Ben called. "Have a seat." He spent a few seconds staring at the computer screen before turning his attention to her. "The magazine crew will be leaving the island this afternoon on the three o'clock ferry. I'd like you to take them to the dock. You can go back to your usual routine tomorrow."

"No problem. Did they tell you why they're leaving early?"

"Nope. All I know is they'll be checking out of the hotel this afternoon." He turned his attention back to his computer.

Brittany walked back to her apartment, resisting the urge to check on Erika. She didn't want to interrupt her meeting with Peter. She detoured to an area with better cell phone reception and sent her a text. She wanted her to know she could count on her for support, but she also wanted to convince her to stay on the island for a while longer. She stopped at the market to pick up a few supplies since she hadn't shopped in a while, thanks to all the dinners with Erika.

She picked out a few items she knew Erika liked and hoped she could talk her into coming over for dinner. She made herself a tuna sandwich and pulled out her vacuum. She might as well put her time off to good use.

She checked her cell phone several times before she put it away, placed the potential dinner in the refrigerator, and went to dress for her trip to the ferry. She hoped against hope that Erika wouldn't be one of the ones leaving. Surely she'd have said something if she was going, right? Not that she really owed Brittany anything, but after the closeness they'd developed, she thought that maybe… She sighed and shook her head. There was only one way to find out.

Brittany waved to George as she pressed the horses toward the hotel. The group was waiting outside with their equipment stacked on large luggage carts. Brittany smiled at the photographer she'd seen with Erika, who smiled back but was more concerned with her kit than anything else. They boarded the coach and hotel employees loaded their baggage and gear. Erika wasn't with them.

They traveled slowly through town and toward the dock and the group pointed and smiled as they passed landmarks, probably enjoying the ride because they weren't working and could relax. Brittany drove the coach back to the stables after dropping her riders off at the ferry. She searched the hotel entrance and surrounding area for Erika to no avail, so she put the horses away for the night and headed home. Erika had to be around here somewhere. There was no way she could have left the island without Brittany seeing her. Still, the niggling uncertainty played with her mind.

She unlocked her door and jumped at Erika's voice behind her.

"May I come in?"

"You bet." Brittany held the door open and followed her inside, relief flooding her.

Erika settled on her couch, and Brittany liked seeing her there. "I picked up some nice stuffed chicken breasts today. Can you stay for dinner?"

"Sounds great." Erika stood and pulled her down next to her. "It'll give us time to talk."

"You look better than this morning."

"Thanks. I feel much better. I'm still unsure of my future in modeling, but Peter left for New York, and I believe he'll do whatever he can to find something for me."

"The magazine group is gone. I just dropped them off." Brittany slid closer to Erika.

"Yeah. Peter left on the two o'clock ferry."

Brittany asked the question she'd wanted to all day but feared the answer. "How much longer will you be staying?"

Erika turned and held her stare. "I'm not sure. I need to wait and see what Peter might find for me. But I talked to the Grand Hotel and they'll let me extend my stay for two more weeks. I guess I lucked out that they weren't booked for the whole summer yet, but I'll have to change suites. Oh, and I may need to go clothes shopping. The magazine group took all the clothes I wore for the photos. It wasn't in my contract to keep them."

Brittany grinned. "No problem, Ms. James. We'll go into St. Ignace or Mackinaw City and find you some nice non-designer outfits, right off the rack. I'll get the chicken started. Help yourself to anything. I have water in the fridge and wine in the cupboard." She finished the meal preparations and settled on the couch next to Erika.

"Thanks for the invitation. I'm feeling off kilter, so it's nice to look forward to a home cooked meal and company." Erika sipped her water and propped her feet up on the coffee table.

"I'm happy to have you here. I can only imagine how you're feeling."

"I'll be hounding Peter daily for sure, but it'll be nice to spend a little more time with you."

"That sounds perfect. We can plan a day off the island for some shopping, and I'm allowed to take a few days off as long as there are people available to cover for me. I think I better check on dinner."

"I can help."

Brittany removed the chicken from the oven while Erika set the small kitchen table. She paused and attempted to define the feelings the domestic scene elicited. Contentment? The heat from the oven combined with the scent of the baked food. The microwave ping indicated the green beans were finished steaming. It could've been any normal day for her preparing an evening meal, but Erika James, the famous model, was in her kitchen setting the table. She set the roaster on the stovetop and turned to watch Erika retrieve two water glasses from the cupboard. It wasn't Erika posing for the camera, it was Erika here with her because she wanted to be.

Erika caught her staring. "What? Am I doing something wrong?" She rested her fist on her canted hip and grinned.

"Not at all. I'm just glad you're here. Oh, I almost forgot the wine. I have a bottle of Michigan's ice wine."

"It sounds different."

"I'm not a big drinker, but I like this wine. It's a lucky year for it, too. The grapes are picked frozen, so the growers depend on an early freeze in December or January. It's a popular Michigan wine." She opened a bottle and set it on the table happy to be able to offer something new to someone who'd tried just about everything.

They ate in comfortable silence for a few minutes. Erika spoke first. "This chicken is delicious." She took a sip of wine. "And so is this wine."

"Glad you like it."

"How're your parents doing?" Erika asked.

"They're managing. My dad has bad arthritis, so he no longer works. Mom's doing all right. They keep busy with their garden." She wasn't about to tell Erika about her financial support of her parents. They hadn't been able to work in years, and she helped as much as she could. But that was private, and a little too intimate. "How're yours?"

Erika sighed. "They're good. I talked to my mom last month. They retired and moved to a ranch I bought them in Arizona a few years ago to get away from the snow."

"Sometimes, I like the idea of no snow. Especially on the island in January and February, although the island is beautiful in the winter. It's like a fairyland covered in a white blanket. Do you get to visit your parents often?"

"I haven't been able to for a while, but I suppose I will if Pete can't come through with something for me." Erika took a drink of wine. How would she tell them?

"Here's to Pete finding you work." Brittany held up her glass for a toast.

They clinked glasses and sipped their wine. "Shall we sit on the couch?" Erika asked.

Erika carried their plates to the sink and Brittany refilled their wine glasses. They sat, as if by design, with their feet on the coffee table and their thighs touching. Neither moved away and Brittany spoke first. "I'm glad you came by today. I was worried about you."

"I was kind of worried about me, too. It really threw me to be dropped so suddenly. Peter thinks it was because this is a new magazine and they didn't have enough experience to know how to handle it. Anyway, they claim to have what they need for their issue, and Pete will make sure I'm paid for what they contracted. I suppose it could be their inexperience that led them to cancel their planned American Parks series. It would have been fun, I think." Erika took a deep breath and expelled it.

"Learning about modeling and photo shoots the last two weeks has been really interesting. Do you have a favorite place you've been to for a shoot?"

"I think I always enjoyed each place in its own way, especially the first time I go there. Once we had a series for a designer set in Egypt. We were there for what seemed like forever. It was hot and dry and sand was everywhere. I coughed for days after we were finished. I hope I don't ever have to go back there."

Brittany chuckled at the face Erika made. "I've read about deserts, and I don't think I'd like it much either. Hopefully, Peter will find you something here in the United States."

Erika set her glass on the end table and cupped her face in her hands. "I may be upset about my future, but I'd be more upset if I lost you after finding you again." Then she kissed her.

Chapter Twenty-four

Erika arrived back at the hotel after dark. She had two more days in the same suite before she had to move. She didn't mind. It would be nice to see more of the hotel. She'd miss riding around the island with Brit, but they could have dinner together and do things on her day off. She realized she had no idea when Brit had days off. She'd figure it out tomorrow. She didn't have anything else to do with her time now. She squeezed back tears. She believed Peter would do his best, and she crossed her fingers it would be good enough. If she didn't hear from him soon, she'd try calling her friend and fellow model Pat in New York. She trod through the entryway and through the hall to her room. The day she'd left New York for this verdant island, she'd been working nonstop, racing against time to outrun her biological clock.

Now, as she faced the very real possibility of the end of her career as she knew it, she admitted to being tired of the constant pressure to maintain the illusion of perfection. But tired was too weak a word, she decided, as she changed into her nightshirt. Weary was closer. Exhausted, drained, disillusioned. Those were nearer to her condition as the end loomed. And surely that meant something. Maybe it was time to move on, to find something that made her happy. She wished she had an idea what that might be. A lifetime of working to be the best model in the world had brought fame and a lot of money, but why did she feel that happiness had eluded her? She crawled into bed and pulled the covers over her head.

Her conversation with Brit about their parents disquieted her. She'd set hers up with an enormous bank account and bought them their sprawling ranch in Arizona. She sensed her motives for such generosity went beyond gratitude for their support. Tightness in her chest told her it was something more visceral. She craved their approval, the way she always had. She lived with a constant whispering voice inside her asking what they would think or say about her decisions. The small voice bellowed when she contemplated accepting *Naturalé's* offer. She drifted into sleep, hoping dreams of Brit's sweet kiss before she left her apartment would sooth the raging uncertainty in her gut.

Erika sat back on one of her parlor chairs and rested her bare feet on the other. She held her coffee cup in both hands and watched seagulls soar over the water. Their shadows, cast by the morning sun above, traveled over the swell of the waves like fish following their path. She couldn't remember when she'd had time to sit without waiting for Kathy or another stylist to arrive and ready her for work. It unsettled her yet freed her mind to wander, and as they always did lately, her thoughts turned to Brit. She'd have to get her work schedule so they could make plans for their shopping adventure. She finished her coffee and rose to take a shower and review her wardrobe.

She smiled at her two pair of designer jeans. She had one pair of shorts and several T-shirts, a bathing suit, and her collection of Victoria's Secret underwear. She probably wouldn't need anything else, really, but she looked forward to spending the day shopping with Brit anyway. She made a mental note to let Peter know she'd like the clothes she wore for the photos next time to be included in her contract. She shuddered when she remembered that next time might be an unclothed event. She chose her blue denim jeans for the day and slipped on a T-shirt. Maybe she'd pick up a Mackinac Island T-shirt in town. She grabbed a sweater and went to look for Brit.

The stables were quiet when she peeked in the door. A gate squeaked so she entered and waited. George appeared from around the corner and smiled. "Hey there. I didn't expect to see you here, Ms. James. Everything okay?"

"Everything's fine." She coughed to expel the lie. "Is Brittany working today?"

"She is. She should be back any minute."

Erika turned to leave until the hotel's omnibus rolled up the hill with Brit seated on the front bench. She raised her hand to wave but quickly lowered it, unsure if it was allowed to distract the driver. Her question was answered when Brit looked at her and smiled. She watched her guide the two draft horses to the unloading area and climb off the coach.

"Good morning. This is a nice surprise," Brit said.

"Good morning. I came looking for you, and George told me you'd be back soon." Erika stood grinning, feeling a little silly at being so glad Brit was there. Brit looked sexy in her starched white shirt and black vest, coat, and top hat. She nearly gave in to her desire to kiss her in the middle of the street. "Will you be free for dinner later?"

"I'll be free as soon as I take care of the horses." She leaned toward her but stopped, looking confused before she backed away slightly. "You can watch if you promise to stay at a safe distance."

Ericka didn't try to hide her excitement. "I'd love to. I understand there're probably insurance restrictions." She followed close behind Brit, anxious to get closer to the horses.

"Hey, George," Brit said. "I'm showing Erika how we settle the horses in the stables."

George waved his assent and grasped the lead of one of the horses while Brit gripped the other. Erika watched as they led the horses into their stalls, amazed at how quietly, almost eagerly the huge horses entered them. She could tell they'd done it many times. "Do they ever give you any trouble going in?"

"Not usually. They know the routine and they know where their food is. They usually go directly to the grain bucket, and as long as we're consistent with them, they're content." Brit stroked the horse's neck when she spoke.

"May I pet him?"

"Sure." Brit stepped aside to let her get close enough to run her hand along his back. His skin twitched under her touch and his short tail swung as if to brush away a fly.

She watched him grab a mouthful of hay from the bag hanging in the corner and chew for a minute before reaching for another. He shifted his weight from one foot to another, and she flinched and stepped back wondering how long it took Brit to get comfortable around these massive animals. They were quiet, non-judgmental hulks. They cared about gentle touches and voices, and nothing about appearances. So unlike the experience Brit had after her accident. It was no wonder she loved it here. She chuckled when she realized this big boy couldn't care less if a world famous fashion model was standing in his stall in fear of being crushed.

"Shall we go get some lunch?" Brit asked.

"Sounds good."

"All right if we stop by my place so I can change first?"

"Of course." Erika followed Brit along the same path they'd taken to the spot from which they'd watched the sunset. She paused to reflect on the memory of safety and caring in her arms. She added comforted and aroused when her warm body pressed against her back. She watched Brit stride in front of her as she followed her. She could be who she was with Brit, beneath the mask of Erika James. And it was enough. She'd try to show Brit how beautiful and valued she was beneath her scars of the past for as long as she was on the island. Her next thought felt like a slap in the face. She'd be leaving for New York as soon as Peter found her work, and Brit would be on her own again.

Chapter Twenty-five

Brittany unlocked her apartment door, aware of Erika close behind her. She fumbled with the doorknob. Her hand shook and butterflies fluttered in her belly. She stepped inside and tossed her keys on her end table. "Help yourself to anything you find in the fridge. I'll just be a minute." She turned to face Erika and the butterflies increased their tempo.

"Go change. I'll be fine."

Brittany disrobed quickly and hung her work clothes in her closet before heading to the bathroom to wash her face. She gently patted her scars dry and applied sunscreen and light makeup before slipping on her jeans and a T-shirt. She hesitated in front of the mirror on her way out. Her skin discoloration and scars would never disappear, and Erika had to see it. What did she really think?

"Ready?" Brittany asked, pushing away the unwelcome thoughts.

"Sure. Where're we going?"

Brittany hadn't thought about where they'd go. "We could go to the Gate House or walk downtown."

"Let's walk downtown and see what goodies we find. Then we can stop at the Gate House to eat."

"Sounds great." Erika pulled her closer. "I'd like to find a T-shirt."

Brit stepped back and held out her hand. "Let's go look at T-shirts."

Erika grabbed her hand and kissed her quickly before turning toward the door.

Brittany enjoyed walking with Erika instead of just being her chauffeur. She wanted to hold her hand as they walked into town but reminded herself there were cameras everywhere these days. She contemplated her options when Erika surprised her and took her hand.

She interlaced her fingers. "Is this okay?"

"It's more than okay. It's wonderful." If Erika didn't mind being seen with her, she could deal with a few stares.

"Let's go in here." Erika pulled her into one of the stores.

Brit shared a grin with the cashier as they watched Erika flip through T-shirt after T-shirt. She held one up against her and looked their way. They nodded in unison and she added it to her growing pile on the end of the table. She grabbed two more and held them up for inspection. Brittany pointed to the one in her left hand and the cashier to the one in her right, so Erika put them both on her pile. She picked up several more and hesitated before she turned and carried her treasures to the checkout counter.

"Will that be all?" the cashier asked.

"Yes, thank you." Erika replied and handed over her credit card.

Brittany watched and tried to look serious when Erika joined her. "Shall we try a few more stores before they close?"

Erika looked sheepish when she answered. "No. Seven Mackinac Island T-shirts are probably enough." She laughed and Brit laughed with her. "They're not all for me." She pulled one shirt out of her bag. "Here. This one's for you." She held it up against her. "It's your color. And"—she pulled another matching style but different color shirt out and held it up—"it matches mine."

Brittany blinked back tears as she accepted the gift. This T-shirt was special because Erika had thought of her when she bought it, and because it matched one of hers. It felt weirdly romantic, and it was a gesture no one had ever made before. "Thank you." She clutched it to her chest.

"Shall we wear them to dinner? It's casual at the Gate House, isn't it?"

"Yes, it is." Brittany held Erika's hand all the way back to her apartment.

They changed quickly and headed to the restaurant. It was more crowded than Brittany had seen it lately, even for a weekday, but they only had to wait for a few minutes before they were seated.

"This is comfortable, and I imagine the food's good." Erika turned in her chair and perused the room. "It has a bar, too."

"Yeah. You can get a percentage off your bill if you're staying at the Grand Hotel, also." Brittany realized Erika wouldn't care about that as soon as she said it. It was going to take her a while to get used to being with someone rich. That thought surprised her. Erika would be leaving for New York eventually. Maybe soon. Then what?

"Cool." She looked at the menu and decided. "The roasted chicken salad sounds great. And, since I get the discount, I'm buying."

Brittany didn't argue. She'd spent more on food since Erika had been there than she had in the entire month prior. They ordered their meals and Erika had a glass of wine.

As always, their conversation flowed easily. Brittany talked about some of the odd hotel guests she'd met over the years, and Erika fascinated her with tales of the foreign countries she'd been to. Brittany looked at her watch.

"I think Sadie's Ice Cream parlor is still open. Would you like to stop in or save it for another day?"

"Let's do it tomorrow."

"Sounds good. Let's go relax for a while." Brittany took her hand and led the way back to her apartment.

They settled on Brittany's couch to watch the late evening news. She wrestled with her desire to ask Erika to stay overnight, but she had only one bed. She could offer to sleep on the couch, but she realized her desire to have Erika there was because she wanted to feel her next to her, and there was no way she was ready for where that might lead if they slept in the same bed. Erika stirred next to her and Brittany sat up and stretched.

"I guess I'll head back to the hotel. Sorry, I almost fell asleep," Erika said.

"Do you want me to walk you back?" Brittany stood and yawned.

"I'll be fine, but thanks." Erika reached for her hand and pulled her close. She cupped her face in her hands and pressed her lips against hers.

Brittany's body reacted before her mind registered what was happening. She pulled her against her and followed Erika's lead with her lips. She used the same pressure but parted her lips slightly. She whimpered and moved her hands to cradle Erika's head. The need to feel her everywhere overwhelmed her senses. She needed something she couldn't define, but her body throbbed, and she felt herself grow wet. It was a new feeling, and she liked it. She drew away but held on to Erika's waist. They were both breathing hard.

"I think I better go now." Erika gave her a peck on the lips and left, giving her a quick, sweet smile before closing the door behind her.

Brittany dropped back onto the couch. She was aroused and unsure what to do about it. She wanted Erika's touch, not her own. Flashbacks of her pinned to Erika's door and the feel of her body against hers triggered another flood of wetness. The new feelings and emotions she'd begun to experience since Erika had returned to her life began and ended with her. What would she do if Erika left? When. When Erika left. She forced aside her fears and refused to think of the future, as if she had some control over it. She plodded to the bathroom to wash her face and brush her teeth before bed.

CHAPTER TWENTY-SIX

Erika sat back in her chair, people watching in the expansive dining area. She thanked the server when he refilled her coffee cup and cleared away her breakfast dishes. She watched a couple finish their meal and lean closer to gaze into each other's eyes. She drank her coffee and switched her attention to a lone woman seated against the wall. Was she alone, or waiting for someone? A formally dressed man and woman stood to leave. Were they vacationing and making a stop for breakfast before heading to an opera? She chuckled at her musings. It had been many years since she'd had time to just sit and ponder nothing. She thought of it as wasting time. Her mother's words echoed in her mind.

Never waste your time. You must remember people will be watching you. You have to always smile, wear your makeup, and present yourself with grace and elegance. What would people think if you looked sloppy or lazy?

She shook her head to dislodge the unwelcome reminder of life. She replaced it with gratitude for her parents' concern and support. She knew her mother's words came from a place of love and worry for her future, but she didn't want to think about her future now. Her life's focus had been perfection. To be the best, the prettiest, the top model in the world and it seemed as if it were crashing down around her. She checked her watch, paid her bill, and went to her room to wait for Peter's call.

She made herself a cup of coffee and settled into a chair. Her thoughts turned to Brit and she decided to test her cell reception. She sent her a text telling her she was thinking of her and wanted to buy her dinner. She finished her coffee and began to worry. No word from Peter. She fantasized he was busy reviewing new contracts from magazines. She pulled out one of the magazines she'd picked up and reviewed the articles. She checked out the latest models and scowled at their youthful faces and figures. She tossed it aside and decided to go for a walk. Her cell phone pinged before she left the room. She picked up her phone, and read the text. *Dinner later sounds great. I get off work at three. Let's make it about six.* She smiled, remembering their previous evening and heated kiss. She sensed Brit's innocence and remembered her words regarding their first kiss. The last thing she wanted to do was take advantage of her and she vowed to keep her hands, and her lips, to herself that night. She checked for a call from Peter before she slid her cell phone into her back pocket and left her room.

She started to head toward town, but changed her mind and proceeded uphill toward the fort. At least she hoped it was the way to the fort. How long had it been since she needed to find her own way anywhere? She picked up her pace and realized the time off her workout schedule hadn't set her back too badly. She'd never been a runner, but she loved a brisk walk, and this beautiful island was a perfect place for one. She followed the road until she reached the fort, where she stopped and took a picture with her phone. She continued along the road enjoying the adventure on her own. She couldn't remember the last time she'd had time entirely to herself, especially out in public. The lack of fans had been disconcerting, but today, it was incredibly freeing.

She waved at a horse and rider who ambled past in the opposite direction and stopped to enjoy the view from atop a hill overlooking a wooded area. She took another picture and checked her watch. She never lost track of time. It was something she could never afford to do. She was required either to be posing for a shoot or preparing for one. She decided she rather liked this down time, but she told herself it was only temporary. Just a short vacation before her next job. She turned to head back to the hotel but continued past it once she got there in hopes of seeing Brit near the stables. She hiked to the back of the building and found George at a small picnic table having lunch. "Hi, George."

"Ms. James. Hello. What brings you out here?" He waved to the empty seat across from him. "I assumed you'd be heading back to New York by now."

"No. My agent's in New York trying to line something up for me, so I'm kind of waiting for him." Erika straddled the bench seat, unsure if she should stay and interrupt his lunch break.

"Ah. I hope you're enjoying your time here. I know it's done wonders for Brittany." He took a bite of his sandwich and a swallow of iced tea, but his gaze stayed on her, the little laugh lines around his eyes crinkling.

Erika had no idea what he meant and scrambled for a way to ask without sounding nosy. "She's been a great driver. I've enjoyed listening to her knowledge of the island."

George held her gaze for a time before speaking. "I remember when Brittany first started working at the stables. She was a shy, self-conscious kid, but with a heart of gold and a will the likes of which I'd never seen. We have a few stable hands working here, and I swear Brittany can outwork them all. I could tell she'd been hurt badly in her young life, but she refused to talk about it." He took another bite of his sandwich and remained quiet.

"What did you mean by it's done wonders for her?" Erika believed it was Brit's choice to tell George it was her that had hurt her, so she kept that to herself.

"I'm sure you noticed the scars on her face. Brittany was burned as a kid and spent time in a burn unit. She's self-conscious about her scars and avoids people when she can, so I try to take over the carriage driving duty. Since she's driven your group around, she's come out of her shell a bit. Yesterday and today, she volunteered to drive the omnibus to the dock. She used to avoid that as often as she could. I think seeing that you didn't make a big deal about her scars has helped heal her inside." George finished his sandwich and stood. "I better get back to work. Are you going to be around for the Lilac Festival?"

Erika had read the ads for one of the biggest events on the island. "It starts the seventh of June right?"

"Yeah. It's a lot of fun."

"I'll see what my agent has to say. Thanks, George." She hiked back to the hotel, hoping to hear from Peter soon.

Watching George eat his sandwich had reminded her she hadn't had lunch. She didn't want to have to talk to Peter in a room full of other diners, so she ordered a cup of soup and a salad from room service.

She finished her lunch and laid all the pamphlets she'd gotten from the hotel out on the bed. The Lilac Festival looked like fun, but June was a couple of weeks off. She hoped to be back in New York getting ready for photo shoots by then. Part of her hoped for that, anyway. The quieter part of her soul had enjoyed this morning's solitude and looked forward to a simple local festival where she wasn't the star of the show. She shook her head. That part needed to be shut down, at least until she was really ready to retire. And she wasn't. Not yet.

CHAPTER TWENTY-SEVEN

"Thanks, Barb. I feel a little silly, but I appreciate your help." Brittany had stopped at an area with good cell phone reception to call for a bit of emotional support.

"No problem. Just remember to protect your heart, my friend. You deserve honesty and respect. The love and the other *stuff* we discussed will come naturally, if it's meant to be. Just make sure it feels right. Never go along with something because you think you should. If she cares about you, she'll respect that."

"Okay. I think I'll be okay. I don't know what will happen or what I want to happen, but I know I want to kiss her again, so that will probably happen." She felt like a ten-year-old searching for words to convey her feelings.

"Take care and be careful. It might feel overwhelming, so remember, you have a right to slow things down if you need to."

Brittany disconnected the call and drew air deep into her lungs. Her friend Barb had experience she was willing to share. She helped Brittany define what she was feeling after Erika's kiss.

Brittany knew the mechanics of lesbian sex from the novels she'd read, and movies and TV were full of heterosexual sex. It was the intensity of the feelings when Erika kissed her or their bodies pressed together that she never could have imagined from any outside source. Experiencing it turned out to be so much more powerful than anything she'd ever known.

She pointed the horses toward the stables with a sense of courage. She might be inexperienced, but at least she'd confirmed that she was having a natural reaction to being close to Erika.

Brittany didn't see George when she arrived back at the hotel, so she parked the coach, unhitched the horses, and put them in their stalls by herself. She left him a note before leaving to let him know she was back and hurried home to shower and change. She carefully reapplied the makeup on her scars and examined her reflection. The pigment had changed and evened out over the years but the damage remained. Whether other people saw it as clearly as she did, she'd never know. Some days it was all she could see when she looked at herself. But Erika wouldn't have kissed a freak, right? She pushed aside her reservations, surprised at how easily she could, and dressed quickly.

She slowed her pace on her way back to Erika's room to give herself time to think. Maybe they needed to talk more about the past. She could tell her feelings for Erika were growing, and if they were going to spend more time together, she needed to make sure she kept her emotions in check. Barb's encouragement and gentle warning echoed in her mind. Did she need to protect her heart? Erika was waiting for Peter to find her more work, but he'd encouraged her to take the nude photos job. What if she left for New York and never looked back? What if she considered their reunion just a short stop along the expressway of her high-speed life? Her insecurity grew the closer she got to the hotel, and she took a series of deep, settling breaths before she knocked on the door.

Erika opened the door on the first knock. "Come on in."

She stepped aside and her warm smile chased away Brittany's reservations. "Did you think about where you wanted to eat?"

"I took the liberty of ordering the prime rib. Then I decided on hazelnut cake for dessert. It should be here in about fifteen minutes. Okay with you?"

"Sounds good to me." Brittany sat across from Erika in what she now considered her chair. "I'd like us to talk tonight, if it's okay with you."

"Sure." Erika turned to face her, looking concerned.

"I guess first of all, do you know how much longer you'll be here?" She tried not to fidget.

"That's a good question. I'm waiting to hear from Peter. I'd hoped it would be today, but he hasn't called yet. He's trying to get me work besides the *Naturalé* one I told you about. I guess I'm not sure how long I'll be here." She sighed. "I have this hotel suite for another week and a half, so I think I'll stay that long unless Peter finds a magazine that needs me right away."

"I guess that answers my question." She swallowed hard. Could she make the most of their time together and ignore the possible loss? What choice did she have? "I think Ben will let me have a few days off before the Memorial Day rush, so let's plan some excursions. I'll talk to him tomorrow. I'd love to take you to a place I visit off the island." Brittany decided not to obsess about how long Erika would be back in her life. One thing she'd learned in therapy was to take things a day at a time, and this situation was no different.

Their conversation was interrupted by the food delivery, and Brittany realized she was hungry now that the knot in her stomach had unraveled. There were still plenty of questions, but she wondered what the point of asking them was. Erika didn't have any real answers. She hoped she could count on Erika staying another week and a half and she'd see where things stood then. She'd protect her heart one day at a time.

Chapter Twenty-eight

Erika finished her coffee and watched the rain fall. Raindrops hit the window and created individual streams against the backdrop of the distant water. It was like a painting, beautiful and sad. She rose from her window seat to refill her coffee cup and check her watch. The rain might be affecting Brit's work schedule. They had plans to rent bikes that afternoon, but the longer the rain fell, the more likely she figured their plans would change.

She struggled to push aside her growing distress about Peter's lack of communication. He'd promised a call with information good or bad, but she hadn't heard a word from him since he'd left. She sent him texts and hoped they'd gone through. She considered flying back to New York to hunt him down but she was enjoying her time with Brit and when she did go back to work, she'd miss her more than she wanted to admit. She had to get back to work. Who would she be if she couldn't work? Another question unsettled her nearly as much. The thought of leaving Brittany behind made her ache inside. But what could they really have, beyond these few special weeks? She paced the length of the room a few times before she sat on the end of her bed. She closed her eyes and meditated for a few minutes to settle her angst. She concentrated on her breath and finally reached a place of calm when a knock at the door intruded on her serenity.

"Come on in, Brit." Erika called out from the bedroom. She wasn't expecting anyone other than Brit, so she took a moment to stretch and fully center herself before going into the other room. She smiled when she turned the corner.

Brit stood holding two bags in front of her. One from Ryba's fudge and the other from a pasty store. "Since it's so icky outside, we can have lunch here. Do you like pasties?"

She looked adorable in her jeans and new T-shirt, holding the bags up in front of her before setting them on the table. "I do. It sounds great." She gave in to her desire to kiss her, which happened every time they were together lately. She cupped her chin with one hand and slid her lips across hers, but didn't anticipate the intensity of her body's response when Brit pulled her close so the front of their bodies met. She stood two inches taller, but Brit had no trouble holding her up when her knees buckled.

"Are you, okay?" Brit sounded out of breath. "I'm sorry. Did I squeeze too hard?" She held her at arm's length.

"No, no. Not at all." She stroked her cheek to give herself a moment to collect herself. "I just wasn't expecting my reaction."

Brit grinned and looked pleased as she took her hands and kissed her knuckles. "I needed to feel you against me. It's an incredible feeling."

"I agree. Shall we eat while the food's warm?" She pulled the plastic silverware out of the bag and set the pasties on the table and tried to ignore her shaky hands. "It's been years since I had one of these. I don't even remember where it was." She retrieved two bottles of water and sat next to Brit.

"It was probably in England. The pasty is associated with the Cornish people in the United Kingdom."

"It was in England, now that you mention it. Where did you learn that?"

"I like to hang out in the library when I have time. I read it somewhere. So, did you like that I pulled you into me when we kissed?" Brit surprised her with her change of subject.

"Yes, I did. I liked it a lot, but it surprised me. I don't ever want to do anything that makes you uncomfortable, but I hope you'll do that again." She finished her pasty and sat back in her chair.

Brit opened the bag of fudge and handed her a piece before she took one. "Would you like to go to the carriage museum today instead of riding bikes? It's indoors, and I think it's a pretty cool place."

"Let's do it." She looked forward to seeing the history of carriages but wasn't sure it would be enough to distract her from the feel of Brit's body against hers when they'd kissed. And she wanted it to happen again, soon. Her sexual encounters with women were usually quick and simple, and she hadn't had to wait to enjoy someone in a long time. The anticipation, the sense of old-fashioned courtship, was nice.

Erika enjoyed the carriage museum more than she'd expected. The antique coaches and carriages on display varied in shapes and sizes. She listened to Brit talk about the designs and their purpose. Brit had taken her hand somewhere during their stroll, which surprised her but made her smile. She glanced at the few couples seated at small tables sharing conversation and a cup of coffee. A few looked their way, smiled, and turned away. This was a new, and pleasant, experience. She had gotten so used to being in the spotlight and recognized wherever she went, she'd never had the opportunity to know what it was like to blend in. To just be another tourist on vacation. It had bothered her just a few days ago, but now, on her own, she liked the peace of it. She squeezed Brit's hand, causing her to turn toward her and smile. She looked comfortable as they continued through the building and the end of the display. "Can I buy you a cup of coffee?" she asked.

"Sounds good." She led them to one of the small tables in a corner away from the growing crowd trying to escape the rain.

She watched Brit for a moment before asking, "Are you okay being here with all these people?" She remembered how Brit ducked her head and turned away quickly when she'd first arrived on the island and George's words about her coming out of her shell since.

Brit offered a small smile and shrugged one shoulder. "I figure I'm with the most beautiful woman in the place. That's probably who they'll stare at instead of me."

Erika smiled to hide the edge of pain the simple words sent through her. She knew she was beautiful. She'd been told that her whole life and had been groomed to make it her life's work to take advantage of it. Her outer shell was the example of perfection in the modeling world, and it had defined who she was since childhood. She sat back in her chair and allowed the familiar, but unexpected, disappointment to wash over her. She'd begun to believe she and Brit shared a connection and feelings beyond skin deep. Maybe she misjudged her instincts. Maybe Brit enjoyed the shell, but knew from their shared past that what lay beneath it wasn't all that nice.

Brit frowned and tipped her head. "What's wrong? Did I upset you?" She took her hands in hers across the table and looked distressed. "Do you want to leave?"

Erika shook her head, certain the threatening tears would fall if she spoke.

"You look so sad. I did say something, didn't I?" Brit looked close to tears, too.

"I'm okay." How could she tell Brit to look deeper, to see her for more than just a pretty face? It had to come from her belief there was more to her worth seeing, and Erika had tried to show her that she wasn't that same spoiled, angry teenager anymore. But what if Brit couldn't see that? What if their past would always lay between them?

Chapter Twenty-nine

Brittany tried to concentrate on the carryout menu Erika handed her, but her thoughts strayed. She could tell she was upset about something but couldn't figure out what. They were enjoying the day, and then sadness shadowed her like a cloud. Brittany mentally went over everything she said but couldn't figure it out. She'd been trying to figure out what to do or say to cheer her up since they'd returned to Erika's room to order dinner. She tossed the menu aside and pulled Erika into her arms. "Please, tell me what's wrong. I can't stand to see you upset."

Erika sighed and pulled her into the bedroom, pushed her onto the bed, and dropped next to her. She rested her head on her shoulder and placed her arm across her body.

Brittany froze, unsure what she was supposed to do. She instinctively wrapped her arms around her. They lay still until Erika's warm tears soaked her shirt. She pulled her closer and kissed her temple. "What's wrong? Please talk to me."

Erika sniffled and Brittany reached to her bed stand for a tissue. She blew her nose.

"I'm sorry, Brit. I'm just so afraid I'll never work again. Peter hasn't contacted me, and you called me beautiful, so that's probably all you see when you look at me, and I'll probably never work again. I'm nothing without my looks." She snorted, trying to get her breath, then began to cry again.

Brittany blinked a few times trying to make sense of Erika's words. She wrapped her arms around her when more tears rolled down her cheeks. "Why do you think the only thing I see when I look at you is your beauty? You're beautiful inside and out to me. You're gentle, generous, and caring. I saw you pay twice for those T-shirts you bought, and I watched you with the horses. I noticed your hesitancy at first, but anyone willing to push past their fear to get close to a horse shows a courageous and gentle heart. You've become important to me, Erika. You're scared that you won't get more work and go back to New York, and I'm scared you will."

Erika covered her face with her hands. A deep frown creased her smooth forehead. "I've been holding all this in for so long, I guess I just had a meltdown. I'm sorry I'm being so sensitive."

Brittany imagined Erika had been holding the fear of not being good enough deep in a corner of her heart for her whole life. She remembered their first kiss as twelve-year-olds. Erika had been pushed hard by her parents to be the best, the prettiest, the most graceful, the most mature. They'd put up with her friendship with Brittany, but she'd always known they wished she was prettier, more in Erika's league. And then the accident had happened, and everything had changed. "I've got an idea." She sat up, took her hand, and tugged her off the bed. "Let's run away from home."

Brittany walked quickly, never letting go of Erika's hand as they followed the path to her apartment. She pulled her to the couch once they entered, pleased to see a smile spread across Erika's face. "Sit for a minute. I'll be right back." She went to her bedroom closet and retrieved a small suitcase. She set it on the couch between them and opened it.

"Oh my gosh." Erika reached for the pad of drawing paper underneath the puzzle pieces. "I can't believe you still have these."

Brittany laughed. "My mom gave this to me when I moved. I had no idea she'd kept this stuff." She picked up the box of drawing pencils, took one, and handed one to Erika. "Shall we draw pictures?" She moved the coffee table and put the drawing pads on the floor. Together, they sprawled out, pencils in hand, and sat quietly drawing for a few minutes before Brittany stood to get two bottles of water. "Do you like Cornish hens?" she asked.

"I do." Erika looked up from her drawing.

"I've got a couple in the refrigerator. Shall I put them in the oven?" Brittany was happy to see Erika look relaxed and smiling.

"Sounds good to me." She stood to look out the window. "I like that we won't have to go back out in the rain. It looks like it's letting up a little, though." Erika settled onto the couch and picked up her pencil when her phone pinged. She scrambled to pull it out of her pocket and stared at it for a minute. She looked up and shrugged. "It's finally Peter. He texted me to let me know he's trying, but *Naturalé* still wants me, and I should seriously consider it. The same thing he's been saying for weeks." She leaned her head back on the couch and closed her eyes.

Brittany could see Erika struggle to stay composed, but she didn't have any more memory-filled suitcases to offer. She sat on the couch next to her and rested her arm across her shoulders. Erika leaned against her and remained quiet. She tried to think of comforting words but couldn't come up with any. Telling her at least Peter had gotten in touch sounded lame. Erika had a big decision to make, and she hoped she'd have the strength to support her, whatever she decided.

❖

"You didn't have to walk me back, you know." Erika grinned and squeezed her hand. "But I'm glad you did." She tossed her room key on the table and went to the bar. "I'm going to have a glass of wine. Would you like one?"

Brittany hesitated. Maybe the wine would help her sleep and keep her from obsessing about Erika leaving. "Sure, thanks." She took the offered glass and held it up for a toast. "To drawing pictures."

Erika smiled and their glasses clinked. She took a sip before speaking. "Thank you for today, Brit. I appreciate your efforts to cheer me up. I'm sorry, again, for my breakdown."

Brittany took her hand and led her to the couch. "You don't have to apologize for anything. I was thinking. What about endorsements? I see models in magazines and on TV recommending makeup and face creams and shampoos. You could do something like that, couldn't you?" She stopped talking, certain she'd overstepped her boundaries.

Erika set her glass on the end table. "Thanks for the support. I'm still holding out hope that Peter can find me something, even in a new magazine like the one we just finished here. I'm sure he's looking into endorsements too. I'll try to refrain from panicking until I'm sure there's cause." She slid her hand behind her neck and pulled her into a kiss.

Brittany set her wine glass on the end table and leaned into the kiss. She rested her hands on Erika's thighs. They were solid and strong, like Erika. The muscles flexed under her fingers and she forced herself to remember to breathe. She pulled her down on the couch until she was lying on top of Erika, and their legs intertwined. The length of Erika beneath her, her breasts against hers, caused her nipples to tighten and her center throbbed. She lost herself in the feelings, surprised by their intensity. She feared passing out when Erika skimmed her lips with her tongue. She became aware, through a haze of feelings, of Erika squirming beneath her. She instantly pushed away, fearing she was hurting her, but Erika shifted beneath her and turned to the side. She found herself trapped between Erika and the back of the couch, and she never wanted to be set free.

Chapter Thirty

Erika was torn between giving in to her intensifying desire and rolling off the couch. Brit murmured, and her resolve not to go too far weakened. She kissed her harder and groaned when Brit responded by meeting the kiss with her tongue. She rolled over, pinning Brit beneath her on the couch. It would only take a small move to cradle her breasts in her hands, and she shifted so her knee and thigh rested between Brit's. A little pressure and she could send her over the edge, and she wanted to. But she wanted more with Brit. She wanted a shared experience. Brit meant more to her than a one-night stand, and she'd be going back to New York as soon as Peter found work for her. She kissed her softly one last time and carefully slipped off the couch. She worked to collect herself and sat on the floor until Brit rested her warm hand on her shoulder.

"Are you okay?" Erika asked.

"I don't think I can stand, much less walk, but I suppose I'm okay," Brit said.

Erika stood to retrieve their abandoned wine glasses and sat next to her. She took a sip to calm herself before speaking. "I didn't expect that. I'm sorry if I took you by surprise."

"But it was a pleasant surprise." Brit beamed. "Please don't feel as if you need to say you're sorry, because I'm not. I love feeling you so close to me." She finished her wine and set the glass down. "I should be going, I guess. I've got to work in the morning. Before

I forget, though. Remember I told you there was a place I wanted to take you off the island?"

Erika nodded, not entirely trusting her voice yet.

"I volunteer at the burn unit at Community General Hospital every so often. Would you like to go with me? The kids would absolutely love to have a famous model visit."

Erika hesitated. She'd love to see the facility she'd been helping to support for the past twenty years. It was her personal atonement for her role in Brit's torment after her accident, though she'd never mentioned it. "I'd love to go with you. Do you think we'd have time for some shopping as well?"

"The day after tomorrow I have time off and we'll make a day of it." Brit kissed her quickly but hesitated. She pulled her against her until their bodies melded and kissed her, lingering on her lips. She held her until their breathing returned to normal before leaving. Her smile was bright and she looked so happy.

How could Erika hurt her again?

Erika changed into her nightshirt and poured herself another glass of wine. She sat by the window to gaze at the water. She struggled with her feelings for Brit. Tonight could have been a huge mistake. She didn't want to lead her on and give her false hope for their future because she didn't know what that looked like. She had feelings for Brit, she knew that, but they both had lives so far removed from each other, and she couldn't see how it would end. What if Peter found work for her tomorrow? She could be halfway around the world by the end of the week, with no way of knowing when she'd be back in this part of the country. The pang of anxiety surprised her. She wanted to work. She needed to work. But where did that leave them?

Long distance relationships didn't work. Or, at least they didn't work for her. Not knowing when you'd next see each other, only speaking when there was time. No, that wasn't a relationship, and it wasn't one she'd subject Brittany to. This had to stay what it was. A wonderful, romantic flirtation that would end with Erika leaving and Brittany moving on with her life.

Erika shook out the wrinkles from a blouse she found in the bottom of her suitcase. She smoothed her hands over it after she put it on until she felt comfortable enough to wear it to the dining room. No one paid attention to her here, and that meant she could afford to not be perfect. It was a novel feeling that surprised her. Was she letting go of her need for the intense attention of modeling? Could she accept being out of the limelight if Peter didn't find her work?

She drank her coffee while deciding what to do until Brit got off work and settled on a walk into town, grateful the rain had stopped overnight. She put a tip on the table and left. She waved to the owner as she passed the fudge shop and waved again to the owner of the T-shirt store. A large magazine rack inside caught her attention. She perused the publications until one cover stood out. "Smooth bronze skin, charcoal brown eyes, and perfect smile." Peter's words echoed in her mind. She bought the magazine, took it to a shady area with a park bench, and sat to read it.

"I'll be damned." She read and reread it. The photo featured Peter with his new model. The photograph showed him grinning broadly with his arm wrapped around the nineteen-year-old. *The upcoming, exciting, new, young model from blah, blah blah blah.* She began to toss the magazine in a trash bin but changed her mind at the last minute and stomped back to the hotel.

She tossed the magazine on the table and sat on the couch for a few minutes to calm down and collect herself before she tried to call Peter. She had no hopes of the call going through, but she had to try. She waited as it rang several times. She was about to disconnect when his voice mail came on. "Peter. What the *hell* is going on? You're supposed to be looking for work for me. I just found you in a magazine with that new model. I know you have to keep working and take care of yourself, but please call me back, or text, and let me know what's happening." She disconnected the call and left for a long walk.

Erika returned to her room sweating and exhausted. She'd walked as fast as she could up and down the hills of the island, unsure how far she'd gone, but she had kept walking until she finally reached a place of calm. She didn't know what she would do if Peter abandoned her. Was he even looking for work for her? Had he given up on her and decided to give all the main jobs to his new star? No. She had a contract with him. She couldn't fathom that he'd turn on her that way, but the thoughts wouldn't go away. She stripped and stepped into the shower. She turned the water on hot and allowed it to melt away some of her distress. She put on a clean bra and pair of Victoria Secret's panties and wrapped herself in one of the hotel's plush robes. She made herself a cup of coffee and picked up the magazine to do a further review.

Half an hour later, Erika became aware of her rumbling stomach. She'd missed lunch so she called to order some food and dressed while she was waiting. She finished her lunch and checked the time. Brit was due in an hour, but they hadn't made any firm plans. She hoped she'd be up for a quiet evening. Maybe she could talk her into another picnic by the water. That sounded soothing, and she needed soothing.

Chapter Thirty-one

Brittany dropped onto her couch exhausted. George had to leave early so she had taken two full carriages on island tours. She reflected on the fact that she'd been comfortable on the carriage runs and hadn't felt anyone staring at her. Was she becoming more comfortable with herself, or had she been overly sensitive until now? She didn't mind that she had to clean all the stalls alone, but she looked forward to seeing Erika and had hoped to leave early. At least she had the next day off. She rose to grab a bottled water and drank the whole thing. It had been a long day, and she hoped Erika would agree to a quiet meal by the water. She took a quick shower and dressed and grabbed her jacket before heading out the door.

She passed across the Grand Hotel porch, smiled and nodded at the few folks enjoying the late afternoon. Only a couple of weeks ago, she wouldn't have considered being this visible to so many people. She reflected on her newfound courage. Was it Erika's reemergence in her life? She accepted who she was on the inside, and it caused the inside scars to fade and made the outside ones less important. She peeked inside at the diners who'd be dressed in formal wear in a few hours. Erika would be completely comfortable seated with them. She'd traveled the world and eaten at expensive restaurants in Paris and who knew where else. The fanciest place she'd ever eaten was an Italian restaurant with Barb. Erika was rich, famous, and beautiful, and she was a hick from a small town who spent her days with horses. But Erika still had that little girl who'd tried to run away from home inside her, and Brittany could see her emerging a little more each day.

❖

Brittany sensed Erika's anxiety as soon as she stepped into the room. She took her hand and led her to the couch. "Did something happen today?" She pushed aside her own fears to concentrate on Erika's answer.

Erika handed her a magazine folded open to a page with a picture of Peter with his arm around a young, beautiful model. She read the caption and understood the cause of Erika's anguish. She scrambled for words of solace but could only shake her head. "What does this mean?" She had no idea how the modeling industry worked and maybe Peter had always been an agent to more than one model.

"It means he's dumped me for this youngster." She stood and paced.

"Can agents represent more than one model at a time?"

Erika sat next to her. "They can. They work on a commission basis, and he's been my agent for years. I suppose since he can't find more work for me, he needs to take care of himself. The agency has probably encouraged him to move on." Erika rested her head back on the couch. She looked crestfallen. "He and I have been together for my whole career. He's probably as upset for me as I am for myself. He can't force a magazine to take me on." Erika's look of defeat tore at her heart.

She slid her arm behind Erika and pulled her into her arms. "Is there anything I can do?" Erika's huge sigh and snuggle into her embrace was her answer.

"Is it all right with you if we eat while we sit by the water again?" Erika asked.

"I like that idea. Did you order anything yet?"

"No, but it won't take long." Erika picked up her phone and ordered the food before she returned to her position in her arms.

"I took the omnibus on two tours this morning," Brittany said. "I actually felt comfortable doing it, and I think it has a lot to do with you."

"Me?" Erika sat up and faced her.

"Yeah. You accept me for who I am and how I look, and I believe it's given me the courage to put myself out there and overcome my uneasiness."

"I'm glad you're more comfortable, and I'm happy if I played a part in it. You are a beautiful, amazing woman." Erika cupped her face with one hand and the deep kiss she intended turned into a quick peck at the sound of knocking at the door. Erika jumped up to get their food.

Brittany set the food and utensils on the table between the parlor chairs, then turned the chairs so they faced the window overlooking the water while Erika poured two glasses of wine.

She turned to serve their meal. "This looks great. I figured we could watch the water from inside tonight."

"Prime rib again sounded good to me, and I hoped you'd like it," Erika said. They ate in comfortable silence, watching the water in the distance.

"Thanks for the dinner. I'm absolutely spoiled." Brittany rested her arm across Erika's shoulders after they settled on the couch.

"You're welcome. I appreciate you stepping in to set it up."

"It's the least I could do since you're willing to share it. These past couple of weeks with you have been really special. You're special."

Brittany slowly pressed her lips against Erika's and cradled her face with her hands. She began tentatively until Erika's quiet murmurs emboldened her to graze her tongue slowly across her lips. She moaned when Erika's tongue met hers and they circled each other. She wanted more but pulled away to catch her breath. They sat quietly holding each other for a few minutes before she rose to leave. Erika didn't seem to want to push for more, and Brittany wasn't sure how to move to the next stage, though her body was screaming for her to. She didn't think it was her, but maybe Erika was too upset about her future. "I'll see you tomorrow. Get some rest tonight." She kissed Erika lightly before opening the door, and didn't miss the thoughtful and somewhat sad look in Erika's eyes as the door shut. What did it mean?

She ambled along the path home. She'd had a long day and should be exhausted, but her time with Erika had energized her. She stopped to watch the moonlight sparkle on the water for a moment and to try to sort out her feelings. She knew she cared about Erika and knew the feeling when they kissed was sensual desire with Erika at the heart of it. She tried to figure out how she'd feel if Erika left and never came back. The pang of sadness, like a slap to the face, brought tears to her eyes. Barb's words echoed in her mind again, but she feared it was too late to protect her heart. She went to bed looking forward to their trip to the burn unit in the morning, but uneasy about the necessary conversation regarding their future.

Erika went to bed with Brit on her mind. She was becoming precious and the time they spent together, more special. Her lifestyle had never allowed her to date anyone seriously, and she'd never met anyone she'd wanted to date long-term anyway. Her modeling career always came first, but for the first time she had someone special in her life. She worried she'd hurt Brit when she left, but she pushed away the terrifying small voice that murmured her career was over so it wouldn't happen. Her throat tightened and she forced back tears. She was nobody if she wasn't modeling. Erika James was the model called first. Requested before the others. Her growing physical relationship with Brit concerned her. Brit's tentativeness was fading, and her kisses were becoming more impassioned. She needed to nip this in the bud but knew her heart had a different idea. She drifted off to sleep hoping for a resolution in her dreams.

CHAPTER THIRTY-TWO

The morning sun glittered off the water and looked like small lights moved along by the waves. Erika drank her coffee and waited for Brit to arrive. She looked forward to their day trip off the island, but her growing idea of taking Brit with her to New York waned when she realized this serene, peaceful scene was one of the reasons Brit lived on the island. She'd made a comfortable life for herself here and probably wouldn't want to leave. She finished her coffee and tried Peter's number. She tapped her foot as nervous tension streamed through her body. She was about to give up, thinking the call hadn't gone through, when he answered.

"Hello, Erika. Did you get my text about *Naturalé*?"

"I did. Did you get my message about you and that model in the magazine?" Peter was short and to the point, so she would be, too.

"Yes. I need to work, too, Erika. I'm sorry that I haven't found you anything yet, but I'm still trying. But you don't have much time left to decide about the nude offer. They won't wait forever."

Erika clutched her phone until her fingers began to cramp. "All right. I just want to make sure you haven't written me off for that new model." She held back her tears.

"I haven't, Erika. We've been together for years. I'm really trying for you."

"Okay. My cell phone works well from here, so I'll call you next week with my decision."

"Sounds fine. Listen, Erika. I'm sorry, but you're not the first model to be in this position. You're still gorgeous, but as you know, youth and beauty sell. These magazines only worry about their bottom line, not the model's careers. They're on a constant search for fresh, young faces. I'm sorry. I won't stop looking, though, and I'll let you know if anything pops up." Peter disconnected the call without so much as a good-bye.

Erika loosened her grip on her phone and sat frozen in place. She struggled to process the idea that her only option was to take her clothes off. She was still stunned and fuming when Brit arrived.

"Ready for our adventure?" Brit looked excited. She held up an insulated bag. "I packed us some water and snacks, but I thought we could have lunch in Mackinaw City."

Erika relaxed and vowed to stay positive. She didn't want this special day ruined and she pasted on a smile to cover the hurt and betrayal she felt at Peter's blunt words. She'd enjoy Brit's company and take things a day at a time. "Sounds good." She grabbed her sweater and followed Brit out the door.

"You look a little sad today." Brit reached for her hand without taking her eyes off the road as she drove. "Is it about Peter and his new model?"

So much for not focusing on it. "I've never been in this position before. I've had time off between shoots, but never because I had nothing scheduled in the future." She traced circles on the window.

"It'll be okay. Even if Peter doesn't find you work, you're beautiful, smart, and financially stable. You can find something to do. Something you're passionate about. People switch careers all the time now. Maybe it's your turn." Brit squeezed her hand before releasing it and gripping the steering wheel.

Erika considered Brit's words. She'd been told she was beautiful her whole life until it became the only way she identified herself. What was she supposed to do now that her beauty wasn't enough? She didn't know how to do anything else. What other passions did she have that could translate into a career? She squashed the threatening panic and vowed to enjoy her day with Brit. She'd worry about her future later. "Where are we going first?"

"I thought we'd start with the burn unit."

"Sounds good." Erika smiled.

Brit parked in the visitor's lot at the hospital and Erika followed her through the halls to the burn unit. Joanne sat at her desk with her attention on her laptop when they entered her office.

"Brittany, it's good to see you again." Joanne looked up and smiled.

Erika laughed at her surprised expression when she stepped from behind Brit. "Oh my gosh, Erika!" Joanne rushed to hug them both.

Brit looked surprised but remained quiet.

"It's good to see you again," Erika said.

"I can't believe you're both here." Joanne looked back and forth between them.

"Erika just finished a photo shoot on the island and we hoped the kids might like a visit." Brit glanced at Erika, clearly a little puzzled. "Shall we gown up?"

Erika had traveled to the unit several times when she first began to donate funds, but she'd forgotten how intense the experience was. The children's pain was well managed for the most part, but their fear and loneliness filled the room. She watched the transformation on their faces when she and Brit introduced themselves. She understood why Brit traveled often to spend time with them. She'd been here after her own tragic experience, and she was an example of healing for the kids. She followed Brit to each room before they left and did her best to encourage the patients.

"Thank you for stopping by today. The kids will be talking about it for days. It gives them something to focus on besides their situation." Joanne hugged them both with tears in her eyes.

Brit took her hand as they left the building. "I always feel grateful after I spend time here. I hope it was okay for you."

"It was. I've been donating to the clinic for years, but donating money is much different than your time. I'm glad we did this today. Thank you." Erika stopped walking and turned to kiss her. "You're special."

Once they got to the car, Brit turned toward her. "Why didn't you tell me you'd been to the burn unit before? And that you were a donor?"

"I don't know. I guess I wanted to surprise you." She shrugged slightly. "I think I was a little embarrassed, too. I admit my motivation was my guilt for my behavior toward you in school. I was trying to make up for it somehow, so when I found out which hospital you'd been in, I made sure I started to support it as soon as I could." She scuffed at a stone, unable to meet Brit's eyes.

She shivered when Brit traced her ear with her finger. "You're special, too."

Chapter Thirty-three

Shall we go into Mackinaw City?" Brittany started the car and waited for Erika's answer.

"Sounds good to me. After lunch can we go shopping?"

"Absolutely." Brittany hated shopping, but Erika looked so excited, she didn't have the heart to tell her.

Erika hopped out of the car as soon as it stopped. The area was full of people strolling on the walkways and going into the many shops. She watched Erika peruse the area while she locked her car and walked toward her.

"This place is great." She took Brittany's hand and pulled her into the first store. "Look." She held up a T-shirt similar to the seven she'd purchased on Mackinac Island, but with Mackinaw City printed on it. She bought two and handed her one as they walked to the next building, which advertised Tilley hats. "I've always wanted one of these." She tried several on before buying the first one. "Would you like one?" she asked.

"Thanks, but I already have one. It's similar to the one you bought."

"Do you want to check out a couple more stores before we have lunch?"

"If you don't mind. I haven't had time to just browse through shops in years."

Brittany grinned. "Let's do that. Then there's a little place around the corner that has great fish and chips."

Brittany followed Erika as she wandered through several more shops and helped her juggle her bags to the small restaurant.

Erika leaned back in her chair at one of the tables on the outside patio. The umbrella blocked the afternoon sun and gave them an opportunity for some people watching. "This has been a wonderful day," Erika said.

"It has. I'm glad you agreed to it. Did it help distract you from your work stuff?" Brittany hoped for a positive answer.

"It did. I've decided to take things one day at a time. Maybe something will come up instead of the nude option. In fact, I have a friend and fellow model who recently retired. I'll give her a call and pick her brain for ideas."

"That sounds like a good plan. It's all we have, one day at a time. Maybe your friend can help you figure out what you can do next." Brittany took a deep breath remembering how, overnight, her life had changed forever. She was home expecting a spaghetti dinner and the same evening was lying on a gurney in the hospital emergency room. Her plans for school the next day faced a six-month delay. She knew about one day at a time.

"I've had fish all over the world, but that was as good as any I've eaten." Erika sat back with her hands on her flat belly.

"I'm glad you enjoyed it. I stop here whenever I can." She finished her iced tea and stood. "Ready to go?" Brittany was ready for Erika's request for more shopping.

"Is it all right with you if we sit a bit longer?"

"Sure." She sat and ordered two more iced teas.

"I'd like to talk." Erika wrapped her hands around her glass. "I didn't tell you everything Peter said this morning. He told me he couldn't find any more work for me. His words were they 'search for fresh, young faces.' He's taken on that new model, and I'm left with *Naturalé* or nothing." Tears welled in Erika's eyes and she looked away.

Brittany searched for words of consolation. She couldn't tell Erika what to do, but her feelings for her induced her to try to come up with a solution. She needed to convince Erika that she was capable of having a life beyond her modeling career. "You said you have a model friend, but are there other models you could contact to see if their agents have extra work?" She had no idea what she was talking about, but Erika's tears made her want to try.

"I'll check it out, but agents are the ones who find work. It's their job and what they get paid for."

Brittany was glad to see Erika's tears had subsided but she still looked so lost. "Shall we help support a few more retailers before we head home?"

"Are you offering shopping therapy?" A smile crept across Erika's face.

"If it helps." Brittany took her hand and pulled her out of her seat. She could put up with a few more stops to keep Erika smiling.

"I think I'd rather just go back. Can we plan another day to go through the fort and lighthouse, too?"

"Sure. Let's head home." Brittany kissed her quickly before starting the car. She mentally considered options Erika might find usable, but without knowing the industry, she was hesitant to suggest any. Unwelcome advice could be a good way to lose a friend, but Erika had opened up about it, right?

The trip back to the island took less time than Brittany would've liked. They'd sat close and held hands on the ferry and they slowed their pace the closer they got to the hotel. She sensed Erika's mood improving, and she hoped she'd been a part of cheering her up. She worried about the decisions she'd have to make about her future and the nude magazine and how much stress it caused her. She walked her to her hotel room and didn't resist when she pulled her into the room and into her arms. Erika pushed her up against the closed door and pressed her body against hers while she kissed her. Every nerve in her body tingled, and she gave in to the feeling as she kissed Erika back with fervor.

She stepped away. "I've been wanting to do that all day." Erika chuckled.

Brittany collected herself enough to speak. "It sure was nice," was all she could think to say.

"Would you like something to drink?" Erika asked.

"No, thanks. I'm good." Brittany sat on the couch mostly to relieve her shaky knees.

Erika joined her on the couch and leaned on her.

"Do you think you'll be hungry soon?" Brittany asked as she slid her arm around her.

"Probably. What do you have in mind?"

"I've got some homemade lasagna in my refrigerator, if you're interested."

"That sounds great," Erika said. "I'll just change and we can go."

Brittany missed her as soon as she left the couch. What would it be like when she left for good?

"Homemade lasagna. Did you make it?" Erika took her hand as they walked.

"I did. I like cooking. I cook a lot in the fall to fill the freezer for the winter. I took it out this morning before I left hoping you were a lasagna fan."

Erika stopped walking and tugged her off the path. "Look." She pointed to the seagulls soaring in circles above the water. Their calls grew louder as they passed close to the shore and quieted while they ascended toward the clouds. A gentle breeze rustled the young spring leaves on the water's edge and brought the scent of the water as the swells washed onto the shoreline. Erika wound her arm around her waist and pulled her close for a few minutes before she spoke. "This is a beautiful spot."

"It's one of my favorites." Brittany gently squeezed her hand. "You've probably seen the shores of Greece. I bet this doesn't really compare."

"I have. And Ireland, and Italy, and Australia, and many others, but this shore has become my favorite." Erika looked wistful as she gazed over the water.

Brittany waited for her to say more, but she remained quiet. "Of all the world's shorelines and coasts you've seen, why is this one your favorite?"

She smiled and raised their joined hands to kiss her fingers. "Because you're here with me."

Chapter Thirty-four

Erika watched Brit slide the lasagna pan into the oven, then retrieve a large plastic salad bowl and fill it with greens from the refrigerator. She was as efficient in the kitchen as anyone she'd ever seen. "You're pretty good at that." She sipped her wine and winked.

"I've been cooking since I was a kid. Mom and Dad always worked, so I started dinner nearly every day."

"I remember. It was pretty cool, so I asked my mom if I could start doing that, and she freaked out. She said I couldn't take the chance of hurting myself." Erika froze. "Oh, God, I'm sorry, Brit. I didn't think before I spoke." She set her glass down and wrapped her arms around her.

"It's okay. I got over being sensitive about it long ago."

She picked up her glass and took a drink, considering her next words. "I never did find out what happened to you. Do you mind telling me?"

"No, I don't mind. The lasagna's done. Shall we talk while we eat?" Brit set the food on the table.

Erika filled water glasses hoping the heavy topic wouldn't be disturbing dinner conversation.

Brit took a bite of food and swallowed before speaking. "My mom worked late on Fridays at the diner, so I was starting dinner. I had a pot of water boiling, and I reached for the spaghetti on the top cupboard. I couldn't reach them, so I pulled one of our wooden kitchen chairs over to the stove and stood on it. It just happened to be the one with the wobbly leg, so it tipped when I reached the box of spaghetti. I slid off, and the box caught the pot handle as I fell." Brit stopped speaking, and a look of fear passed over her face. She took a few bites of food and sat quietly for a moment before continuing. "It dumped on me, and I lay on the floor going in and out of consciousness for about an hour before my mom got home. It's funny, well, not funny, but my mom always told me to remember to put a little oil in the water so it wouldn't boil over. It sure didn't keep it from tipping over. The doctor said the oil was probably the reason I sustained third degree burns." She took a bite of food with a trembling hand.

Erika couldn't imagine the pain and fear she must have experienced. "It must've been awful. I'm so sorry that happened to you." She reached to hold Brit's hand.

"Thanks. I spent three months in the burn unit. You've seen what that's like, and it took another three months of healing and learning to care for my scarring on a daily basis at home. I missed about six months of school."

"I remember when you got back." She tensed with guilt. "And then we compounded your pain with our taunting and teasing." She released Brit's hand.

She bent her head and Brit stepped behind her chair and wrapped her arms around her. "That's all in the past. It's a new day and we have a lot to be grateful for."

Her breath was warm against her ear and she quaked with desire. She placed her hands over Brit's but resisted repositioning them to her breasts. Brit had just relived a traumatic event in her life, and she didn't want to take advantage of her vulnerability. Brit hesitated before she returned to her seat.

"This was a wonderful day." Erika settled shoulder to shoulder with Brit on the couch after they'd cleaned the dinner dishes.

"It was. I'm glad you were here to share an important part of my life." Brit snuggled into her side when she put her arm around her. "My visits to the burn unit help me continue to heal emotionally and remind me to maintain an attitude of gratitude. Those kids remember the terror of whatever happened to them. Then, they have to go through the pain of being torn away from their family. The critical ones see the walls of plastic surrounding them as their future. They don't understand about a sterile healing environment. All they know is that they're scared, in pain, and trapped. They believe they'll be there forever, and I suspect the younger ones feel as if they're being punished for causing what happened to them. Their days and nights blend together, and if it weren't for the nurses checking on them, they'd believe they were alone in the world. And the flashbacks linger for a long time." Brit wiped away tears with her hand. "I like to think when I visit and they hear what happened to me, it helps them know there will be an end to their suffering. They'll get out of there eventually, grow up, and have a life worth living. Does that make sense?"

Erika wiped tears from her own eyes before attempting to answer. "It makes a lot of sense. Thank you for sharing all that with me." She kissed her forehead and pulled her close. The story Brit relayed was probably her own, and Erika's tears rose again when she pictured young Brit trapped inside a sterile plastic world.

"How about a movie?" Brittany rose from the couch and opened a cabinet lined with several DVDs. "I've got comedies, romance, and probably every movie Meryl Streep is in."

Erika looked at her watch, surprised to see how late it was. "It's almost eleven o'clock. I should go." She stood to stretch.

Brit rested her hands on her hips. "I have a new T-shirt you can use to sleep in."

Erika noticed the slight quiver of Brit's fingers, and her shy smile made up her mind. "Well, it is late, and it's a long walk back to the hotel."

Brit took her hand and led her to the bedroom. "You know where the bathroom is, and I have a pair of shorts that will probably fit you." She set a pair of jersey shorts and her new T-shirt on the bed. "Oh. I sleep on the left side of the bed. Are you okay with that?" She fidgeted with her hands while she looked away.

"It's fine, sweetheart. Do you have an extra toothbrush?"

Brit opened a closet and retrieved a towel, washcloth, and toothbrush with a tiny sample tube of toothpaste. “Let me know if you need anything else.” She handed her the pile.

Erika slid into bed after her shower. Brit faced away from her and breathed softly. She suppressed her stirring desire. Brit probably needed to feel safe and cared about, not lusted over. She could wait and see what feelings developed between them. If there was time before she had to leave. She nestled against her back and enveloped her with one arm. A feeling of fierce protectiveness was the last thing she remembered as sleep overtook her.

Erika woke to the scent of bacon. She sat up confused until memories of last night and Brit’s disclosure of her accident washed over her. She reached for Brit but the sheets on Brit’s side of the bed were cold. She rose and stretched before heading toward the smell of breakfast.

“Good morning, sleepyhead.” Brit smiled and flipped the pieces of bacon. “Are scrambled eggs and bacon okay?”

“Are you kidding? It sounds wonderful and smells even better.” She spotted the full coffeepot and poured herself a cup. “What time do you have to work today?”

“I’m going in to help George clean stalls in about an hour. I’ll be done for the day after that unless Ben calls me in for something. You want to go back into town for more shopping later?”

“You say shopping, and I’m there.” She grinned, set her coffee cup on the table, and wrapped her arms around Brit from behind. “You doing all right this morning?”

Brit turned in her arms and kissed her lightly. “I am. Thank you for listening last night. I hadn’t told anyone about that day except my therapist, since it happened.” She shivered.

“I hope it helped to talk about it. I’m grateful you trusted me enough to tell me.” She stepped away and sat at the table. “Did I hear bacon and eggs?”

They finished eating and Erika cleared the table and washed the dishes while Brit got ready for work. She sat on the couch to finish her coffee.

"Before I leave, I have something for you." Brit handed her a key on a Mackinac Island key chain. "You're welcome to stay as long as you like, or go and come back. I should be done by one o'clock." She kissed her quickly and left.

Erika leaned back on the couch to assess her feelings. She'd never had anyone serious in her life. Never anyone who'd given her a key to her home. She smiled and reveled in the feeling.

Chapter Thirty-five

"Good morning." Brittany grabbed a broom and began to sweep the barn floor where George was working.

"Good morning." He scooped one more shovel full before he stopped to turn toward her. "Did you have a nice day off yesterday?"

"I did. It was another volunteer day at the burn clinic." She leaned on her broom. "How's your wife doing?"

"Good. She's getting anxious about our daughter heading to college this fall. Empty nest syndrome I think they call it." He mimicked her stance by leaning on his shovel.

"How long have you two been married?"

George looked thoughtful. "It'll be twenty years in August." He smiled. "I picked a good one with her."

"How'd you know, George? That she was the one."

"That's the question of the ages, my friend. All I can tell you is from the very beginning we fit. We laughed together, enjoyed the same music and movies, and boy can she cook." He grinned and tipped his head. "You all right?"

"I'm fine. A little tired from my day off. Let's get these stables done." She began to sweep in earnest and considered George's words. He hadn't asked why she wanted to know about his wife, and she was unsure herself. Erika's smile, tender touches, and her kisses caused stirring in a place she was pretty sure had been reserved for Amy years ago. She feared their time together might be ending soon and guilt rose like bile in her throat when she hoped Peter didn't find work for her. It would mean her life as Erika James was over, but she feared it would mean the death of Amy as well. They were clearly intertwined, and it wasn't fair of her to want to deny something so integral to who Erika was. But she couldn't sweep away her own feelings, either. This relationship stuff was incredibly complicated. She cleaned the last stall and said good-bye to George before leaving.

She'd given Erika a key to her apartment with hopes she'd be there when she got home. That anticipation was a new feeling for her, and she wished she knew what it meant. She decided to follow her old standby and take things a day at a time.

Brittany followed the path to her apartment without giving in to her desire to swing by Erika's hotel room to see if she was there. She hoped to find her at home. She pulled her keys out of her pocket as she got to the door but put them away and opened the door. Erika put her arms around her and kissed her. Brittany pulled her closer and caressed the firm muscles of her back. The feel of her breasts pressed against hers sent shivers of longing to her core. She decided to enjoy having Erika in her arms and let her take the lead as to where things went. A cold empty space took over when Erika pushed out of her arms. "I sure like coming home to you." Brittany kissed her.

Erika took her hand and guided them to the couch. "Are you done for the day?"

"Yep. I'm all yours."

"If you haven't eaten, maybe we could go to the Gate House for lunch on our way to town." Erika looked as if she was struggling to hold back her excitement.

"It sounds good, but let me take a shower and wash the horse smell off before we go." She kissed her quickly and retreated to the bathroom.

She showered and put on clean clothes, then stood before the bathroom mirror. She applied sunscreen and hesitated before applying her makeup. Erika had spent the night in her bed and called her sweetheart. She'd seen her without makeup. She studied her face and tried to see what Erika had. The years had dulled the shock and pain of seeing her own deformity, but she ought to feel exposed and self-conscious that Erika had seen it, but she didn't. Somehow, Erika had gained her trust, and Brittany liked it. She finished quickly and returned to the living room where Erika lay stretched out on the couch reading a magazine.

She stood for a minute, overwhelmed by a sense of peace. As if this were all planned. Erika looked content, and she enjoyed the view for a moment.

"I'm ready when you are." Erika grinned when she caught Brittany staring at her.

They left and headed toward the restaurant.

Brittany wasn't surprised at the crowds in the Gate House. Memorial Day was close and it meant more visitors arriving to enjoy the island. They took seats at a table for two and ordered lunch.

"You didn't hear from Peter this morning, did you?" Brittany asked.

"No. I don't expect to. We left it that I'd call him with my decision. I'll give him a call Monday."

Erika looked sad so Brittany dropped the subject.

"Are you doing okay today? You relived some painful memories yesterday." Erika stroked her hand from across the table.

"I am. I think it does me good to remember. It happened and it changed me forever, but I've also healed, grown, and made a life for myself. You being here has helped, too."

"I'm not sure how I helped, but I'm glad you think so."

"I never thought I'd see you again, and I carried the pain and resentment of your betrayal inside for years. Your apology and explanation has helped."

Erika looked like she was going to speak but remained quiet.

"I didn't ask you if you slept okay last night."

"Like a baby." Erika grinned.

"Good. I sure conked out." She wondered what might have happened between them if she hadn't.

They finished their meal and she took Erika's hand as they ambled past the shops.

Erika pulled her into the first store they passed. "What do you think?" Erika held up the fifth sweatshirt for her opinion.

"I like it." Brittany smiled and gave her a thumbs-up. She enjoyed seeing Erika's enthusiasm. She looked happy and it surprised her how important Erika's happiness had become to her. She people watched while she waited for Erika to make her decision. She scrutinized the other shoppers and passersby. Nobody paid attention to a scar faced woman shopping with a beautiful fashion model. Had they all changed or was it her perception?

She chuckled when Erika took her arm and led her out of the store wearing her new sweatshirt. "You might be a bit warm in that."

"It'll be okay for the walk to the hotel. I like it." She ran her hands up and down the sleeves. "It feels great."

"Excuse me! Hello. Are you Erika James?" A grinning, heavyset woman rushed toward them waving a magazine over her head. "Please could I have your autograph?" She glanced at Brittany and continued to try to get Erika's attention.

Erika turned toward the woman and smiled. "Of course." She signed the frayed magazine and chatted with the woman.

Brittany stepped into a nearby store and watched the exchange. A small part of her wished she'd introduced her. But as who? *This is my friend whom I've kissed several times but will be leaving when I go back to New York.* Erika was glowing as she engaged her fan. She smiled and listened to the woman as if she were the most important person in the world. Erika was really good at connecting with people. So unlike her.

"Sorry for the interruption," Erika said as she stepped into the store and looked around.

"No problem." Brittany forced a smile. "More shopping or shall we head back?"

"I'm ready to go back to the hotel."

Brittany noted a melancholy look in Erika's eyes as she walked her to her hotel room. She had a feeling Erika needed some time on her own, and she knew she did. She snaked her arm around her waist and pulled her close. "I'll see you later for dinner." She released her and headed home.

Chapter Thirty-six

Erika's thoughts spun like a top when she returned to her hotel room. Brit had given her a key to her home. Her sanctuary. That meant a lot to her, and she wanted to be worthy of her trust. Brit hadn't asked her to move in with her, obviously it was too soon for that, but was that what she expected at some point? She needed to decide about her future. The fan who'd recognized her verified she was still popular and a huge part of her was convinced Peter could find her work if he tried harder, but she needed to be realistic. He'd done his best, and twenty years was a good long career for a fashion model. She plopped into a parlor chair and gazed out the window. She hated to consider *Naturalé's* offer. She didn't want to do a nude spread now, and she never wanted to before. But if could lead to more work maybe she ought to try it. She hated this back and forth uncertainty.

Brit's words of encouragement came back to her. It was true she was financially stable, but what Brit didn't understand was she didn't know how to be anything but a model. It was all she knew and all she was. What else was she passionate about? She hadn't had time to cultivate other interests. And now there weren't any to lean on. She hated feeling so perplexed. She began to pace, becoming more agitated with each step. She left her room, intending to walk until she cleared her mind and made room for answers.

She started uphill toward the fort and continued until she was out of breath. She spotted a shady area with an open bench and sat. She watched a few people walk past and two trotted by on horseback. One of the carriage tours rolled by and the group on board waved and chattered. She waved back and forced a smile. She leaned forward with her elbows on her thighs and cradled her head in her hands. *What the hell am I going to do?* A warm hand on her shoulder startled her.

"Sorry. I didn't mean to disturb you, but I was worried about you. You looked down when we left the store and worse when I dropped you off at the hotel. I thought you might need some time on your own, but then I thought maybe I was wrong and it would have been better for you to talk it out. Now you look miserable. Can I do anything?" Brit sat next to her with their legs touching.

"I wish you could, sweetheart." She leaned back on the bench.

"Is it Peter? Did he upset you?" Brit looked intense.

"No. I haven't talked to him." Erika figured this was as good a time as any to ask about Brit's intentions. "I'm concerned about what my future's going to look like. I hate feeling in limbo, and I have no idea how to tell my parents." She didn't know how to approach the subject of the key.

"I'm sorry you're so upset. I know you can do whatever you set your mind to. You're intelligent and beautiful, and I know your parents love you and are proud of you." She kissed her lightly on her cheek.

They were nice sentiments, but they felt empty when she had nothing to attach them to. And talking about her fears about losing her career, yet again, seemed pointless. Erika leaned toward her. "Why did you give me a key to your apartment?"

Brit leaned away and cradled her face in her hands. "Did I upset you with that? I'm sorry, you don't have to keep it. I like having you there, and I wanted you to have an alternative to that hotel room. I didn't mean to push you in to anything."

Erika felt like a jerk. She knew Brit's intensions were innocent, but she had no idea how to express her concerns, and she'd unintentionally hurt her. "Oh no. No, Brit. You didn't upset me. I was surprised, that's all, and I didn't want…" She turned her head and kissed one of Brit's palms before continuing. She assessed her feelings before she spoke again to confirm the sincerity of her words. "Never mind. I have to give up the hotel room next Wednesday. I could just leave tomorrow and stay with you until then. If you'll have me."

Brit's wide grin encouraged her. "Definitely."

Erika's problems weren't solved and she knew she was falling for Brit, which didn't make anything easier. But spending a few more days and nights on the island with her would be no hardship. At least, not in the short term.

❖

Erika pulled her suitcase out of the closet and opened it on the bed. She packed her few essentials and called the hotel laundry to make sure she didn't have anything left there. She packed everything she had hung in the closet and considered the wet bar but changed her mind. She could pick up a bottle of wine at the store if she wanted one. She sat in one of the parlor chairs and watched the water through the window. She'd miss this view, but there were many gorgeous views from the island. This was a beautiful hotel, as nice as any she'd ever stayed in around the world. She looked forward to staying in Brit's small apartment because she was there. A luxury hotel was no match.

She carried her suitcase to the checkout, settled her bill, and began her walk on the path to Brit's. She was halfway there when Brit surprised her.

"Did you think I'd let you carry your suitcase all the way?" Brit gave her a quick kiss and grabbed her bag.

"Thank you. I'm sure I could've managed it." She snorted.

"I've got a chicken roasting in the oven. Does that sound okay?"

"It sounds great. I was going to grab a bottle of wine from my room, but it felt like stealing. Do you want me to pick one up at the store?"

"I've got a bottle of white wine, if you'd like."

"Good, because I'm not sure where the store is." She took Brit's hand, thinking how boring their conversation sounded and how perfect it still was.

Brit opened the door when they arrived and Erika shook off her unexpected shyness. She was never shy. She'd shared hotel rooms with other models before, but never lived day to day with anyone. She took a deep breath and stepped inside. This was different from anything she'd experienced, and she looked forward to every minute of it.

"Is everything okay?" Brit asked.

"Yeah. I've never done this before. Lived with anyone I mean, even temporarily."

"Hey." Brit wrapped her in her arms. "You can leave anytime you want. I'm not taking you prisoner."

"I don't want to go anywhere." She snuggled into Brit.

"I need to check on dinner. Why don't you go unpack?" She squeezed her before heading to the kitchen.

Ericka took her suitcase to the bedroom. She opened the closet door and smiled. Half of the wall-to-wall closet was empty, and several wooden hangers hung empty for her. She hung up her few items and looked for a place to put her suitcase. She planned to keep her underwear in it until she noticed the bottom drawer of Brit's dresser open and empty. She shook her head and grinned. Brit wanted her here. And not because she was a model, or because she wanted anything from her. Just because they were sharing something special. It was exhilarating. And terrifying.

Chapter Thirty-seven

"Dinner's ready," Brittany called from the kitchen. She went to look for Erika and found her putting her Victoria's Secret underwear into the drawer she'd emptied for her. "Glad you found things okay." She leaned against the doorframe.

"Thank you." Erika set her suitcase on the floor in the closet and closed the door. "It's great. Did you say dinner was ready?" She strode to her and pressed her body against hers.

She kissed Erika then held her at arm's length. "The chicken will get cold, and the wine warm." She pulled her to the table.

Erika speared a piece of chicken, a carrot, and a piece of sweet potato with her fork and stuffed it into her mouth. "This is fantastic. You're a good cook."

Brittany drank her wine. "Thanks. Do you think you'll be comfortable here? It's not exactly the Grand Hotel."

Erika swallowed before speaking and reached for her hand. "I want to be here, Brit."

"Okay, good. I believe you, it's just I know you're used to fancy hotels and room service." Brittany began to worry she'd made a mistake inviting Erika to stay with her, but she wanted the opportunity to get closer to her, especially if she planned to go back to New York.

"Honestly, sweetheart, I get tired of traveling and staying in hotels. It's nice to feel like I have a home." She crammed another forkful of food into her mouth. "And this is definitely a home cooked meal."

Brittany breathed a sigh of relief. If Erika called her sweetheart again she might invite her to make this her forever home. Now all she needed to figure out was the sleeping arrangements.

The day they'd been to the burn clinic and she'd told Erika the details of her accident had been emotionally upsetting but cathartic as well. She'd felt exposed and vulnerable, but in Erika's arms, sheltered and protected. She'd delighted in her presence next to her all night. She thought that Erika had sensed it, too, and they'd spent a quiet, peaceful night sleeping together. Was that why she'd asked her to stay with her? Her own neediness or something else? Something deeper and more vital? She had no idea when Erika would return to New York, but she was certain she'd leave behind a hole in her heart.

After dinner, Brittany put her teapot on the stove and retrieved two cups. "Chamomile or green tea, honey?" she called from the kitchen.

Erika entered the kitchen barefoot, wearing a sleeveless T-shirt and panties. Her smooth bare legs looked longer without pants on. Brittany blinked and tried but couldn't speak.

"Chamomile, please. Can we drink our tea in bed? It's been an emotional day, and I'm about to crash." She took her cup and headed to the bedroom.

Brittany picked up her cup and followed her. Her sleeping question had been answered. Erika sat on the right side of the bed with her pillow supporting her back. Her watch and cell phone were on her nightstand, and she held her cup with both hands as she took a sip. She looked entirely relaxed and at home, and Brittany quivered. "I'll be right in to join you." She set her cup on her nightstand and went to the bathroom to change. She returned within five minutes and copied Erika's seated position with her pillow at her back and cup in hand. Was this what George meant when he told her he and his wife fit? That things were easy and just fell into place?

"I'm glad you agreed to stay with me. I like having you here." Brittany sipped her tea and hoped for a positive response.

Erika adjusted her pillow so she could rest her head on it before she moved close and placed her hand on her belly. Erika's hand was hot and her muscles jumped involuntarily. She never wanted it to end. "I like being here with you." Erika slipped her hand under her T-shirt and drew small circles on her stomach inching upward until she lightly stroked the underside of her breast.

Brittany set the cup on the nightstand with her shaking hand and whimpered as tendrils of need wound through her. The tendrils coiled like a spring, and she craved release when Erika squeezed her nipple between her fingers. She tugged her hand against her breast and bucked her hips searching for relief until the tingle of the gentle orgasm unfurled from her center to her toes. She lay on her back, still clasping Erika's hand until she caught her breath. Brittany heard Erika's soft chuckle and felt her smile against her neck before she kissed it.

She stretched out, gently slid her arm over Erika, and drifted into sleep to the melody of her breathing.

Brittany awoke and turned toward the warmth of Erika. She slept on her side with one arm under her pillow, the covers tucked under her chin and over her shoulder. She shifted to her back slowly so as not to wake Erika and stared at the ceiling. She'd taken the day off to spend time with Erika, but she wasn't used to sleeping past six o'clock. She glanced at the clock radio, surprised it was seven. She didn't know what time Erika usually woke. There were many things she didn't know about her and she hoped they'd have enough time together to learn. She closed her eyes and ran through possibilities of things they could do with their day. They'd talked about going back to Mackinaw City and touring the fort and lighthouse. She ran the ferry schedule through her mind and began to plan their day.

"You're mumbling." Erika turned on her back and stretched. "What time is it?"

"Seven o'clock." Brittany struggled to focus when Erika's bare leg pressed against hers. Feelings from the previous evening surfaced. They were under the covers. It was quiet and private. If she turned to face her, she could reach most of her body, but she didn't know if that's what Erika wanted. She knew what she wanted, but she wasn't certain how to begin. Memories of Erika's touch launched an ache and a flood of wetness between her legs.

Erika remained quiet but turned toward her. Her fingers were soft and warm. Her touch was gentle enough to tickle as she glided them down her neck to trace her collarbone to her shoulder and down her arm. She interlaced their fingers and squeezed gently before she moved their joined hands to the waistband of her panties. Her grip tightened and her breathing became ragged as she pushed lower.

Brittany raised herself onto her elbow to continue the exploration Erika offered. Her soft curls were slick with her wetness, and she was hot. Erika fisted the sheets and pushed her center against her fingers. Brittany pressed her fingers against her and, going by instinct, stroked her stiffening clit. She grew wetter and Brittany slowed her pace to catch her breath. Erika grumbled and released the sheets to push harder. Brittany reached inside her own panties and touched herself. She mirrored her caresses with Erika's on herself until they were both writhing, and Erika stiffened and shuddered as she thrust Brittany's middle finger inside her. Brittany's orgasm rippled through her, surpassing anything she'd ever read about and nothing like she'd imagined. Her clit was so sensitive, she was certain she'd come again if she touched it, but the emotions encasing her heart seized her attention and threw her off balance. She'd never been so overwhelmed with feelings. They spun through her, jumbling her thoughts. The softness and heat of Erika's skin and the scent of her arousal generated a longing so foreign yet so intense that she trembled with need. She wanted her. All of her. Body and heart. Her reflection was interrupted by Erika's insistent mumble.

"Mmm. I need you naked." Erika tossed her own panties and tank top to the floor.

Brittany stripped and drew Erika on top of her so she straddled her with her knees. She cradled her breasts in her palms and brushed her nipples with her thumbs. Erika covered her hands with hers, and she felt her wetness against her stomach as she moved above her. Brittany gently squeezed Erika's nipples and thrust her hips as she lost herself in the beauty of her climax and tumbled into her own.

Chapter Thirty-eight

Erika's body felt like lead, and she loved it. She kissed Brit softly, but coherent speech eluded her. She snuggled into her arms and drifted into contented sleep. She awoke when the bed shifted when Brit got up. "Where you going?"

"Sorry. Nature calls."

Erika rolled to her side and placed her hand on Brit's side of the bed. Her body heat reminded her of her warm touch. Her instant excitement when their legs touched took her by surprise. She'd lost control and had to have her. She sat up, worried she'd taken advantage of the situation. She didn't think Brittany had ever been with anyone before, but she might be wrong. She would have stopped if Brit hadn't wanted to go any further, wouldn't she? She swung her feet off the bed and stood as Brit returned.

"Are we getting up now?" Brit's grin eased her tension.

"I just started to worry that you were okay." She wrapped her arms around her and squeezed.

"Oh, I'm more than okay." She put her hands on her waist and began to move her feet.

"Are we dancing?" Erika stepped closer and swayed along with her.

"Yeah. Dancing with joy." Brit kissed her. "Is there someplace you'd like to go today?"

Erika seriously considered taking Brit back to bed and having her way with her for the entire day. Her better sense took over when she reminded herself she might be heading home soon. She didn't want to hurt her by getting too involved, then leaving. Her stomach dropped. She'd have to figure something out with Peter. Maybe she'd get a spread with a travel magazine here on the island. She put her dilemma out of her mind. They were going to spend the day together. One day at a time.

❖

"You were right about this view. It's magnificent." Erika sat next to Brit on one of the benches at the beach below the lighthouse. She sat quietly watching the gulls soar across the waves with the view of the expanse of the Mackinac Bridge in the background. "Thanks for letting me hit all those shops." She held up her bag of assorted items.

"No problem. I like seeing you happy." She took her hand and kissed it.

Erika shifted in her seat and pulled her to sit next to her. She leaned against her, remembering their morning and their closeness. Her reticence to have sex again seemed ages ago. The line had been crossed. No reason to deny them what they both wanted. "Can we go back now?"

"Sure. Are you okay?" Brit looked concerned.

"I just have an urgent need to be alone with you." She kissed her hard, not caring about people around them.

Brit took her hand to tug her off the bench. "Let's go."

On the ferry, Erika rested against Brit's shoulder, and then she held her hand as they walked to Brit's apartment. Erika touched Brit's trembling hands when she fumbled with the key to unlock the door. She wanted her desperately but going slow wasn't the end of the world. Brit was endearingly nervous, and she wanted her at ease. "It's a beautiful afternoon. Let's walk by the water before we go inside."

Brit looked surprised, but relief passed over her face as she smiled. "I have another place I'd like to show you. Come on."

Erika followed her along their usual path to an overgrown trail she never would have noticed. Brit walked ahead of her moving branches aside as they hiked. She caught the scent of the water and the sound as it splashed against the shore. Brit took her hand as they broke through the brush, and she sucked in a breath when she caught the first view of the Straits. The Mackinac Bridge stood in the distance as the only reminder of the human presence in this unspoiled environment. Words escaped her for a long moment as she took in the view. She imagined the explorers the first time they stumbled upon this scene, who must have been awestruck. Even minus the bridge. "Wow."

Brit put her arm around her waist and drew her close. "This is my favorite spot on the island. It's my special place where I come to think and restore my serenity. I've never seen another person here."

"Thank you for sharing it with me."

"We can head home anytime you'd like."

Erika reflected on her earlier intensity and desire to take Brit to bed. The desire still smoldered, and she believed the feeling was mutual. "I'm ready. Can we come back here for a picnic one day?"

"I think that's a good idea." Brit took her hand and led the way back to the main path. This time, she unlocked her apartment door with steady hands. "I'll start dinner soon. Pork chops sound good?"

"Sound great. I think I'll go to that spot where I had good cell reception the other day and try Peter's number. I'll be back soon." She kissed her and left.

She found a bench and sat to make her call. She hoped for strength and clarity before trying his number. She tapped her foot as she waited, unsure if she hoped he'd answer or get his voice mail.

"Hello, Erika."

"Hi, Peter. Any work for me yet?"

"I thought I made it clear that there wasn't. *Naturalé Mag* is it. Can I tell them you're available?"

"Listen, Pete, I have an idea. What about a travel magazine? Like the one I just finished with here. Surely there must be others. I shouldn't have to tell you that."

Peter's loud sigh gave her the answer. "No, Erika. I'm sorry. I've tried every angle for you. I even looked at a few of the European magazines. Like I told you, they want fresh and new. I'm flying out tomorrow to San Francisco. Leave a yes or no answer with my answering service by Friday. Again, I'm sorry, Erika." He hung up.

She stared at the horizon, aware that he was truly done with her. He didn't sound empathetic, he sounded irritated. Clearly, he had better things to do and he expected her to quietly fall in line. What was she going to tell her parents? Slowly, she made her way back to the apartment, trying to plan for a conversation she hadn't imagined having to occur. She sniffled and found a tissue in her pocket to blow her nose before she reached Brit's. She pasted on a smile before she opened the door and entered. She wouldn't ruin any of their remaining time together by crying over what she couldn't have. Not in front of her, anyway.

CHAPTER THIRTY-NINE

Brittany rested her feet on the coffee table as she watched the news, but her thoughts strayed to Erika. Calls to Peter never seemed to go well, and though she wasn't going to give her opinion, she thought Erika might be better off without him. She went to the kitchen and filled two wine glasses. They'd either be celebrating or drowning their sorrows. She carried them into the living room to wait.

Erika opened the door a few minutes later and called out. "I'm home."

She searched her face for an idea of how things went, but she couldn't read Erika's expression. She handed her one of the wine glasses. "Good news?"

"Not really." She sat on the couch and took a drink of her wine. "He gave me an ultimatum. *Naturalé* or nothing. Nothing new."

Brittany took Erika's glass and set it on the table before enveloping her in her arms. She kissed the corner of her mouth and stroked her hair. "It'll be okay. I was thinking while I waited for you about the burn unit. We could both become more involved and volunteer on a regular basis. I thought of something else, too. We could always use more help with the horses. I'm sure, if I talked to Ben, you could work part-time in the stables." She tried to look hopeful, but her sad face told her it wasn't working.

Erika reached for her hand. "I appreciate your efforts, Brit, but I've lived my whole life being told my only value is my looks. I've been groomed to be the most beautiful, and my life has been in front of a camera. I just wouldn't know who I was if I wasn't a model. And if I'm not…well, I'll have to figure out what it is I want to be."

She looked so sad Brit had no idea what to do. "Is there anything I can do or say to help? I feel useless."

"Let's have another glass of wine for dessert."

Brittany carried the glasses to the living room. "I'm not sure if wine makes anything better, but it can't hurt."

Erika took a drink and set it on the table. "I don't have to decide anything until Friday, so where're we going tomorrow?" She leaned against her.

Brittany retrieved a folder from her file cabinet and opened it on the coffee table. "I've got this great map of Mackinac Island. Is there any place you'd like to see?"

Erika studied the map for a few seconds and pointed to an area just outside of town. "What's up there?"

Brittany looked through her folder and found a tour that included the area Erika had pointed to. "That's a scenic area of the island that's a little far to walk from here, but we can take a carriage tour. In fact, I kind of like the idea of being a passenger for a change."

"Cool. We'll do it tomorrow. Does it say what time the tour starts?"

"Eleven o'clock. We can have breakfast, throw some snacks and water in my backpack, and go." She was warming to the idea of riding instead of driving for a change. And Erika's smile and enthusiasm helped ease her worry.

"Okay. We've got tomorrow all set. Shall we watch TV for a while?" Erika asked.

Brittany put her maps away to give herself time to figure out her feelings. She'd been hoping for the possibility of making love, but she wasn't sure how to make it happen. Was it only this morning Erika had clenched her hand and moved it to offer her the precious gift of herself? She craved Erika's touch now. Maybe she was teasing about wanting to watch TV, maybe she regretted their earlier closeness, or maybe she was so upset about the ending of her career, she couldn't think of anything else. Out of maybes, she returned to her seat on the couch. "Anything you'd like to see?" She picked up the remote as she spoke.

"Well, actually…" Erika kissed her. "It's getting late." She kissed her again. "Maybe we should go to bed."

Brittany's heart pounded. She pulled Erika into her arms and kissed her. She would've been content to stand in the living room kissing Erika until they could no longer stand, but Erika broke the connection and led her to the bedroom.

Erika pushed her onto the bed and straddled her waist with her knees and Brittany grasped her hips. She followed her movement as she crossed her arms and slowly lifted her shirt over her head. She traced her fingers over the swell of Erika's breasts above her lacy bra and forced herself to breathe when she unclasped it and tossed it aside. She glided her fingers over her soft pale skin to circle her areolas and firm pink nipples. She relished the weight of Erika's breasts in her hands when she leaned over and braced herself on either side of Brittany's head. Her nipples tickled her palms and she took them between her index and middle fingers. She gently squeezed and Erika gasped and sat up. Erika covered her right hand with her left and slid her own hand past the waistband of her jeans and panties to touch herself.

Brittany inhaled a ragged breath as she watched Erika's face as her orgasm overtook her, and she collapsed to lie next to her. She gathered her in her arms and held her as she mumbled unintelligibly. They rolled over on the bed and Erika wiggled out of her jeans and panties. As much as she loved having Erika naked, being fully clothed herself seemed wrong. She lifted off her T-shirt and unbuttoned her jeans, aware of Erika watching her. They were both breathing hard by the time Brittany finished undressing and they pressed together with lips joined and legs intertwined. She thrust her center against Erika's and released a groan when Erika ground against her. Erika slipped a hand between them, slid a finger inside her, and Brittany lifted off the bed, urging her deeper. She clung to Erika as her orgasm engulfed her and she shivered with aftershocks.

Brittany shifted to be able to reach Erika, overcome with the need to touch her everywhere. She traced her fingers down her neck to her breasts. She circled a nipple with her finger before using her tongue and slipping her middle finger inside Erika. She became dizzy with the scent of her arousal and awestruck by her silkiness and the strength of her contractions as she came. Brittany reluctantly withdrew her hand and encircled Erika in her arms. *Mine* was her last thought as she fell asleep.

Chapter Forty

Erika lay wrapped in Brit's arms and snuggled closer as she drifted in and out of sleep. She didn't want any thoughts bombarding her. Brit stirred and held her tighter. There was a two-inch difference in their height, but lying naked in each other's arms, they fit together perfectly. She tried to remember the last time she'd spent a whole night with anyone and came up blank. There'd been an Italian beauty she'd met while on one of her shoots in Rome, but she'd slunk out of the hotel room at some point while she slept. Erika found out later that the woman was married to a male high-ranking government official, making her decision to make herself scarce quickly a great idea. But she loved waking next to Brit, and that was wonderful and scary. Brit had been hurt too many times in her life, and she didn't want to be the one to hurt her again.

She looked at the clock and turned over on her back.

"I can feel you thinking." Brit placed her hand on her belly and drew small circles with her fingers.

"Keep that up and you'll feel more than my thoughts." Her hips rose, an involuntary request for more.

"Are you all right?" She continued her finger doodling.

"I'm fine. Go lower." Her breath caught as Brit started figure eights moving closer toward her mound. "Please." She grabbed the sheets and pushed into Brit's touch.

"Close your eyes."

Erika turned toward Brit, unsure what she had in mind, but decided she liked the game. She shut her eyes and waited. Her left nipple responded to Brit's warm breath on her breast then the flick of her tongue. She squirmed and pushed her chest up, needing more. Then Brit blew softly on the side of her neck and tracked moist kisses and light nibbles toward her shoulder. She tried to remain still and anticipate what came next, but intense desire replaced surprise when Brit took her left nipple in her mouth and sucked gently. She grabbed her head and pulled her against her.

"No fair. I get to choose what comes next." Brit sounded breathless.

Erika released her grip. "Please continue."

The mattress dipped as Brit shifted and Erika's body tingled in anticipation. She didn't have to wait long before Brit's body pushed against her side. She moved so her leg pressed against Erika's center. Erika responded to the pressure by grinding against her thigh, hoping for more. She wasn't disappointed when Brit moaned and apparently gave up on the game. She kissed her and slid her pussy against her leg while pushing her thigh into her.

Erika clung to Brit as they rode out their orgasms together.

After her breathing returned to normal, she turned to her side and pushed her butt back against Brit. She squeezed her hand when she draped her arm over her and interlaced their fingers. "This feels nice."

"It feels better than nice. I don't suppose we could just stay in bed all day." Brit moved their joined hands to her breast and shifted closer to her back.

Erika gasped at the contact. "That's tempting." She wanted to call her lover, or sweetheart, or any other endearment, but uncertainty tore at her. She had to go back to New York. She had to do and be the person she was groomed to be. She couldn't walk away from the spotlight without trying harder. She blew out an exasperated breath.

"You okay?" Brit rose on her elbow and kissed her shoulder.

"Yeah, I'm okay. Just not used to lying around in bed, I think."

"How does oatmeal sound for breakfast?"

"Do you have raisins?"

"Absolutely."

"Sounds good to me." She wrapped her arms around Brit and hugged her before swinging her legs over the side of the bed. "Okay if I get in the shower first?"

"Sure. I'll get the coffee started."

Erika stepped under the hot spray and considered her options. How could she take some control? She used the body wash Brit had left for her. The scent reminded her of Brit, and confusion surfaced as emotions swamped her. She couldn't deny her feelings for her went way beyond friendship, and she'd all but invited her to stay so they could see where this took them, but who would she be here? It was a beautiful island, but except for finding Brit, it could have been a vacation. A getaway from her hectic life. The only life she'd ever known. The life that defined her. Would Brit be able to stand the fast-paced life of New York? If her next job was *Naturalé*, where would that leave her? She finished her shower, dressed, and went to find Brit.

"I just finished the oatmeal. You can go ahead and eat if you want. I'll just be a few minutes in the shower." Brit picked up her coffee cup and headed to the bathroom.

Erika settled at the outside table with her coffee. She pulled out her phone, surprised it looked like it had nearly full reception. She decided to try her friend in New York. It either would work or it wouldn't, but she was tired of waiting for Peter. It surprised her again when the call went through on the first try.

"Hello, Erika. Are you still on location in Michigan?"

"Hey, Pat. I am. I'm glad my call went through. The cell reception isn't too good here. I'm calling to see if you have any info on job openings." Erika tried not to hold her breath as she hoped for a positive response.

"As you know, I retired a few years ago, but I try to keep up with things. My ex-agent calls me if he hears of an opening for a mature model. Sorry there hasn't been anything lately. But I'm pretty much happily retired. Why are you asking? Doesn't Peter have anything for you?"

"No. He's pushing me to do a nude shoot, but I really don't want to. He tells me it's my only option. I'm getting tired of hearing that, so I called you."

"I'm sorry I can't be of more help. I'll certainly keep my eyes open for you. I can make a few calls, too."

"Thanks, Pat. You can reach me on this number. Take care."

"You, too, and good luck."

Erika blew out a breath. She'd hoped Pat would know of something. She sipped her coffee amazed how much more settled she felt just from trying to take matters into her own hands.

❖

"Ready?" Brit asked as she slung her backpack over a shoulder.

"Ready for today's adventure." Erika took her hand and glanced at the sky as they walked. "It almost looks like it's going to rain."

"The weather forecast is for a cloudy day, but no rain. We'll be in the enclosed carriage anyway."

They followed the road to the waiting area where four Percherons were hitched to a large coach. Erika looked closer and counted at least fifteen seats. "Wow. This is a big wagon."

Brit chuckled. "It's made to hold up to twenty people and it goes pretty much around the whole island, which is a grand total of eight miles."

They boarded and took seats toward the back. A middle-aged couple climbed aboard and argued over where to sit.

The woman stopped a few feet from them and gasped. "Harold look. Harold! It's Erika James, the model." She rushed toward them, dragging Harold behind her.

Erika smiled and offered her hand in greeting. "Hello."

"Oh, I can't believe it's you." She turned to Harold, who looked like he'd rather be anywhere else. "This is my husband, Harold, and I'm Elizabeth." She pulled out a crumpled piece of paper and a pen from her huge purse, and handed them to her. "Could I have your autograph? I've seen you in Vogue magazine. You're beautiful, and I love the outfits you choose. They're perfect for you."

Erika thanked her and signed the paper. People recognized her. She had to keep modeling. She sat back and waited for the tour to begin. When Brit took her hand, she squeezed it and prayed she could figure out a way to keep her in her life and still continue her career.

Chapter Forty-one

Brittany watched the woman fuss over Erika. She looked thrilled to see her, and she'd never seen Erika look happier. This woman recognized her and obviously loved seeing her in the magazines. But Erika didn't have any magazines requesting her, and she couldn't imagine how devastating that must be for her. It wasn't like an athlete aging out of their chosen sport. They could become coaches or sports announcers. What did retired fashion models do? She'd read about a model who'd married an NFL quarterback. She did some acting and was involved in charities, but she also had children. Erika had the option of posing nude or finding something besides modeling. She hoped she could help her find her way but questioned what she had to offer. She took her hand and kissed the underside of her wrist.

The older couple wasn't obtrusive but made sure to include Erika in their conversation whenever they could. Well, the woman did, anyway. The man looked about as interested as a plastic bag in the wind. The tour of the most secluded area of the island was beautiful, and it let Brittany focus on the area instead of the instability of her emotional life. The tour ended at the gift shop, and the woman waved enthusiastically as they left, shouting that she couldn't wait to tell her friends who she'd spent the morning with. Erika laughed and waved back.

"Can we go into the gift shop for a while?" Erika asked.

"Of course. You never know what treasures you might find." She followed Erika through the store and helped her carry her selections.

"Are all those gifts?" Brittany asked. Erika had purchased two coffee mugs and two shot glasses displaying images of the Mackinac Bridge.

"Yes. Gifts for me. Would you like one?" Erika held up a cup and glass.

"No, thank you. I already have a few. Did you enjoy the trip today?" Brittany asked.

"I did. This is a beautiful place." She took her hand as they walked home.

"I have an idea for tomorrow. Since we couldn't do it the day it rained, would you like to rent bikes and go see Fort Holmes? It's about a two-mile trip from here, then there are a bunch of stairs to climb. It's located on the island's highest point. Three hundred and ten feet above Lake Huron."

"That sounds fun. I haven't ridden a bicycle in years."

"I'm having a cup of tea. Would you like one?" Brittany set her backpack on a chair and headed to the kitchen when they made it back to her apartment after a leisurely stroll.

"Yeah. Thanks. Can we sit out back? I want to tell you something."

"That's a great idea. You go ahead. I'll bring the tea out in a minute." Brittany loved sitting outside at her small table. It gave her a clear view of her bird feeder, and she could count on a gentle breeze this time of year. "Here you go." She set the full cups on the table and sat across from Erika. "So, what did you want to tell me?"

"I called a friend of mine in New York today. She's a retired model but keeps up with the industry news and gossip. I asked her to see if she could find me something, and she said she would. I'm hopeful, but mostly I feel like I'm at least being proactive instead of sitting and waiting for Peter."

"Great." Brittany took her hands in hers. "I can't imagine how hard it must be for you. We'll keep positive thoughts that something breaks." Brittany swallowed the lump of distress at the thought of Erika leaving. But she'd probably leave anyway, either for the nude photos or something else. She forced herself to remember to take things a day at a time. They were together now enjoying a beautiful day.

"This is nice." Erika leaned back in her chair and tipped her face to the sky. "I love seeing the expanse of blue sky."

"Me, too. Remember when we used to lie on our backs in the grass and make up figures out of the clouds?"

"I do. It was the only time I was able to escape the pressure of focusing on my future." Erika looked sad.

"Look at that one." Brittany pulled Erika from her chair and wrapped her arms around her from behind. She pointed to the sky. "I think it's a dragon."

Erika shook her head. "It's a seahorse. And the one next to it is a donkey."

"I see it. Yep, a donkey." She turned Erika in her arms and kissed her with all the emotions flowing from her heart. She kissed her until they were both breathless.

Erika pulled away and began to cry. Brittany put her arms around her and held her until she stopped. She didn't know what to say, but she figured it was less to do with anything to do with them, and mostly to do with the career decisions she faced.

Erika sniffled and stepped out of her arms. "I'm sorry. I don't know why I got all blubbery."

"I certainly hope it wasn't my kiss." She smiled, hoping to lighten Erika's mood. "It's okay. You've got a huge decision weighing on your mind. You're allowed to break down occasionally." Brittany stroked her hair and longed for the words to make things easier.

Erika looked up with bloodshot eyes. "You saw that woman today. She recognized me immediately and wanted my autograph. I like it, and I always have. I don't know if I can give that up."

"I understand. I do. It's just, you've become important to me, and now that I've found you again after all these years, I don't want to lose you. It's selfish, I know."

"Oh, my sweet, Brit." Erika stroked her face.

"Would you like to go for a walk with me before dinner?" Brittany hoped to show Erika more of the beauty of the island to help convince her to stay.

"Let's walk. It's a beautiful afternoon."

"I just need to put on more sunscreen first." She hurried to the bathroom and refreshed her sunblock. "Okay." She held open the door for Erika, hard-pressed to imagine what her apartment would feel like without her in it.

Brittany took her hand and led her to an area just outside of town. One of George's friends owned a livery stable and had invited her to stop by anytime. She decided this would be the time. "I think you'll like it, but if you don't, that's fine." Erika wore a pair of jeans and a blouse so she figured she'd be okay with what she had planned. They both wore sneakers, but the horses at these stables were easy to ride, so she wasn't worried.

"Here we are." She stood next to the sign about trail riding.

"Are we going to ride?"

"Yep. These are docile animals. They're used to being ridden so we shouldn't have any trouble. What do you think?"

Erika threw her arms around her neck. "I think it's fantastic."

"Okay." Brittany made sure the horses were the tamest in the stable before she watched Erika mount hers and she settled on the other.

Brittany followed the route they were told to take and watched Erika closely. "You having fun?"

"I'm having a ball. Thank you so much for this!"

"I know you've always loved horses, and I hoped you'd like a ride." Brittany delighted in seeing Erika so happy and in being the one to bring her the happiness.

"This is really special. You're really special," Erika said. "I've loved everything we've done here."

They passed several other riders going the opposite way and waved. Brittany thought about how far removed this must seem to the world-traveling Erika James. She could only hope it was enough to make her consider staying longer. "Thank you," Brittany told the owner as they walked away after the ride. She took Erika's hand as they walked on the path. When they reached her special place overlooking the water she turned and framed Erika's face with her hands. "I needed you alone for a minute." She pressed her lips against hers and whimpered when Erika pushed her against a tree. She grabbed her ass and ground her center against Erika's. She moaned and slipped her hand under her shirt to push up her bra and fondle her breast. Brittany's knees gave out and Erika held her up against the tree. She muttered between breaths. "Home. Please. Now?"

Erika took her hand and pulled her along the path, and her desire intensified the closer they got to her apartment. She'd never known this powerful need. She feared it could only be assuaged by Erika and wondered how she could survive if she left.

Chapter Forty-two

They tossed their shirts and bras aside as soon as they stepped inside. Erika pushed Brit onto her back on the bed, eager to feel her next to her. She grabbed the front of Brit's jeans, unfastened the button, and slowly lowered the zipper. Brit raised her hips, and she pulled her jeans and panties down to her knees in one motion. Her blond curls glistened with evidence of her arousal and Erika lowered her head to feast. She ran her tongue along her slit and flicked it on Brit's hardening clit, then slowed to gentle circles. Brit grabbed her head and bucked her hips. She stiffened and whimpered, and her guttural sounds morphed into words. "Oh yes!" she cried out and shuddered before falling back onto the bed. Erika crawled up next to her and held her until her breathing evened.

"Amazing." Brit's voice cracked, and she cleared her throat before she kicked off her pants.

Erika slid off her jeans, held Brit close, and reveled in the feeling of peace and rightness of their joined naked bodies. "This is wonderful." She rolled over onto Brit and nuzzled her neck.

"Mmm, yeah." Brit enfolded her in her arms, and she ran her hands along Brit's sides and over her ass. "You're beautiful."

Erika watched Brit's eyes flutter closed. She kissed her lightly on the lips and carefully slid off the bed. She put on Brit's robe and hugged herself, imagining being wrapped in Brit's arms. She wasn't in front of any camera now and she could feel the sincerity in Brit's words. She meant something more to her than just a beautiful woman, and that was something special, something not to be thrown away. But she couldn't have it all. So what had to give?

❖

"Sorry, I fell asleep. You seem to have knocked me out, but I woke up and missed you." Brit sat next to her on the couch. "I like you in my robe. It's sexy." Brit cupped her chin and brushed her lips across hers. "Are you all right?"

"I'm fine." That sounded lame, and she knew Brit would never buy it.

"You don't look fine. What's the matter?" Brit's hand warmed the spot where it rested on her thigh.

"I think I'm just tired." She immediately regretted her words. They had been keeping busy, and she'd loved every minute of it, but she wanted to spend as much time with Brit as she could before she had to leave to face her future.

"Have I pushed you? Am I trying too hard to keep us busy? I don't believe you're all right. What's going on? Please talk to me."

She took Brit's hand between hers and drew it to her chest. "No. You haven't pushed me. I've enjoyed every minute of our time together. I'm just scared, Brit. I don't know what my future holds, or if I even have one. I've never been in this position. I feel lost." She held back tears, angry with herself for allowing her uncertainty to interfere with their private time.

Brit kissed her neck before she sat back and spoke. "None of us know what our future holds. We can hope things go the way we planned, but we can't really know how they'll work out. I've decided we have to let things go and live our lives. Things work out the way they're supposed to. I'm going to get a cup of tea, would you like one?"

"I'll go with you." Erika followed her, unwilling to lose a minute of their time together.

They took their tea to the outside table while they watched the birds. Brit spoke first. "Are you still up to the bike ride tomorrow?"

"I think so. Can we decide in the morning?"

"Sure. That sounds like a good idea."

Erika relaxed into the quiet time with Brit. She savored the warm breeze and the sound of the rustling leaves. She rarely had time to sit and do nothing but enjoy nature. Her schedule had her visiting some spectacular settings, and she'd enjoyed meals with various people over the years while overlooking an ocean somewhere in the world. But it didn't matter where she and Brit were, their connection came naturally. The difficulty of connections and the emptiness of the relationships she had wasn't something she wanted to return to. But maybe she could change that, if she wasn't moving so fast?

"You're worried, aren't you?" Brit asked.

Erika had no answer. Worried was an understatement. She didn't have the energy to try to explain it, but she'd find a way after she'd figured out her next step. Brit deserved it. "Is it all right if we just relax quietly tonight?"

"Of course, honey."

"Tomorrow's your last day off, isn't it?"

"Yes. It's getting busy on the island so we have several carriage rides a day. The Lilac Festival is coming up in a couple of weeks and kids get out of school. It's super busy here during the summer months." Her voice trailed off, and Erika was sure she was holding back her request for her to be with her for the lilacs.

"We have all day tomorrow. Maybe we'll be up to riding." Erika stood and stretched. "I believe I saw some Ryba's fudge in the kitchen earlier. Shall we have some?"

Brit grinned. "Definitely."

"There are two pieces. One for you." She set Brit's piece on a napkin on the table. "And one for me." She took a bite.

"You know," Brit said. "Ryba's is only about a ten-minute walk from here."

Erika wiped her mouth with a napkin. "Let's go."

They held hands as they walked to the fudge shop. The owner was inside, about to turn over the sign to its closed side, but she opened the door when she saw them. "Come on in, Brittany. It's good to see you."

"Hi, Sheila. We just ran out of our supply of fudge. This is my friend Erika, and she loves your fudge as much as I do."

"Good to meet you, Erika. I'm glad you like our fudge. How much do you two want?"

Erika walked along the display cases filled with the many varieties and chose several kinds. "I'd like an extra-large piece of the plain, too. Thank you." She paid for the fudge and took Brit's hand when they got out to the street.

"Thanks for buying all the fudge. And thanks for getting extra plain. It's my favorite."

"I know." She kissed her lightly. If only the rest of her upcoming decisions would be so easy.

Chapter Forty-three

Erika shifted next to her, and Brittany reached to touch her. It amazed her how quickly she'd gotten used to waking next to her and having her in her daily life. She'd be going back to work, but having Erika to come home to filled an empty space she'd never been aware of. She rolled over, pressed against Erika from behind, and listened to her soft breathing. All the years and painful memories between them melted away, leaving two adults with a natural connection. Erika scooched back closer to her, and Brittany tightened her grip around her waist. Her arousal flared, but another, more vital feeling surfaced and she pulled Erika even closer.

"Is it time to get up?" Erika mumbled.

"If you want to. It's seven thirty." Brittany rolled to her back. "I was planning on making breakfast sandwiches this morning. Canadian bacon, a fried egg, and a slice of American cheese on a toasted English muffin. Sound good?"

"Are they done yet?" Erika chuckled.

"I'll get the coffee started." She kissed her quickly and got out of bed before desire took over and breakfast turned into lunch.

"I'll get in the shower then." Erika sat on the edge of the bed and stretched.

Brittany watched her for a moment to enjoy the rise of her breasts as she raised her arms. She remembered their weight in her hands and the smoothness of her skin.

She sliced two oranges in half and squeezed them into juice glasses when she got to the kitchen. She took one to the bathroom, slowly opened the door enough to see Erika was in the shower, and set it on the bathroom counter. She soundlessly closed the door and went to finish making breakfast.

"We have an orange fairy on the loose." Erika set her empty juice glass in the sink and then kissed her. "Thank you."

"You're welcome. I set places on the outside table for us. It's a beautiful morning."

They finished eating and sat drinking coffee and watching the birds in companionable silence. "I've been all over the world, but I can't think of a time I've been more content." Erika looked far away.

Brittany smiled inwardly. Maybe Erika was going to stick around after all. "It's a serene place to live. The town gets crazy busy in the summer, but we're far enough away from the main road to be quiet most of the time."

"I like that we can walk to Ryba's, too," Erika said.

Ryba's probably wouldn't be enough to keep Erika here, then she realized Erika could order fudge from New York or anywhere else in the world if she wanted to. "What do you think about bike riding today?"

"Two miles, you said?"

"Yes."

"Well, with all the fudge I've been eating, bicycling would be a good idea."

"Okay. Fort Holmes, here we come."

Brittany strapped on her backpack and led Erika to the bike rental in town. They rode toward the fort in silence at a leisurely pace and passed other bikers and a few riders on horseback. Brittany spoke when they got close to the fort. "It's a pretty cool place with lots of history. You'll be able to read about it on the plaques. Let's take a water break." She handed Erika a bottle of water from her backpack and grabbed one for herself. "The fort is going to be on our right." They watched one of the carriages pass and waved at the occupants before continuing their ride. She reached for Erika's hand when she climbed off her bike and held it for most of the climb to one of the most spectacular views on the island. Erika read the plaque aloud when they reached the top. "The fort was built in 1814 by the British and refurbished several times throughout the years. This place is fantastic. I love it."

Brittany had been to the fort several times, but watching Erika see it for the first time made her realize how much she wanted to share more with her than just landmarks and fudge. Time had always been fleeting and precious, but never more so than now with Erika. Now it became everything. She followed her around the fort, chatting about this and that, but mostly just enjoying being there with her.

Brittany was glad they'd packed a lunch since they'd gotten a late start to their day. She wouldn't have changed it. Their time together seated at her outside table meant the world to her. She could have stayed there all day. Tomorrow Erika would make her decision to stay or go, so they had today to pretend like everything was perfect. "Shall we have a picnic lunch here overlooking Lake Huron?"

"That sounds good to me," Erika said. She settled on one of the benches and enjoyed the view of the sun sparkling off the water below them. A sailboat glided across the waves in the distance. The serene picture contrasted with her roiling emotions. She turned her face toward the breeze and took a settling breath.

Brittany spread the paper towels she'd brought on the bench between them and retrieved their sandwiches and water. "There. We're having a picnic with the seagulls."

"This was fantastic. Thank you for suggesting it." Erika reached for Brittany's hand.

"It is pretty special to be here with you. I'm glad you enjoyed it." Brittany squeezed Erika's hand gently and took a bite of her sandwich.

They finished eating and enjoyed the panoramic view for a few minutes before packing their paper towel and empty water bottles in the backpack. They held hands on the way down the stairs to their bikes and began the trip back to town.

"Anything you'd like to see while we're in town?" Brittany asked.

"Nothing could top what we just saw. Can I buy you dinner at the Gate House?"

"Sounds good to me." Brittany would've said yes to anything that kept Erika close to her.

Chapter Forty-four

Erika reached for Brit and looked at the clock. Two in the morning. Brit slept quietly next to her and a feeling she couldn't ignore washed over her. She had to make a decision later, but she feared it had already been made for her years ago when she was told by her parents to pack her suitcase for modeling school. Twenty years was a good run for a model, she knew that, but how could she give up who she'd been all her life?

She rolled to her side and wrapped her arm around Brit. She closed her eyes and dozed until Brit's fingers brushed her nipple. She instantly throbbed and grew wet. She loved Brit's touch. She'd gotten bolder the more time they'd spent naked together, and she could imagine how much more intense their lovemaking could get. If she stayed. Maybe Brit could come to New York… She dismissed the idea quickly when she envisioned Brit sitting in her Manhattan apartment while she was off to a shoot. She'd hate it. Brit was used to trees and open spaces. She was settled on the island with her work and her quiet life, but maybe a visit in the winter would work.

She turned to her back and dragged Brit on top of her. Brit's thigh pressed against her center and the beginning tingle of her orgasm moved through her. She squeezed Brit's thigh between her legs to gain control, then raised her head to kiss Brit. She caressed her back and slid her hands to grip her ass while Brit squirmed above her. She let go and pushed against Brit, and they clung to each other while they rode out their climaxes together. Brit mumbled something against her shoulder.

"Did you say something, sweetheart?"

Brit turned her face away from her shoulder to speak. "I said this is the way to wake up in the morning."

"Mmm. I agree."

Erika watched Brit get ready for work. It was so different from what she went through for work. She put on a pair of jeans, a Grand Hotel T-shirt, and a pair of boots. She took a little more time putting makeup on her scarred face. There was no makeup artist to help, but she was expert at it. No one came to mess with her hair, to check that clothing still fit, to tell her how to smile or what to feel. She got dressed and went to work. Erika couldn't fathom how that would feel.

She went to the kitchen and set the table before checking on Brit's progress. "When you're done, come on in the kitchen."

Brit entered the room and a smile lit up her face. "Wow. You made omelets."

"And toast." Erika held up the toasted pieces of bread like trophies.

Brit pulled her closer. "I'll miss you today."

"I'll miss you, too. What time do you get off?"

"At three. I'll see you then." She kissed her again.

They finished breakfast and Brit turned to her before going out the door. She looked like she wanted to say something but just kissed her again and left.

Erika went back to bed after Brit left. She hugged Brit's pillow, inhaling her scent. She hoped for her body heat, but it was too late. Her side of the bed and her pillow were cold. She lay and stared at the ceiling longing for an easy answer. But none came.

She took a shower and put on a T-shirt and a pair of shorts. There was no point in delaying the inevitable. She put her cell phone in her pocket and headed out the door. She went directly to the area where she'd been the last time she'd talked to Peter and punched in his number. She considered disconnecting the call when she got his voice mail, but remembered he was in California, probably busy with his new model. She swallowed the lump in her throat and left a message.

"Okay, Peter. Tell *Naturalé* I'm available, but please get me the best contract you can. I don't want to do this, so at least make sure I'm well compensated." She disconnected the call and broke into tears.

She didn't know how far she'd walked, but she intentionally chose uphill roads. If she was going to have to take her clothes off for the camera, she didn't want any flab. She returned to Brit's apartment breathless. Her phone pinged before she could open the door, and she read the message, surprised that a text came through.

Erika. Good decision. I'll get you the best contract I can. They want you for their fall issue, so the shoots will begin next weekend. I'm sending a chartered plane to the island to pick you up tomorrow. Saturday at 11a.m. See you in New York. Peter

Erika opened the door and fell onto the couch. Tomorrow. Her stomach clenched, and she choked back more tears. She'd have to tell Brit tonight. She checked the time. Brit would be home shortly, so she opened a box of macaroni and cheese. It was almost done when Brit opened the door.

"I'm home." She called from the living room.

The sweet, simple words made Erika's stomach drop and she closed her eyes against the storm of sadness sweeping through her. She put the food in bowls and set them on the table with spoons, then went to greet Brit. She pulled her into her arms and kissed her. "I'm glad to see you. Dinner's on the table."

"I could get used to this." Brit followed her into the kitchen. "Thanks for cooking." She retrieved two bottles of water from the refrigerator and sat at the table. "I might smell like horses, but I'm hungry, so I hope you don't mind." She took a bite of her food and swallowed.

"Didn't you have lunch?"

"George brought me some meatloaf. His wife is an excellent cook. But mucking out the stalls is hard work."

Erika shifted in her seat and took a spoonful of food, trying to look as relaxed as if she'd sat at the kitchen table and had dinner with Brit for years. "I went for a walk this morning up that steep hill toward the Grand Hotel. About how far do you think that is?"

"It's probably a good mile. You didn't have any trouble with it did you?"

"No. But it was a good workout."

"You're in good shape. Oh, before I forget. I talked to Ben this morning. He told me he could always use extra help. You could work part-time in the stables and train to drive a carriage, if you wanted to." Brit looked hopeful.

Erika scrambled for a response as her stomach felt like it was turning inside out. She should tell her now, but it would spoil their evening. She managed to finish the food on her plate but couldn't find any words that wouldn't feel false. The truth hurt too much. She was too weak to say no. To quit and step away from the spotlight. She managed to look up with dry eyes.

Brit finally filled the awkward silence. "Would you like to go into town and check out the few stores you haven't been to yet?"

"That sounds great. I guess you've figured out I love to shop." She pushed past the cowardice knotting her stomach to paste on the smile she reserved for times she had to pretend everything was fine.

Chapter Forty-five

Brittany watched Erika hold up a sweatshirt and put it back, then pick up another one and put it back. She hadn't bought anything after being in two stores, which seemed unusual based on their past shopping excursions. She wondered if Erika had already made the decision to leave, or if she was still deliberating. She could ask, but she wasn't sure she wanted to know the answer, so she decided to enjoy whatever time she had left with Erika. She smiled and gave a thumbs up to the latest shirt she held up. Erika took it to the counter and paid for it, but she put it on instead of putting it into a bag. The evening had cooled off substantially, and they picked up their pace back to the apartment. Brittany couldn't bring herself to talk about plans for the weekend or even the next day. Erika walked silently beside her, seemingly deep in thought. She hoped they were thoughts about how to tell Peter she was staying.

"Wow, it got cold outside." Erika stepped inside and wrapped her arms around her.

Brittany kissed her and held her close. They stood by the door quietly hanging on to each other.

"Let's make some hot tea and cuddle under the covers," Erika said.

Brittany pushed her an arm's length away. "You get the cups. I'll start the water boiling." They settled on the bed with their steaming mugs and sipped tea. Brittany was struck by the domesticity of the moment, and she never wanted it to end. She started to ask about Peter's call but decided to wait until Erika was ready to talk about it. "You warm enough now?"

"I am. There's nothing like cuddling to warm up." Erika set her cup on the nightstand and snuggled against her.

Brittany finished her tea in one gulp and placed her cup on her bedside table before she enveloped Erika and stroked her hair. She noted the beat of her own heart, knowing it would continue even if Erika left, but never again with as much happiness. She held Erika until her breathing evened, and she lay asleep in her arms.

She woke folded in Erika's arms and didn't want to move. She checked the time and reached to shut off the alarm before it went off. Erika tightened her hold, and she settled back. But she had a busy day ahead of her at work, and she hoped Erika would update her on her *Naturalé Mag* decision before she had to head out. She nestled deeper into the safety of Erika's hold until she moved. "Good morning." She slid her fingers into Erika's hair, enjoying the feel of its silkiness. She kissed her lightly and watched her eyelids flutter open. She smiled and all thoughts of work fled.

"Good morning." Erika's touch on her neck was gentle and warm. "Is it time to get up?"

"Sorry. I'm driving the omnibus this morning. We're beginning the busy time now, especially on weekends."

"I'll scramble some eggs for us if you want to get in the shower. I need time to talk this morning." Erika turned away and looked near to tears.

Brittany realized she'd made her decision to leave and felt it like a splinter to her heart. "I won't be long." She dragged herself out of bed and trudged to the bathroom. As soon as she turned on the shower, her own tears flowed. She stepped under the spray and turned her face to allow the water to cascade over her still sensitive scarring. The discomfort wasn't enough to dull the pain growing in her heart. She quickly finished and dried her hair to begin the process of braiding it.

Erika was dishing the eggs on the plates when she entered the kitchen. "Just in time." She looked up and smiled. "Your hair looks beautiful. Is that a French braid?"

"It is. I usually wear it this way for the summer since I never know when I'll need to drive the big carriage." Her words were flat and she saw Erika flinch slightly.

They sat at the table and Brittany took a bite of eggs and swallowed without tasting a thing. "So, you've made your decision, haven't you?" She set her fork down and took a sip of coffee.

"I have." Erika looked down at her untouched breakfast. "I'm trying to figure out how to make you understand why I need to do this. It's who I am. I'm nothing, empty, a nobody if I'm not modeling. My whole life has been about being Erika James. I don't know who or what else to be." She raised pleading, tear-filled eyes.

"You're the only one who can make the decision, Erika, but you're still Amy Jansons to me, no matter what you call yourself. My friend, my lover. I can beg you to stay, but your happiness is as precious to me as you are, so I have no choice but to let you go if that's what you choose." She willed her tears not to fall by forcing her thoughts to redoing her makeup. "It's not like I didn't know you might go. That you'd have to, because your life is there, not here. I guess I just let myself hope…" She shrugged.

"Oh, sweetheart, I don't want to hurt you, I never want that, but I have to give this a try. It could lead to more offers. I just have to." Erika covered her face with her hands.

"You even said you never wanted to do nude photos. You said you didn't want it to be the last thing you did. And what about us? I thought we had something special. A connection. You never even suggested I go to New York with you. Even for a visit." She sighed, unsure what else to say. If Erika didn't feel the same way it was probably best if she did leave. "When do you go?"

Erika looked up and sniffled. "This morning at eleven. Peter's sending a plane for me."

"So soon." Brittany stood and moved toward the door, needing some space. "So, we don't matter to you at all? Am I just another quickie on your way through life? You're ready to leave and never look back? Never come back?"

"Oh no, Brit. No. I care about you, but I have to see where this leads, and I have no idea where work may take me from one day to the next. I can't just give up. Please don't ask me to."

She was surprised when Erika rushed to her, and because she could do nothing else, she wrapped her arms around her and kissed her. "I love you," she whispered in her ear. "Don't ever forget that." Then she released her and walked out the door. This time, Erika wouldn't be waiting when she got home.

❖

Brittany stopped outside the stable to collect herself before seeing George. She pasted on a smile and strode to the carriage, but it looked as if George had polished and readied it already.

"Good morning," he called as he appeared from around a corner.

"Hey, George. Thanks for getting her ready for me this morning." Brittany rested her arm on a wheel as she spoke.

"No problem. There wasn't much to do. You could wipe down the seats again, though. Bit dusty." He leaned on the other wheel and narrowed his eyes. "You feeling okay? You look a little down."

Brittany considered it a good thing she only looked down, because she felt miserable and heartbroken. "I'm just a little tired today. I was up late."

George nodded and patted her hand as he walked past. "Let's get the horses."

Brittany prepared one of the large draft horses and led it to the front of the carriage while George took care of the other. She made sure they were harnessed and ready to pull the coach before she wiped down the seats with disinfectant and climbed onto the driver's seat. "See you later." She took the reins, pushed aside her anguish, and concentrated on her job.

She picked up the luggage and passengers from the dock and dropped them off at the hotel after offering her usual informational discourse. Everyone looked happy and excited for an adventure on Mackinac Island. She doubted she'd ever look happy again as she waved at the riders and thanked them before she led the horses back to the stable.

She checked her watch. Almost noon. Erika would be well on her way to New York. She wished she hadn't taken her heart with her.

CHAPTER FORTY-SIX

Erika watched Mackinac Island get smaller through the window of the plane. The tinier it looked, the bigger the hole in her heart became. She read the safety and emergency procedure booklet several times to distract herself. Maybe she could find a magazine stand in the Chicago airport to offer Peter options. She stuffed the information sheet back where she found it, leaned her head back, and closed her eyes. It was Peter's job to find her work. She could bring him every magazine in the world, and he'd still tell her there were no other options. She'd look anyway. It eased the turmoil roiling in her gut.

Erika would have enjoyed the view of the water and treed landscape out the window if she hadn't felt so lost. She went wherever and whenever the agency sent her. Brit was right. She'd told Peter when she began modeling that she wouldn't take her clothes off, and here she was on the way to do just that. Tears welled when she thought of Brit. She'd looked so dejected and she was the cause. It was the second time in her life that she'd hurt her badly. Maybe it was time to try something for herself. She just had to figure out what that could be and how it could include Brit. If she'd even speak to her again. She thanked the pilot for a smooth trip when they landed and followed the directions to the terminal to wait for her flight to New York. The first-class passengers were called first, so she took a seat close to the front of the boarding area. She spotted a shop with magazines next to the restrooms and decided to take care of business after buying a few copies of things to flip through on the plane.

She checked her makeup after washing her hands and was about to toss the paper towel into the bin when a woman exited one of the stalls. “Erika James? Is that you?”

Erika turned and smiled. “Yes. I’m Erika James.”

“I can’t believe it. You’re Erika James standing here with me.” She pulled a folded magazine and a pen out of her purse. She opened it to a page with Erika’s photo and pushed the pen and the three-year-old magazine toward her. “Please, could I have your autograph?”

“Thank you for asking. What’s your name?”

“Joleen. Gosh, you’re even more beautiful in person than in the pictures.”

“Thank you, Joleen.” Erika inscribed her note and handed back her magazine and pen. “I appreciate you keeping that magazine all these years.”

“I think you’re the best. You always wear my favorite designers. I think I have every magazine you’ve been in. Oh, this is so exciting. I can’t wait to tell my daughter.” Joleen continued to chatter as she left the room.

Erika grinned. An adoring fan was just what she needed to help her move from wretched to only miserable. She made a mental note to tell Peter about Joleen and Elizabeth. People still recognized her. He had to let all the fashion magazines know.

She returned to her seat to await her flight home. As soon as the word entered her mind, she realized within the fleeting time she’d been with Brit, she’d felt at home. She’d be going back to an empty, expensive apartment alone. Was that a home? She boarded the plane and took her seat with a heavy heart.

Erika plopped into her favorite chair after the porter brought in her bag. She didn’t have the energy to unpack yet, but she opened her suitcase and pulled out a Mackinac Island T-shirt and the carefully wrapped pussy willow branch. She searched her cupboards for an appropriate vase, put in the stem, and set it on the mantle of her gas fireplace. She traced a finger along its length and fought back tears at the memory of the surprise gift. She gave up the struggle and allowed them to flow when Brit's words of love reminded her she'd walked away. Was it really love? Brit hadn't been with anyone to fully understand her emotions, had she? Erika was a first crush, a blip on her dating radar. Now that she had more confidence, surely she'd bounce back like one did from a first crush. No matter what she told herself, it sounded an awful lot like justification.

She returned to her chair, covered herself with the T-shirt, and thought of her and Brit shopping and sitting at her backyard table. Should she call Brit to let her know she got in safely? Would she want to hear from her? Ever again?

She ordered Chinese food from her favorite restaurant and called Peter while she waited for the delivery.

"Hi, Peter. I'm back in New York."

"Great. I let the magazine know you'd be available, and they've put you on the schedule to start this week. Did you have a smooth flight?"

"I did. I'm tired but back. I wanted to let you know that I had a woman on the island recognize me and ask for my autograph. Then, in the Chicago airport another one. People recognize me, Peter. Tell *Vogue*, *Elle*, and all of them. I'm still popular. You'll tell them, won't you?" She hated the desperation in her voice.

"I will, Erika. I promise I'll do my best. I've worked hard for you throughout the years and I'm not giving up now. I'm sorry, but I keep getting 'we're looking for new, fresh faces.' Get some rest, and I'll be in touch."

She paid for her food when it arrived and put the bag in her kitchen. She stood for a moment looking at the stainless steel appliances and the spotless countertop and floor. She'd loved this apartment when she moved in. Her cleaning service kept her refrigerator and bar stocked, so she didn't have to worry about shopping. She had a dining room table, but she couldn't remember when she'd used it. There was no small, well-used wooden table with worn edges and comfortable chairs with homemade cushions embroidered with rooster heads. She opened a carton of food and a bottle of wine and sat back in her chair to eat. She took one bite and put it aside to send Brit a text.

I wanted to let you know I got to New York safely. I hope you're doing okay. Erika

She hit send and hoped it went through. She ate her dinner without tasting much and wondered if Brit liked Chinese food. She turned on the TV and searched for an interesting program. Her thoughts turned to evenings spent with Brit sharing a meal, talking, and enjoying each other's company while watching the evening news. She flipped through channels and settled on a talk show hosting celebrities. She finished her meal and contemplated appearing on the show. Would it keep her in the spotlight? She sighed deeply, wondering where her life was headed. She knew she was facing a major change. She just wished she knew how it all would end. She finished her meal and switched the channel to a news station before going to bed.

The next morning, Erika woke disoriented. She reached for Brit, but there was no Brit, no body heat, nothing but cool satin sheets. She curled into a fetal position to squeeze away the emptiness. How could she have gotten used to the right side of the bed and waking next to Brit in such a short time? Surely you didn't fall for someone that fast? Loneliness was something she'd never experienced. Had she been too busy to recognize it? She did now. She missed Brit. She missed everything about her. What she could do about it was a question she didn't know how to answer.

She went to the kitchen to check for breakfast food. She found eggs and dismissed them. It was the last breakfast she'd shared with Brit. She searched the cupboards and found a box of quinoa. *Perfect.* Nothing to remind her of Brit. She ate breakfast seated in her living room and watched the morning news. She checked her phone for a text from Brit and went into her office to check her email. She wasn't one to be on the computer all day, but she had some friends who liked to send notes and connect on Facebook. She waited for her computer to boot up, surprised that she'd been away for three weeks and hadn't missed it. She sent a note to one of her fellow models asking her if she knew of any last-minute openings. Sometimes agents overbooked and had to find fill-ins, and sometimes models got sick. She checked her social media accounts and responded to a few comments. She still had fans in real life and online.

She shut down her computer and stepped onto her treadmill to begin her workout routine. She was still on her first half mile when her phone pinged with a text from Peter.

Erika. I talked to Naturalé last night. They're excited to have you onboard, but they've moved their schedule up a few days. I'll know more tomorrow, but they've already rented a studio somewhere in New York. I'll send you info and the schedule as soon as I get it. Peter

Erika shut off her phone, then turned it back on so she wouldn't miss a call or text from Brit. She continued her workout. All she could do now was wait.

Chapter Forty-seven

Brittany watched the gulls glide over the water and dive when they spotted their next meal. The weekend had turned cloudy and rain threatened. The sky was dark, like her mood. She watched for a few more minutes before she headed home to an empty apartment. She reminded herself it was the same apartment she'd had before. She divided her life now between before Erika and after. She didn't like the after much. She missed her. She'd gotten used to sharing meals, her bed, her life. She hoped Erika found what she was chasing. She knew it wasn't more fame or fortune she was after, it was her identity as a supermodel. It was who she'd been her whole life and she'd grown to enjoy the attention, the travel, the money. All of it. Would they talk again? Or would Erika disappear into another memory, a time together that ended, once again, in pain? They'd dismissed the idea of being together in some kind of long distance thing, but maybe they shouldn't have. The thoughts went round and round, and Brit did what she could to distract herself so they'd tumble to a stop.

She stirred the pot of beef stew she'd defrosted that day and sat on her couch to eat and watch the evening news. Was Erika watching whatever version she received in New York? She looked at her phone and considered for the tenth time responding to Erika's text. But it didn't sound like she expected a reply. She was thoughtful enough to let her know she was safe, and she was grateful, even though it felt pretty final. She finished her meal and decided she didn't care about whatever was happening in the world and shut off the TV. She put the leftovers away and washed the dishes before heading outside.

She didn't want to have to explain the tears streaming down her face to anyone passing by, so she settled on a secluded bench. When she was comfortable no one was close, she blew her nose, and punched Barb's number into her phone.

"Hi, Brittany. How're you doing?"

"Hey, Barb. Do you have time to talk?"

"I do. If I didn't, I'd let it go to voice mail. You okay?"

Brittany held back her tears to be able to speak. "No. My time with Erika didn't end well. In fact, it ended completely. She's gone back to New York, and I feel lost." Her tears flowed despite her efforts to control them.

"I'm glad you called, my friend. I don't know if there's anything I can say to make you feel better, but I know you well enough to know you're a strong, brave woman, and you'll be all right."

It was worth hearing, even if it didn't ring true right now. "I suppose I will. I've got some experience with that. Thanks for listening."

"No problem. I have an idea. If you can get some time off, why don't you come up here for a few days? I'll talk to my friend Josie and see if she has a cabin available for you. We can do a little fishing and get your mind off things. Do you want to talk about the details now, or tell me when you get here?"

Brittany smiled and shook her head, grateful for a friend like Barb. "I'll talk to Ben tomorrow and we'll chat when I get there. Thanks, Barb."

"Cool. I'll talk to Josie tonight. Take care of yourself. Things will get better. Honest."

Brittany hung up and relaxed on the bench. It had been two years since she'd traveled to see Barb on Drummond Island, and a couple days away sounded good. She had a feeling it would take more than a couple days fishing to get over Erika.

She relaxed on the bench for a few more minutes to absorb her friend's support. She took the long way back home to avoid the routes she and Erika had taken so many times. She walked home slowly searching for the strength and bravery Barb had told her she had. She unlocked the door, stepped inside, and tossed her keys on the counter. She made herself a cup of tea before she sat on the couch and put her feet up. This was the way her days had been before Erika, and she'd been perfectly content. She'd been just fine. All she had to do was figure out how to dull the ache of missing her.

She continued drinking her tea until the silence became deafening, and she turned on the TV. She stared at the television hoping for a distraction, but her mind wandered to Erika. She rolled her empty cup between her hands and realized she'd changed because of Erika. She *hadn't* been fine before. She'd avoided contact with people whenever possible and rarely looked them in the eye. She loved driving the carriages but had shied away from them to avoid contact with people. She'd stayed away from restaurants and crowds because she couldn't take being stared at. She'd seen everyone as a tormentor and had allowed her disfigurement to control her life. Erika had shown her she could be loved for who she was, not what she looked like. Now she had to believe it enough to live it, to keep staying out of the shadows even if Erika wasn't around. She wanted to be part of the world now, not apart from it.

She took her cup to the kitchen and went to change for bed. She lay on her side watching the moonlight cast shadows through her blinds. She turned onto her back and reviewed her work schedule. She'd help George clean stalls and ready the carriages for the day before talking to Ben about taking a few more days off. She closed her eyes and allowed her thoughts to go to Erika again. She'd never had feelings like the ones she'd experienced with her. Cared about. Content. Now she was gone, and it was as if she'd taken an essential part of her being with her. Had she changed Erika at all? Had Erika taken anything with her, other than Brittany's heart?

"Good morning, George." Brittany arrived earlier than she'd planned, anxious to talk to Ben about time off.

"Morning." George polished the front of the omnibus.

"I want to ask you something before I talk to Ben. I know it's a busy time, but would you mind if I took three days off?"

"Of course not. I know you'd make up time if we needed you. You do what you have to, Brittany. Does it have anything to do with that pretty model and why you look so low?"

"She went back to New York. I just need a change of scenery. Do some fishing on Drummond."

"Ah. You go fishing but be sure to bring some back for me." George grinned, then surprised her by enveloping her in a hug. "Heartache is part of life, but it's never a nice thing. You'll be okay."

Brittany held back her tears until she left the stable. She leaned against a wall to collect herself before she went to talk to Ben.

She waited outside his office until he was off the phone. "Good morning, Ben. Could I talk to you for a minute?"

"Sure. Come on in. What's up?"

Brittany was encouraged by his smile. "I was hoping I could get three days off."

Ben looked at her for a long time before answering. "Helen and Joe are back so I don't think it's a problem. When do you want off?" He turned to his computer and brought up the work schedule.

"Monday, Tuesday, and Wednesday."

"Good. If you can be here for the weekend it shouldn't be a problem."

"I will. Thank you, Ben." Brittany felt a little of the despair fall away. For the first time since Erika had left she had something to smile about.

Chapter Forty-eight

Brittany checked off items on her list as she filled her suitcase. Barb would have any fishing equipment she'd need, but she put the small tackle box her father had given her in her suitcase. She stood back to review the scene. Only one more item. She packed two bags of fudge for Josie and Kelly. She shook off the memory of Erika in the fudge shop buying one of every kind and extra of her favorite. Erika was gone, and she had to get on with her life. Still, she wished they were planning this trip together. She reviewed everything once more and left, locking the door behind her.

Brittany walked to the dock to wait for the next ferry off Mackinac Island. She pushed aside the emptiness in her heart and looked forward to a few days with friends. She barely noticed the view of the bridge as they passed it, refusing to acknowledge memories of Erika's enthusiasm whenever she saw it.

She took her time driving to Detour Village to catch the ferry to Drummond Island. She relaxed as they traversed the water, and wished again, that Erika was with her. When would that stop? Granted, it wasn't like it had been any amount of time since she'd gone, but still. The sooner the pain left, the better. She focused on her surroundings instead. She'd forgotten how lush the vegetation and evergreen trees were. She drove off the ferry toward Josie's, determined not to think of Erika while she was there. She pulled into Josie's parking lot, checked into cabin five, and sent a text to Barb before unpacking. She hung up her few T-shirts and extra pair of jeans and put her toiletries in the bathroom cabinet. She sat on the couch and persuaded herself she was content and happy and on vacation instead of running away.

She took a bottle of water to the porch and waited for Barb. She'd only been waiting for a few minutes when she pulled in, parked her cruiser, and hopped out. "Hey. It's good to see you." Barb pulled her into a hug.

"It's good to see you, too." She held her at arm's length and looked her over. "Do you have to work? You're in uniform."

"Nope, I'm off starting now. I've taken a couple of vacation days. I'll go home and change after we make plans over lunch. I'd like to take you to my favorite place. It's not far."

"Cool. It's been a couple of years since I got a ride in your cruiser." Brittany climbed into the front seat and watched the scenery as Barb drove to the restaurant. During the short drive, she gave an abbreviated version of the story about Erika, and how the time had changed her in ways she didn't even really understand yet. Barb listened without interruption and nodded thoughtfully as she parked in front of the restaurant.

They were seated as soon as they went in and Barb pulled her chair out for her. "Would you like some wine?" she asked.

Erika liked wine. "No, thanks. I'll just have a Coke."

They both ordered grilled fish with vegetables and red skin potatoes. Erika would have loved it. *So much for not thinking of Erika.*

"Would you like to go out on the water this afternoon? It's a good day for it," Barb asked.

"That sounds great." Brittany's spirits went up a notch.

"Josie's reserved a boat for us for the duration of your stay, and she's offered any fishing equipment we need."

The server interrupted their conversation and delivered their food.

"So, tell me how you're doing. Really doing," Barb said, looking at her as she speared a potato.

"I'm okay. I miss her. I think this little getaway is perfect. Thank you for inviting me. I hope it'll take my mind off her." She drank her water and ignored memories of dinners with Erika in her hotel room. "It's going to take a lot of time, I'm afraid."

"Have you heard from her since she left?" Barb took a bite of her fish.

"She sent me a text letting me know she arrived in New York. It was thoughtful of her, but I didn't reply. There just didn't seem much point." Brittany didn't tell her how much effort it had taken not to respond and beg her to return.

"It sounds like she had a decision to make, and it doesn't sound like it was an easy one for her, either. Sometimes people come into our lives just to help us with a single thing, like the way she made you see that you're a beautiful woman." She gave her a lopsided grin and wiggled her eyebrows. "The way I look at things, is if something or someone is meant to be, the universe has a way to make it happen. I might be full of baloney, but it works in my life." Barb shrugged and went back to eating.

"That makes it easier to let go of things we can't control. Isn't there some saying about letting love go and seeing if it comes back to you?"

"Yeah. Then it's yours to keep." Barb grinned. "Or something like that."

Brittany finished her meal determined to relax, enjoy Barb's company, and drive Erika out of her mind. Ousting her from her heart was going to be much more difficult.

The sun sparkled off the clear water, and the swell of the waves gently rocked the small boat. Brittany watched her bobber rise and fall as she stretched her legs out in front of her and adjusted her hat to shade her face. The gentle breeze carried the scent of water and freshwater grasses and tickled as it caressed the skin of her arms below the sleeves of her T-shirt. She couldn't imagine a more serene picture, and she relaxed for the first time since Erika had left. She glanced at Barb seated across from her, her fishing line on the opposite side of the boat. She looked just as relaxed.

"This is such a beautiful place. I really needed this getaway." Brittany smiled and tipped her head back to gaze at the few fair-weather clouds.

"I've been going non-stop for weeks and didn't realize how much I needed this break. To tell you the truth, I don't care if I catch any fish." Barb's rod bowed, and her bobber disappeared. She sat up and reeled in a tiny bluegill. She carefully removed the hook from its lower lip, lowered it into the water, and watched it rocket out of sight into the depths of the lake. "We won't get dinner at this rate." She baited her hook and tossed it over the side of the boat. "That reminds me. Josie and Kelly invited us to have dinner with them at the lodge tonight."

"Sounds good." Brittany sat up to watch Barb catch the only fish of the afternoon. "Did you want to stay longer, or try again tomorrow morning?"

"Yeah. Let's do that. If we get out early enough, we might catch a few walleye."

Did Erika like walleye? Brittany smiled at memories of them sharing meals despite her resolve not to think of her.

"I'm glad you could stay with us, Brittany," Kelly said as she set a bowl of greens on the table.

"Thanks. You've done a lot to the place since I was here a few years ago. How's Pogo doing?"

"He's a happy boy. I ride him every day, and he loved the attention when I rode him in the Memorial Day parade this weekend."

"Cool. I'm glad you were able to bring him with you. By the way, how's Josie's gram doing?"

"She's great. She loves living at the assisted living facility, and we bring her home every week for Sunday dinner. It usually means one or two of her friends come with her." Kelly's smile told her it was all good.

"Ready for the main course?" Josie set a platter of hot baked chicken breasts in the middle of the table before she sat next to Kelly.

"It looks great. Thanks for inviting us," Barb said.

They finished eating and relaxed on the couch and chairs in the large room. "I'm stuffed. That meal was great." Brittany chuckled and continued. "It's a good thing you didn't wait for me and Barb to bring dinner."

Barb smiled and shook her head. "We're going to try for walleye in the morning. Maybe we'll have better luck."

Brittany watched Kelly and Josie's body language. Josie only removed her hand from Kelly's thigh when she gestured to speak, and Kelly took her hand and kissed it before she stood to retrieve tea for everyone. They were so clearly connected, and she concealed her sigh with a yawn when memories of Erika's touch flooded her. "Excuse me." She murmured. "I guess all that fishing wore me out. Thanks again for dinner. I think I'll call it a day." She stood and hugged everyone before going to her cabin. It was better than going back to her empty bed at home, but it was still a bed she was sleeping in alone.

Chapter Forty-nine

"You're still waiting on Peter?" Erika's friend Pat asked.

They were people watching while seated at their favorite bistro close to Erika's apartment. "Yeah. Timing is still up in the air."

Pat reached across the table and took her hand. "Are you sure this is what you want? You know there's no going back after you pose nude."

"I've modeled in swimsuits that barely cover anything. This is just another step, right? I just hope it gives me the boost I need to get some more contracts." Erika wrapped her hands around her coffee cup and stared into the street. She didn't believe her own words about "just another step," but she was conflicted. Was it really worth compromising her standards to boost her modeling career at this late stage? "It's so hard to explain. I'm not sure I understand it myself. It's as if there are no other choices. I can't think of anything I'd do if I wasn't modeling."

Pat sat back in her chair. "I'm sorry I couldn't come up with anything to help you, but I'll keep my eyes and ears open. I've been there, my friend. If you remember, I quit when I was thirty-two, and I'm still who I am. I have time now to pursue other passions in my life. I devote time to my charities, and I have a home life. Maybe it's time to consider looking at other options."

What would her parents think, or say, if she no longer modeled? How would they feel about her posing nude? She drank her coffee and for the first time, allowed an inkling of what her life without modeling would be like. Pat was fine and happy, and there was no logical reason Erika wouldn't be, too. But the only part of the scenario where she was happy included Brit. The rest was a blank. She remembered her words about volunteering at the burn unit and working at the stables with the horses. Neither of those held any appeal, not as a career change. She sighed loudly.

"Are you all right? Honestly?" Pat asked.

"I'm fine. It's just that I'm floundering, and I don't like it."

"Tell me if I'm wrong or overstepping boundaries, but this *Naturalé Mag* isn't *Vogue Italia* or *British Vogue.* I've never heard of it. Did Peter check out its credentials? Who's their readership? I guess the bigger question is does it matter to you? You'll be the one that needs to be okay with it."

"Peter wouldn't sign me up with anything pornographic. I'm sure of that. Maybe this is a new magazine featuring mainstream models. Or maybe models over thirty." It hadn't occurred to her to look up the magazine. She didn't like what they were selling, so checking it out wasn't on her radar. In retrospect, that was naïve.

"I only know Peter through his reputation, and it's a good one." Pat paused and twirled her empty cup. "I told you I quit when I was thirty-two, but I never told you the whole story. Only my husband and ex-agent know about this." She toyed with a napkin. "I'd decided to do a nude spread, too. It seemed harmless enough, and my agent told me there were no other options. Exactly what Peter is telling you." A look of pain crossed her face. "It was awful, Erika. The guy I met at the studio nearly raped me. I was able to fight him off enough to escape, but the experience traumatized me for a long time. Maybe this *Naturalé* is legit, but I'd be leery if I were you. Please at least look into it. There's no reason to go in blind." Pat placed her hand on hers, and her eyes were glassy.

Erika squeezed her hand and stood to hug her. "I'm so sorry that happened to you." She held her at arm's length to hold her gaze and show her support. "Thank you for sharing it with me. I don't know what I'm going to do, but I know I've never wanted to pose nude. Especially not for my final work. I think maybe I need to start taking some control." She'd been with Peter from the beginning of her career, and she'd never questioned his decisions. Before now. "I guess I should get home. I've missed my workouts for the last few weeks. Thanks for meeting me today, and I'll let you know what I decide." She hugged her good-bye, trying desperately not to wish it were Brit in her arms.

❖

Erika turned up the speed on her treadmill and pushed herself until she was sweating and breathing hard. She slowed her pace after twenty minutes and stopped. Her energetic workout didn't quell her anxiety. She took a shower and poured herself a glass of wine before calling Peter.

"Erika. Are you all right?"

"Yes. I need to know what's going on. Has the magazine contacted you with a schedule?"

"Not yet. I'm planning to contact them tomorrow."

"What do you know about *Naturalé Mag*? I've never heard of the magazine." Erika took a sip of wine and tried to relax.

"It's a fairly new magazine, similar to the old *Playboy*. It's nothing pornographic if that's what you're worried about. I'd never expect you to do anything like that."

"So, it's a reputable publication that people will read?"

"Yes. I believe it is. It has articles and pieces on travel and all that kind of stuff."

"Okay, Peter. I'm getting antsy waiting, but I'm also not positive I want to do this."

"I understand, but like I told you, there isn't anything else out there. I'll call you tomorrow."

Erika hoped his information was correct, but wasn't sure it would make any difference.

She had one more source for information. Her friend Jean was two years older than her and had been a top fashion model based out of California. She didn't think she was still working, but decided to find out. She logged on to her computer and sent her an email.

Then she decided to look up the magazine and decide for herself. She typed in the name and found it to be a bit racier than Peter indicated, but she wouldn't consider it porn. Still, she flinched at the photo of the model's backside and bare breasts, and another view from the side, her breasts lifting as she stretched toward something overhead. She hoped he'd research it carefully before he contracted with them, but even if they were reputable, she wasn't sure she was going through with it. Pat's advice was sound, and she wasn't about to dismiss it as someone else's experience. She closed down her computer and ordered Thai food for dinner.

She relaxed in her living room chair, turned on the TV, and remembered the evenings with Brit watching the news while cuddling on the couch. She missed her. Would she ever see her again? The thought she might not, nearly doubled her over. She couldn't imagine never holding her again or hearing her words of love. She hesitated. Did she have words of love for Brit, and what did it mean if she did? Pat's mention of having a home life made her wonder how much she'd missed out on. She'd finished her meal and begun to clean up when her phone rang.

"Hello, Jean."

"Hey, Erika. Long time no hear. How're things?"

"There're okay. Could I talk to you for a bit? I'm dealing with frustrations about my future."

"Ah. Aging out are we? I don't mean to be flippant about it, but I do believe I understand."

"I thought you would. There are fashion models working who are over fifty, aren't there?"

"Yeah, but not many, and they aren't necessarily in the big magazines. Personally, I don't see why they do it. I'm finally settled in one place with my husband and a grandchild on the way. I wouldn't trade my life to go back to the grind of high fashion modeling for all the money in the world."

Jean's intensity surprised Erika. "I'm trying to decide if I should do a nude spread in a new magazine."

"Only you can make that decision. But double-check with your agent, because other models I know say that was it for them.

The agencies dropped them afterward, and they got hardly any compensation for taking their clothes off. I haven't heard of anyone who got the bump they hoped for after that kind of shoot. Just be careful."

"Thanks for being honest with me, Jean. I knew I could count on you to be candid. How did you manage to redefine yourself? I mean, could you see yourself doing something besides modeling?"

"I always knew I'd have to quit one day. I modeled because I was considered *model material* by my agency, and I was good at it. I made a good living, and I enjoyed the spotlight, so that was enough for me. It was a job I enjoyed, but I never considered it my life forever."

"I guess that's the difference between us. It seems like more than only a job to me. It's my life. I'm going to have to figure out how to change that." They chatted about a few friends and surface things before Erika hung up. She realized she had a lot to consider and a short time to do it. She went to her refrigerator to get her last piece of Ryba's fudge and allowed memories of her time with Brit to flow as she tasted the sweetness. What would their lives look like if they stayed together?

Chapter Fifty

Brittany woke before dawn. She rolled to her side, reached for Erika, and remembered she was on Drummond Island. Erika was in New York, a million worlds away. She showered, dressed, and ate a protein bar before heading to the main lodge.

Josie finished setting up the large coffee pot. "Morning. Did you sleep well?"

"I did. Thank you. It's peaceful here."

"Kelly's making omelets and pancakes this morning and you're welcome to join us. Help yourself to a cup of coffee. What time is Barb arriving?" Josie filled a coffee cup and sat at the table with her.

Barb entered the room before she could answer. "Good morning. It looks like you've started without me." She grinned and fixed herself a cup of coffee before she sat with them at the table.

"Hey. The gang's all here." Kelly carried plates and silverware to the table. "Omelets for all this morning?"

"You're spoiling me. You don't do this for all your guests, do you?" Brittany asked.

"No. Just for our friends. We're not a bed and breakfast." Josie stood to help and pulled Kelly into her arms for a kiss before they went to retrieve the food.

Avoiding thoughts of Erika was impossible when faced with an example of love like theirs. She'd never forget the feel of Erika's arms around her, her gentle touch, her soft kisses, but remembering was all she had, and it had to be enough.

Brittany and Barb left for the fishing boat after breakfast.

The waters were perfect and they set out with no trouble. They cast their lines and hardly had a moment to talk when the fish started biting.

"There's a catch limit of five." Barb smiled and netted the fish.

"We've only been fishing for an hour, and I've just pulled in my fourth walleye. They're hungry this morning." Brittany was having a ball and realized she hadn't thought of Erika more than twice since they'd been out.

Barb looked out over the water for a long minute and turned back to her. "I'm happy you're having fun. I like to see you smiling."

"I am having fun. Thanks, again for inviting me. I think getting away was exactly what I needed. Even for a day. My heart still aches, and my arms feel empty, but I'll live."

"I'm glad. I think we should make this a yearly tradition." Her rod dipped and Barb grappled for a while before she was able to reel in the biggest catch of the morning. "I guess I'll be cleaning fish today, too."

They cruised along the shoreline once they'd each reached the catch limit to enjoy the quietude of the morning. The mist had dissipated and a few seagulls soared overhead. The clear water stretched ahead of them like a mirror. They glided over the calm water leaving a wake that looked like an arrow pointing the way. She remembered the days standing on the shore with Erika watching the birds and the sunset. They passed an interesting looking pine tree leaning over the water, and Barb steered the boat back toward the lodge.

Brittany took one more look over the water before she followed Barb to the fish cleaning area. Erika would love it here, but she wasn't so sure about the fish. She doubted she'd enjoy the cleaning part, but she wished she could find out.

Brittany and Barb spent the rest of the day visiting with Josie and Kelly. She nearly swooned when Josie started a fire in the fireplace. The evening was cool, not cold, but she didn't care. She imagined huddling on the couch with Erika while they watched the flames dance. She became so caught up in her fantasy she didn't hear Barb call her name. She flinched when Barb waved her hand in front of her face. "Hello?"

"Sorry. Did you say something?"

"We're ready to go to dinner. Do you still want to go?"

"Definitely. I was mesmerized by the beautiful fire." She stood and stretched then followed them out to the car and hopped in the back.

"We're going to one of our favorites. It's just a small family style restaurant with good food." Josie steered her vehicle into the parking lot.

"Tell me about Mackinac Island, Brittany. It's been years since I've been there," Kelly said after they were seated and ordered their meals.

"The Lilac Festival is next week. It'll be packed with people. Have you ever been to it?"

"No, but I'd love to see it." She looked at Josie and her smile would have melted her heart if it had been Erika. "Maybe we could plan it for next year?"

"Maybe we can." Josie picked up Kelly's hand and kissed it.

Brittany had to look away when she imagined Erika doing that to her. She swallowed before speaking. "It would be great if you came. They choose a festival queen and there are sunset cruises and food. There's a dog and pony parade that's a hoot. And the grand parade is awesome. When you know for sure I'll try to take time off to show you the highlights." She pictured herself taking them to the fort and showing them her special spot by the water. The one Erika had grown to love also. She sighed in an attempt to push away the visceral memories of the feel of her in her arms as they gazed out over the straits.

They finished dinner and headed back to the lodge. The fireplace still glowed with warmth. Barb excused herself to go home, and Brittany hugged everyone and went to her cabin. She was tired, but a grain of happiness pushed its way past her loneliness.

She regarded her reflection in the small mirror above the bathroom sink. She gently fingered her scarred cheek and wondered why she hadn't considered it since she'd arrived. She plopped onto the bed on her back and allowed herself to feel the caring and support of her friends. They accepted her for who she was without caring about her disfigurement. It had been a good day.

Chapter Fifty-one

Erika considered her options as she paced herself on her treadmill after breakfast. The words of caution from her friends weren't lost on her. She'd never wanted to take her clothes off for photos. She remembered Brit's beautiful body and her intense reaction to her touch and smiled until the pain of loss punched her in the gut. Brit said they had something special. A connection. Tears welled as she remembered her question about being a "quickie." Had she given her that impression? How could she ever make things right between them?

She finished her workout and a bottle of water before she went to her computer to do more research. She logged on and searched for models over forty. Then she tried over fifty. There were some, and she knew a few, but they could be counted on both hands. Then she logged off and poured a glass of wine. Pat and Jean had a point when they told her a slower paced life gave them time for other pursuits, but she didn't *have* any other pursuits. Only Brit, and she'd probably lost her. Her life's pursuit had been her parents' dream for her, and she admitted it had been a good life. She'd enjoyed her career, even with its pitfalls. She couldn't imagine doing anything else, but realized the world held many options. She just had to find one.

Erika opened the envelope she'd been waiting for since Peter told her he'd put it in the mail. It contained the one-time contract for the photo shoot and detailed instructions for what they expected as well as a map to the location. She looked up the address online. She recognized the address as where models filmed commercials, located in a decent part of Manhattan. At least it wasn't in some gross abandoned warehouse or something. Next, she reviewed the details of the shoot. She was due at ten o'clock sharp the day after tomorrow.

She'd lost count of how many times she'd questioned her decision since she'd accepted the offer. She was used to designer clothes along with a hair and makeup artist. This magazine only wanted her bathed and smiling. They didn't care what she wore because she'd be removing it anyway. They'd supply any garments deemed necessary and apparently hair and makeup weren't an issue either.

She sat back in her desk chair to contemplate her options. Twenty years of modeling the latest work of famous designers, walking catwalks in Paris and Milan, and in two days she might be naked before the camera. She sighed. Much had changed over the course of twenty years. The fledgling internet had expanded to extend around the world. The published magazines had existed only on racks or delivered to subscribers. Now she could count on any photos to be posted online almost immediately after they were taken.

She sighed again. What was Brit doing? Would she ever want to see her again? Her pulse jumped remembering her naked in bed next to her, under her, on top of her.

She called Peter to let him know she received the contract.

"Thanks for letting me know. You should be all set then." He sounded distracted, barely listening.

"Is this it for me, Peter?" She had to know, and it was time to ask the questions.

"What'd you mean?"

"I mean, is this nude spread the end for me? For us?"

He hesitated and gave a deep sigh. "If you mean with the agency, I believe so. There's just nothing else out there for you. I'm sorry, Erika. I thought it might give you one last chance, but if I'm honest…I think it would be your final shoot." Peter sounded genuinely regretful.

Erika paused and took a deep breath before speaking. Her next words would change the course of her life. "Okay. If that's the case, I'm out. I'm done, Peter. Just tear up the contract for this. I won't be there, and I'll mail my request for release from my contract to you tonight. I'm officially retired!" Erika froze when she realized what she'd said. Did she mean it or was she upset and scared? An unexpected feeling of relief emerged.

"Whatever you decide, Erika. We've had a good run, you and I. I've enjoyed working with you. You'll always be special to me, and I hope we can get together and have lunch when I'm in town." He sounded relieved and maybe a little bit saddened by her decision.

"Thanks, Peter. Lunch sounds good. Take care of yourself, and I'll keep in touch." Erika hung up and swiveled in her desk chair. The sense of anticipation took her by surprise. It was a pleasant feeling, and she worked to hang on to it before the fear of the unknown began to creep in. A new concept washed over her as she basked in her new feelings. *She* could decide what she did now. Her life had never been her own. From the time she was a child her life and future had been planned by her parents. Once she signed with the modeling agency, they took control and sent her all over the world for different magazines. She'd never known a life that was wholly hers to control, and she had no idea where to start. But the decision was made, and the next years would be completely her own.

She needed to tell her parents. Her heart pounded in her chest at the realization she had to tell them everything they'd expected of her was over. She hesitated before picking up the phone. Her parents loved her and always wanted the best for her. She knew that in her heart, and she'd appreciated their help and encouragement throughout the years. But she'd become a successful top fashion model because of her own hard work. She was the one posing for the cameras and traveling the world. They'd be proud of her even if she retired. With that thought at the forefront, she picked up her phone.

❖

Erika went to her computer to book a flight to Arizona. She hadn't given her mother any details other than she had some news to share and wanted to know the best time to come for a visit. She reserved a flight and considered her next step. This was a conversation she wanted to have in person. She missed Brit terribly but hesitated to call. She'd never had the opportunity to think of her future in her own hands, so she sat for a moment to absorb the new sense of freedom before she punched in her number. Brit's voice mail answered, and she left a message.

"Hi, Brit. It's Erika. I have a new development in my life, and I'd like to see you. I miss you, and I want us to talk. Please let me know if you're willing." She disconnected the call and cringed at her choice of words, but she had to make the call before she lost her nerve. Now she'd wait. She made herself a cup of coffee and realized she needed food. She made a sandwich and remembered the meals she and Brit had shared.

Chapter Fifty-two

Brittany looked at the small clock on the bedside table, surprised that for the second night in a row, she'd slept through the night. At least thoughts of Erika weren't keeping her up anymore. She hoped it would last once she got home. She put on a pair of shorts and a T-shirt and went to the kitchen. She found a small coffeepot in a cupboard and a few flat coffee-filled filters. Josie probably had a pot brewing in the lodge, but she wasn't ready to interact with them yet. She needed some quiet alone time. She slipped on a sweatshirt and sat on the porch. The birds flitted along the railing and chirped their displeasure at her intrusion into their domain. She rocked in the porch rocker, sipped her coffee, and enjoyed the morning serenity. Erika would love it here. She began making plans to bring her for a vacation until the reality of her life crept in like a thief stealing her happiness. She hoped Erika had found what she was chasing. She doubted their lives would ever intersect again unless she made it happen. But Brittany wasn't enough for her. Her love wasn't enough to entice her to stay, but it was the most she had to offer. It was everything. She finished her coffee determined to deny the threatening tears. She went in to shower and get ready to join her friends.

Josie had the fireplace ablaze to chase away the morning chill when Brittany entered the lodge, and she relaxed in the cozy warmth. "Good morning. That fire feels great," she said.

"I thought it might be nice for your last morning with us." Josie poked the fire before joining her at the coffee pot.

"It is." Brittany settled into one of the chairs facing the fire.

Josie sat across from her and put her feet up on the coffee table. "Barb mentioned you were going through a rough time. She didn't disclose any details, but I wanted to let you know I'm here if you want to talk." She held her cup in both hands and gazed at the fire.

"Thanks, Josie. I find myself in love with someone who lives in New York." Brittany surprised herself by talking about Erika but it was a relief to tell someone. "We had a wonderful few weeks together and then she left me."

"That's hard. When Kelly and I got together, she had a house to sell and a horse to move, but we worked it out."

"I don't think Erika wants to work anything out. She left to try to continue her life as a model. That wouldn't work on Mackinac Island." Brittany drank her coffee and watched the flames consume the logs. It reminded her of the pain consuming her heart.

"Career and love. That can be a tough balance. But life has a way of working things out to bring healing. You're always welcome here, Brittany. Just give us a call." Josie stood and opened her arms for a hug.

Brittany held back tears when she stepped into her arms. She'd spent years after her accident withdrawn and alone. Friends were few, so the comfort and warmth of her friendly embrace touched her deeply. Erika was right. She'd closed herself off, lived in the shadows. How much had she missed by thinking people wouldn't accept her, that they'd all be cruel? She allowed her tears to flow but managed to refrain from blubbering. She sniffled and stepped back. "Thank you for being my friend."

❖

"Good morning, everyone." Barb entered the lodge carrying two large bags. "I brought muffins and scones." She set the bags on a table and Josie went to get plates and napkins. She returned with Kelly, who carried a plate overflowing with grilled Canadian bacon.

"That looks great," Brittany said.

"Help yourself." Kelly positioned the food in the center of the table and they sat to eat.

Brittany soaked in the positive feeling of sharing a meal with friends. They asked for nothing but offered all they had. She looked forward to a time she could reciprocate the hospitality and ached to share it with Erika.

Brittany sat back and sipped her coffee. She checked her watch and wished she had more time to spend with her friends. The two-and-a-half-hour drive loomed ahead of her and it was already noon. They'd been talking, laughing, and eating for hours, and she wouldn't have changed it for the world. She finished her coffee. "I suppose I should get going."

"We'll miss you. Make sure you come back soon," Josie said.

"Thanks for everything. I had a ball."

They took turns hugging her good-bye, and she went to her cabin to pack. This had been a good idea, and getting away had helped, at least a little bit. Now she had to think about what she wanted the next step in her life to look like. She'd hoped to have time with Erika to perhaps share more time together, if not their futures. She pushed that thought aside. Even if Erika wanted to be with her, she was probably projecting her feelings on to her. A one-sided relationship would be unbalanced. She grabbed her suitcase and went to her car.

Brittany watched the wake of the ferryboat as it glided toward Mackinac Island. She smiled, remembering the fishing and the camaraderie of her last few days. She liked having positive memories to refer to when she was having a bad day, and most days would be bad for a while unless Erika came back. She picked up her suitcase and bag with George's walleye, exited the boat, and headed home.

Loneliness washed over her as she entered the empty apartment. As wonderful as it was to spend time with friends, it almost made coming home to an empty place unbearable. No friends meant no one to miss. No one to love meant no one to hurt you. That's how she'd spent years thinking, and it was time to approach life in a new way.

She unpacked and turned on the TV for the evening news and to disturb the quiet. She opened a bottle of water and made a grilled cheese sandwich. What was Erika having for dinner? Had she posed for that nude magazine yet? Was she even still in the United States? All the Erika thoughts were driving her crazy. She checked the time and decided to take a walk to the library. Surely, she could find something to read that would take her mind off her. She grabbed her phone and locked her door behind her.

She started down the same street she and Erika had taken to the fort, so she turned and went the long way. She passed a bench she remembered they'd sat on when they were on a walk. She backtracked to cut through a grassy area until she noticed the tree Erika had pointed out to her as being one of her favorites. She stopped and realized Erika was everywhere. On the island, on her mind, and in her heart. She trudged back to her empty apartment.

She looked at her phone and remembered she'd turned it off to save the battery. She turned it on, set it on her dresser, and plugged it in before heading to take a shower.

Chapter Fifty-three

"Are you all right, Ms. James?" Henry reached for Erika as she stumbled into the foyer.

"Yes. Thank you, Henry. I had to get out for a walk and ended up going much farther than I'd planned." She'd intended to walk around the block to clear her head and find some direction for her life, but had picked up her pace when she kept drawing a blank, and she realized she'd have to figure it out without divine intervention. She'd walked miles and was exhausted from the New York heat already seeping through the city. She checked her phone for word from Brit when she got to her apartment. She'd probably deleted her message without reading it. She couldn't blame her if she did, but it still hurt. Could she ever generate healing between them? She poured herself a glass of wine and went to take a shower.

She stood under the spray until the hot water ran cool. She stepped out of the shower and wrapped herself in her thick terrycloth robe. She turned on the TV for a distraction, but couldn't concentrate, so she shut it off. She poured the wine from her glass into the sink and made herself a cup of tea. She sat back in her chair and began to feel more settled. She'd spent twenty years either posing for cameras or preparing to, and always had another shoot waiting for her. She'd traveled the world and now she was sitting in her apartment, alone, with nowhere she had to be. How did other people change directions for their lives? Most had families and had other interests than the work they'd been doing their whole lives. There was no need to panic. She was financially secure. She could figure out something. She just had to give herself time. She decided to go to bed early and figure out what her next step would be in the morning.

She gave up trying to sleep and decided to see what was happening on Mackinac Island. She typed in her search engine, and pictures of the Lilac Festival filled her screen. Photos of the horse drawn carriage reminded her of Brit, and she began to cry so hard the computer screen blurred. She'd given her up for her work, and she had to live with that. She managed to shut down her computer and crawl back into bed but continued to sob herself to sleep.

Erika woke to the sunrise through her bedroom window edging away the darkness of night. She lay on her back staring at the ceiling as memories of the previous day's events cascaded through her mind. She took several deep settling breaths before she sat up and swung her legs over the side of the bed. Pat had said she was still who she was even after she retired, and she was still, and always would be, Erika James, supermodel. She could do promotional events and whatever else she decided. She was home and safe and had time to figure out the rest of her life and what she'd tell her parents. She put on her robe and slippers and went to the kitchen for a cup of coffee. She opened the blinds in the living room and enjoyed the view that had enticed her to settle in this building. She watched her area of the city begin their day as a few taxis and limos passed on the street below, and pedestrians rushed toward their morning routines. She checked her phone for a message from Brit, but its blank stare indicated it might be too late for them. She might have walked away from the best thing in her life. Brit's love.

She poured herself a bowl of cereal and turned on the morning news. Her life was upside down and her future unclear, but the world still revolved around the sun and politics still ruled the headlines. She finished eating and drank her coffee. She considered the day she'd left for Mackinac Island. She'd been complaining about only having a week off, and now she had the rest of her life off. She had enough money in the bank to be comfortable for the rest of her life. She had this Manhattan apartment. She had friends and parents who loved her. The only thing missing was Brit. How could she fix that?

Chapter Fifty-four

Brittany listened to her voice mail for the fifth time. She couldn't decide if it really was Erika or her imagination playing tricks on her. She wanted to see her, there was no question of that. She didn't know what *new development in my life* meant, but she focused on her final words. *I miss you.*

She debated responding at once or letting Erika wait. She realized the immaturity of that and acknowledged the underlying anger at her for leaving. She decided on a text to give herself time to find words to say to her.

Hi, Erika. I miss you, too. I'm busy with the Lilac Festival this week, but it doesn't matter. There's still time for us to go together...

Brit

She didn't want to sound desperate, but she wanted Erika back in her life. She wanted to find out if her feelings of connection were way off base or if Erika felt something, too. She regretted her angry words when Erika had left, but her hurt had pushed her to lash out. To make her hurt as much as she did. She knew she was naive about relationships and that it took more than just words of love to make them work. Maybe their reunion would bring love. If not, she wouldn't be worse off than she was.

She put her phone in her pocket, finished her sandwich, and headed back to the barn to get ready for the afternoon rush of visitors. She polished the small carriage and helped George ready the omnibus for his trip to the dock. She checked her phone for messages before she went to clean stalls. She worked for a couple of hours and finished brushing the horses for the smaller carriage, then checked her phone again.

She finished cleaning the last stall and fed and watered the horses, then swept out the barn before she checked her phone again. She ran out of things to do before George returned so she went to talk to Buddy.

"Hey, boy. Guess what? I got a message from Erika. She might be coming back. She said she misses me." She watched him ignore her and slowly munch his hay. She checked her phone and filled his grain bucket, then went to wait for George.

She sat at one of the benches and pulled her phone out of her pocket. She set it next to her on the bench while she cleaned and polished one of the harnesses. She finished just as George pulled in with the omnibus.

"Hi, George. How's everything at the dock?"

"It's all good. Pretty busy, that's for sure." He hopped off the carriage and began to unhitch the horses.

"I'll help with that." Brittany finished with one horse while George took care of the other.

"Thanks. You expecting a call?"

"Maybe, why?"

"You were looking at your phone when I pulled in and you've checked it twice since." He grinned.

"Amy…ah…Erika called me earlier, so I'm waiting for another call from her."

"I'm glad she called. You looked chipper this afternoon."

"Chipper?"

"Yeah. I was getting worried about you. You've looked so down since she left." He hauled one of the harnesses to the tack room.

Brittany followed him with the other one. "Can I tell you something?"

George hung the harness on the rack and turned to her. "You probably don't have to, but go ahead." He chuckled.

"I grew up with Erika. Amy is her real name. She became Erika James when she started modeling."

He tipped his head and looked at her, clearly surprised.

"We were both born in Roscommon and went to school together." Brittany's relief at talking about Erika comforted her, but she wasn't ready to get into the mean girl group and her involvement and all the rest. "I hadn't seen her in years, so it was a surprise when she showed up here. So, there's history, you know?" She smiled. She was grateful for his friendship. It felt good to be able to talk to someone.

"I see. History can be awkward, but it can be a great starting place, too. It's great that you were able to reconnect." He bent over to stretch his back. "I'm beat. It's been a long day. You ready to head home?"

"I am." She checked her phone. "Let's do our last walk-through and lock up." Brittany went home without checking her phone once. She was trying not to get overexcited. Getting her hopes up that they could somehow tunnel through the mountain of things that lay between them might be silly. Erika had left her once. She didn't want to be in that position again. Hope might be dangerous, but it felt really good.

❖

Brittany checked her food supply and made a grocery list. Erika had only said she wanted to see her but didn't indicate when. She needed food anyway, so she just added a little extra just in case. She checked her phone when she returned from the store, then put her groceries away and mixed up a tuna salad. She opened a bottle of water and turned on the TV before she sat on the couch to eat and wait for Erika's call. She turned off the television after the news and went to bed to read. She squelched her disappointment at not hearing from her again, but she hadn't said she was going to call back today. She listened to her message again. She wanted to see her, and she had a new development in her life. More importantly, she said she missed her. She'd call back. She just needed to be patient, but that would be a struggle. She drifted off to sleep with Erika's tender kisses and gentle caresses on her mind.

CHAPTER FIFTY-FIVE

Erika did a little happy dance when she read Brit's text. She wanted her to come back. She considered her timeline and wasn't sure she could make it there for the Lilac Festival. It sounded like it would be fun, but she'd booked a flight to Arizona for the day after tomorrow, and she didn't know what to expect when she told her parents the news. She might have to turn around and leave the same day, or it could be fine and they could ask her to spend a few days. She'd take this event in her life one day at a time. She was so excited about Brit's positive response that she texted her a row of kisses before her message.

Need to take care of some things first.

She planned her wardrobe for Arizona and realized she wanted to go shopping. There'd be quite a few things to get used to now that every minute of every day wouldn't be scheduled for work somewhere in the world. The first thing she'd do is update her wardrobe. She called Pat, who loved to shop as much as she did. As she waited for Pat to answer, she allowed herself to feel the excitement of having time to shop whenever she wanted to.

"Hi, Erika. What's up?"

"Feel like going shopping with me?"

"What time and where?"

"This afternoon. About two? I'll meet you at the bistro."

"I'll be there."

Erika began pulling everything out of her closet. She was midway through when her phone pinged. She grinned at Brit's response, which filled her whole screen with kisses. She'd let her know her plans when she was able. She sent kisses back. Words would have to wait until they were together and she could figure out what to say. Texting anything didn't feel right.

Pat wrapped Erika in a hug when they arrived. "It's good to see you again. You look good."

"Thanks. I have news. I'm retired!" She blurted out the words and reveled in the tiny bit of excitement behind them.

"Wow. As of when? We just talked the other day." Pat sat across from her at a small table.

"Day before yesterday. Peter sent me the info on that *Naturalé* shoot. We talked and he told me that was my final option, and if I did it, the agency would probably let me go anyway. So I quit. I really don't want the last photos I ever do to be nude ones." Erika took a sip of her espresso.

"Cool. I'm sorry they couldn't find you other work, but now you're free to go shopping with me!" She held up her cup. "Here's to being beautiful, older but not wiser, and ready for whatever comes next." They clinked their cups in a toast.

Erika juggled six bags back to her apartment after they'd hit every shop along their favorite strip. She checked her phone before she went into the building and smiled at all the kisses on the screen. She replied with kisses and grinned all the way up in the elevator.

She sorted all her clothes, still piled on the bed, and hung them in her closet as she mentally packed her suitcase for Arizona. She stopped halfway through to pour herself a glass of wine and swallow the nervous lump in her throat. She plopped onto her bed and stared at the ceiling. She looked at her cell phone and giggled. Along with the kisses, Brit sent her a note.

Soon????? Along with more kiss emojis.

Erika considered calling her to tell her the news but decided to wait until she spoke to her parents. She replied.

Don't know if I'll make it for the lilacs, but as soon as I can. I'm headed to Arizona to see Mom and Dad first! A ton of kiss emojis followed.

She called Henry to pick up her bags and ordered a car to the airport before she locked her door, took a deep settling breath, and headed to face whatever her parents had in store for her.

She chose a window seat in the airport to watch the planes taxi to the terminal. She turned to observe the people scurrying in various directions toward their destinations. It was a familiar scene from her years of world travel, but different this trip. Few trips had been for anything except photo shoots or promotional events, but this one was strictly personal and, in her mind, the most important she'd ever taken. She thought back to the woman at the Chicago airport who'd requested an autograph. It was exciting to know she was recognized, but she realized her excitement had come from a place of desperation. She would still love to know she had fans out in the world, but her focus was shifting to a future away from modeling. To what, she wasn't quite certain, but at least she was looking forward to it. They called her flight to begin boarding, so she followed the line of people into the plane.

"How was your flight, dear? Did you get something to eat? You look so thin, are you sure you're all right?" Her mother hadn't stopped fussing over her since they'd picked her up from the airport. She'd wanted to rent a car, but they insisted it was only a half hour trip to their house and would give her dad an excuse to drive the Mercedes she'd bought them.

Erika fidgeted in the back seat and smiled every time her mom turned to address her with a question or comment. She looked forward to spending time with her parents but struggled for words to tell them about the new direction in her life.

She took her suitcase to the guest room. She liked the coziness of the smallest of the four bedrooms in the house. It hadn't changed since the last time she was there two years ago except for the addition of a framed photo of her cut from the latest magazine in which she'd been featured. A pang of guilt rippled through her when she realized how long it had been since she'd visited her parents. She washed her face and changed into shorts and one of her Mackinac Island T-shirts before joining them at the dining room table. The three of them seated at a table reminded her of her childhood. Her mother would get home from work before her father and have dinner ready when he arrived. They'd all sit at the table and she'd answer questions about school and what she'd learned that day. She remembered her father's words about how important it was to learn something new every day. After dinner, three days a week, they'd take her to her modeling or dance classes. They'd devoted their lives to her, and now she had to tell them it was all over. She took a breath for courage.

"I have something I want to tell you." Her mother poured glasses of juice for each of them, and she took a sip before continuing. "Do you remember my agent, Peter?"

"Oh, yes. He was a good man," her father said.

"He still is a good man. He's worked hard for me throughout the years, but he hasn't been able to find work for me lately. The magazines all want younger models. His words were they want 'young and fresh.'" She took a deep breath to muster her courage. "I'm trying to tell you that there isn't any more work out there for me. They want new, young, and fresh, so I'm out of the picture. I'm officially retired now."

"You're not working at all?" her mom asked.

"No, Mom. I'm sorry, and I want you to know how much I appreciate your encouragement and all the time and money you spent on my career. But it's over unless I find work on my own. I don't know what I'll be doing now, but it probably won't be fashion modeling. I'm sorry." Saying the words out loud, to the most important people in her life, made them concrete. It hurt, but it was also a relief.

"Oh, honey. You don't have to say you're sorry. I hope you don't think we were ever disappointed in you. We're very proud of you." Her mother drew her into a hug.

Baffled, Erika pulled back to look at her. "But I'm not a model anymore. I'm no longer Erika James, fashion model. I feel like a has-been."

"Listen to me." Her father stood, gently turned her, and held her by her upper arms. "You're still our daughter. We love you, and like your mom said, we're very proud of you."

"Everything you planned for me and expected of me is over." She held back tears. Barely.

"You've exceeded any of our expectations, and you have a right to be proud of your accomplishments," her mother said. "People have career changes, honey. You had twenty years in one, and now you can move on. You've done exceptionally well, just like we knew you would. And you'll be wonderful with whatever you decide to do next."

Erika let her tears fall. "Thank you." She choked out the words. Why had she ever been worried about their reaction? Had she simply projected her own fears and disappointment onto them? It seemed so.

"Come, let's have some lemonade." Her mother put three glasses on the counter, and Erika got the lemonade from the refrigerator.

She excused herself, went to the bathroom to splash water on her face, and collected herself before she returned to sit with them at the table. "I do have some other news." She took a sip from her glass and a deep breath. "Remember years ago when I told you I was struggling with my sexuality and I'd realized I was a lesbian?"

"Of course we do. And we told you we only wanted to see you happy and hoped you'd find someone to love, male or female," her mother said.

"I've become very close to someone in the last few weeks."

"Oh, honey, that's wonderful. Who is she?" her mother asked.

"Do you remember Brittany Yardin from the old neighborhood?"

"She's the poor girl who had that accident. Her parents were upset for years. I remember you two were friends as kids. Why do you bring her up?"

"I had my last photo shoot on Mackinac Island. Brittany lives there now, so we reconnected. She was the carriage driver for me while I was there. She's who I've become close to." Erika wanted to tell her parents exactly how close they were but needed to define it for herself first.

"Oh." Her mother and father shared a look across the table. "We love you and we want to see you happy. Marriage is legal now for everyone and we have three lovely female couples in our church." Her mother patted her hand.

Erika smiled, grateful for their support. "Thank you, both. I'm relieved that you're okay with it. I've never had anyone special in my life before now, so this is new for me."

"I hope you know you can bring her here whenever you want to." Her mother looked excited.

"I appreciate it, Mom. And I will."

Her mom took her hand and her father's. "Does this mean we'll get to see more of you now?"

"Absolutely. I'll figure out what's next for me and we can make plans."

Her dad surprised her by pulling her into his arms again. "You made us so proud. We love you. I hope you'll enjoy retirement as much as I do."

Erika let happy tears fall as she absorbed the feeling of being loved.

CHAPTER FIFTY-SIX

Brittany looked at her phone. The last text she'd gotten was two days ago and she was slightly deflated. Erika hadn't said anything about a specific date, but Brittany had hoped that soon meant, well, sooner than later. She sent another kiss message to Erika and went back to work. It was the last day of the Lilac Festival, and she was driving the Grand Hotel's omnibus in the main parade. She had the harnesses polished and the headdresses fluffed and ready to be mounted on the horses. She checked her phone before she went to the restroom to get dressed. She reflected on her life since Erika. She'd brought love into her life and a confidence she'd never felt before. Today was her debut driving the big carriage in the parade, and her previous fear and shame fled. She touched up her French braid and her makeup and adjusted her tie and hat. She sent one more text to Erika, just to say she was thinking about her, and then she was ready. She went to let George know.

"Good luck, Brittany. You look great. I'm glad you decided to do this. I'm proud of you." George beamed like a proud father, although he was only five years older than she was. "I love driving the big bus in this parade. Wait until you hear the crowd cheering when you drive by." He looked at his watch. "I've gotta go. Enjoy yourself."

"Thanks, George. See you later." She checked her phone before she turned it off and put it inside her vest pocket.

"Thanks for helping me get these guys hitched up." Brittany worked with one of her coworkers to put the harnesses and headdresses on the two draft horses. They double-checked that all was in order and Brittany climbed aboard the carriage and began the trip to the parade route. She waved to the crowds and smiled at the kids being held back from running into the street. She reached the main area and waited for the signal to begin the slow procession through town. She could feel the excitement from the people lining the route and hear the cheers as she began to slowly creep past. The children squealed and pointed at the horses, and she could hear their cries "horsie, horsie." She'd been to many of these parades but sitting atop the Grand Hotel's premier carriage was an experience she wouldn't forget. She vowed to invite her mom and dad next year if she had the opportunity to drive again.

She neared the end of the parade route and got the signal to hold the horses back. She held the reins tightly and scanned the crowd. She caught movement out of the corner of her eye and looked to her left. A Tilley hat shadowed her face, but there was no mistaking the golden-flecked eyes as they held her captive. Her smile warmed her a hundred times greater than the sun. Erika mouthed the words *I love you*, and it took her breath away. She willed the parade to end, no longer caring about anyone else in the crowd except Erika. She was back, and she loved her. She had no idea what their future would look like, but she was determined they'd work one out, together. She parked the carriage and put the horses away in record time, then went in search of Erika. She found her waiting by the entrance to the barn.

Brit grabbed Erika's hand and pulled her into an empty stall. "When did you get here?" she asked.

"About an hour ago. I hope you don't mind, but I put my suitcase in your apartment. I still have a key. I couldn't wait any longer." Erika framed her face in her hands and kissed her. "So much better than text kisses." She kissed her again.

"Let's go home." Brit took her hand and led her to her apartment. She fumbled with the key when they got there. She couldn't believe Erika was there, and because she wanted to be. Here because she loved her. She dropped her keys and picked them up with trembling fingers.

Erika reached around her and supported her hand as she unlocked the door.

They entered the room and Brit locked the door behind them and tossed her hat aside. "Would you like something to drink?"

"I'd like you." Erika led her to the bedroom and pushed her onto the bed on her back. She straddled her, grabbed her hands, and placed them on her breasts. It was a familiar pose Brit would never forget and considered her favorite.

She brushed her thumbs over Erika's erect nipples. Her whimper encouraged her to slip her hands under her T-shirt and push up her bra to feel the weight of her breasts. She squirmed, thrusting her hips in time to Brit's thumb movements on her nipples. Brit traced her fingers down Erika's sides to the waistband of her shorts and shoved them down as far as she could. "Take these off."

Erika rolled off Brit, stood, and pushed off her shorts and panties and pulled off her T-shirt and bra. Brit forced a breath into her lungs. Erika was beautiful clothed, naked she was a Goddess. She pulled off her own clothes, desperate to feel her against her own nakedness.

"God, you're beautiful." She drew Erika close so their breasts touched. Erika gripped her hips and gently pushed her back on the bed. Brit hugged her close when she lay on top of her and shivered with need. Erika pulled up the covers, cocooning them.

"I'm glad you came back to me." Brit kissed her lightly on the lips. "Do you have to leave anytime soon?"

Erika turned to her side and propped on one elbow but kept one hand on her belly. She trembled at the heat of her touch. "I don't have to go anywhere, sweetheart. I'm retired."

"When did this happen?" Brit tried to sit up but Erika's gentle contact held her captive.

"We can talk about all that later. Right now, I want to show you how much I love you." She kissed her deeply, and Brit couldn't have been happier with her answer.

CHAPTER FIFTY-SEVEN

Erika woke to sounds of birds drifting through the open window. She shook off her disorientation and rolled to her side. Brit slept soundly next to her, and she gently slipped her arm over her and snuggled close.

"Mmm. I've missed this." Brit mumbled and scooted back into Erika.

"Me, too." She looked at the clock. "Do you have to work today?"

Brit turned to her back and stretched. "No, but I'm on call in case it gets busier than George can handle. I don't expect it will. Most people were here for the grand finale, the parade, yesterday."

"Good. I'd like us to talk and spend some time trying to figure out a few things."

"Sounds like a good plan. Let's make some coffee and talk while we eat breakfast." Brit sat up and kissed her before swinging her legs over the side of the bed.

"Can I get in the shower first?" Erika asked.

"Sure. I'll get the coffee started."

She refrained from lingering in the shower to enjoy the scent of Brit's body wash. They had issues to discuss. As good as it felt being with Brit, she needed to figure out what came next in her life. The only thing she knew for certain was that she wanted it to include Brit. She wrapped herself in her robe and found Brit pouring their coffee.

"Morning, honey." Brit kissed her and handed her a coffee cup. "I suppose I ought to shower now, too, in case Ben calls me in."

Erika sat outside sipping her coffee while she waited for Brit. The cloudless sky was blue and a slight breeze cooled the summer air. She considered what it would be like to live on this island with Brit. It was one of the things she wanted to discuss with her.

"You look lost in thought," Brit said and sat across from her.

"I'm working on figuring out our future."

"I like the sound of 'our.'" She sipped her coffee and held up a finger before retreating to the kitchen. She returned a minute later with a platter of homemade scones.

"Yum. Did you make these?" She grabbed one and took a bite.

"Yep. Another hobby of mine. They're cinnamon with apple. I also make blueberry and chocolate chip. I keep a supply in the freezer so all I have to do is put them in the microwave."

"You're full of surprises, and I want to find out all of them."

"It might take a long time."

"As long as it takes." Erika grinned. "On a serious note. I want us to discuss our future."

"I'm glad you want one with me. Have you thought about what you might want to do if you're not modeling?"

"Not with any real planning. I'm still known in the modeling world. I have the face and name recognition, and I was thinking last night, that I have valuable knowledge of it. I have a lot of research to do yet, but what do you think about me doing something like a blog about the fashion world?"

Brit took a drink of her coffee. "I like it. Are you thinking of doing interviews of current models?"

"Probably, and offering makeup and fashion tips. Maybe feature a popular model and talk about what makeup she wears or designers she prefers or even little personal tidbits about her life she'd be willing to share." She warmed to the idea the more she talked about it. "It would be something I could do either here or in New York. I'd just need a reliable internet connection." She took a breath and a sip of coffee. It was the first time she'd gotten excited about doing anything for herself, and it felt good.

"I think you'd be great at it. You could use your years of experience to help the newbies."

Brit's enthusiasm spurred more ideas but she needed to find out what Brit thought of their future together. "Do you think you'd be happy living in Manhattan? At least part of the year? My apartment is really nice."

Brit grinned. "If you're there, I'll figure out a way to be there, too. What would work for me would be to spend the winters there. I could still help Ben out at the Grand Hotel in the summer, and do a little part-time bookkeeping, too. I'd have to work out something during tax season, but my business clients could depend on our local CPA in the winter." Brit sipped her coffee and looked deep in thought. "Does New York get a lot of snow?"

"Probably not as much as here!" She shuddered. "Why? Would you miss it?"

"I might, but we're in the planning stage. I'd certainly be willing to try it for a year or two. We could reevaluate yearly. See where we're at and how we feel." Brit reached for her hand and squeezed. "I love you, and I want to make a life with you."

"I'd like that, too. I think yearly reevaluations would be a good thing. And you know there's plenty of money in New York. You could probably pick up finance work there easily."

"Well," Brit said quietly, "I think I'd like to try it. It sounds like a good compromise. And, I suppose that's what relationships are about. Loving each other and compromising."

"There's something else I have to say, Brit." She took both her hands in hers and held her gaze. "I never, ever, thought of you as a 'quickie.'"

"I was hurting and angry. I'm sorry I said that, but I hope you understand that was how it felt when you were willing to just walk away." Brit squeezed her hands.

"I do and it was tearing me apart to leave, but I couldn't figure out another way. I was paralyzed by fear and uncertainty about my future. Remaining in the spotlight was all I could see for myself. But now I can see how restricted I was, and how free I am now. I can do anything, and I want you beside me all the way." She moved to stand behind Brit and wrapped her arms around her. She had to touch her to convey her sincerity. "I want us to be together, sweetheart. In whatever way works for us and for as long as you'll have me."

Brit turned, pulled her into her arms, and kissed her. "Me, too. We'll figure everything out as we go. It'll be our best adventure yet."

About the Author

C.A. Popovich is a hopeless romantic. She writes sweet, sensual romances that usually include horses, dogs, and cats. Her main characters—and their loving pets—don't get killed and always end up with happily-ever-after love. She is a Michigan native, writes full-time, and tries to get to as many Bold Strokes Books events as she can. She loves feedback from readers.

Books Available from Bold Strokes Books

Femme Tales by Anne Shade. Six women find themselves in their own real-life fairy tales when true love finds them in the most unexpected ways. (978-1-63555-657-5)

Jellicle Girl by Stevie Mikayne. One dark summer night, Beth and Jackie go out to the canoe dock. Two years later, Beth is still carrying the weight of what happened to Jackie. (978-1-63555-691-9)

Le Berceau by Julius Eks. If only Ben could tear his heart in two, then he wouldn't have to choose between the love of his life and the most beautiful boy he has ever seen. (978-1-63555-688-9)

My Date with a Wendigo by Genevieve McCluer. Elizabeth Rosseau finds her long lost love and the secret community of fiends she's now a part of. (978-1-63555-679-7)

On the Run by Charlotte Greene. Even when they're cute blondes, it's stupid to pick up hitchhikers, especially when they've just broken out of prison, but doing so is about to change Gwen's life forever. (978-1-63555-682-7)

Perfect Timing by Dena Blake. The choice between love and family has never been so difficult, and Lynn's and Maggie's different visions of the future may end their romance before it's begun. (978-1-63555-466-3)

The Mail Order Bride by R. Kent. When a mail order bride is thrust on Austin, he must choose between the bride he never wanted or the dream he lives for. (978-1-63555-678-0)

Through Love's Eyes by C.A. Popovich. When fate reunites Brittany Yardin and Amy Jansons, can they move beyond the pain of their past to find love? (978-1-63555-629-2)

To the Moon and Back by Melissa Brayden. Film actress Carly Daniel thinks that stage work is boring and unexciting, but when she accepts a lead role in a new play, stage manager Lauren Prescott tests both her heart and her ability to share the limelight. (978-1-63555-618-6)

Tokyo Love by Diana Jean. When Kathleen Schmitt is given the opportunity to be on the cutting edge of AI technology, she never thought a failed robotic love companion would bring her closer to her neighbor, Yuriko Velucci, and finding love in unexpected places. (978-1-63555-681-0)

Brooklyn Summer by Maggie Cummings. When opposites attract, can a summer of passion and adventure lead to a lifetime of love? (978-1-63555-578-3)

City Kitty and Country Mouse by Alyssa Linn Palmer. Pulled in two different directions, can a city kitty and country mouse fall in love and make it work? (978-1-63555-553-0)

Elimination by Jackie D. When a dangerous homegrown terrorist seeks refuge with the Russian mafia, the team will be put to the ultimate test. (978-1-63555-570-7)

In the Shadow of Darkness by Nicole Stiling. Angeline Vallencourt is a reluctant vampire who must decide what she wants more—obscurity, revenge, or the woman who makes her feel alive. (978-1-63555-624-7)

On Second Thought by C. Spencer. Madisen is falling hard for Rae. Even single life and co-parenting are beginning to click. At least, that is, until her ex-wife begins to have second thoughts. (978-1-63555-415-1)

Out of Practice by Carsen Taite. When attorney Abby Keane discovers the wedding blogger tormenting her client is the woman she had a passionate, anonymous vacation fling with, sparks and subpoenas fly. Legal Affairs: one law firm, three best friends, three chances to fall in love. (978-1-63555-359-8)

Providence by Leigh Hays. With every click of the shutter, photographer Rebekiah Kearns finds it harder and harder to keep Lindsey Blackwell in focus without getting too close. (978-1-63555-620-9)

Taking a Shot at Love by KC Richardson. When academic and athletic worlds collide, will English professor Celeste Bouchard and basketball coach Lisa Tobias ignore their attraction to achieve their professional goals? (978-1-63555-549-3)

Flight to the Horizon by Julie Tizard. Airline captain Kerri Sullivan and flight attendant Janine Case struggle to survive an emergency water landing and overcome dark secrets to give love a chance to fly. (978-1-63555-331-4)

In Helen's Hands by Nanisi Barrett D'Arnuk. As her mistress, Helen pushes Mickey to her sensual limits, delivering the pleasure only a BDSM lifestyle can provide her. (978-1-63555-639-1)

Jamis Bachman, Ghost Hunter by Jen Jensen. In Sage Creek, Utah, a poltergeist stirs to life and past secrets emerge.(978-1-63555-605-6)

Moon Shadow by Suzie Clarke. Add betrayal, season with survival, then serve revenge smokin' hot with a sharp knife. (978-1-63555-584-4)

Spellbound by Jean Copeland and Jackie D. When the supernatural worlds of good and evil face off, love might be what saves them all. (978-1-63555-564-6)

Temptation by Kris Bryant. Can experienced nanny Cassie Miller deny her growing attraction and keep her relationship with her boss professional? Or will they sidestep propriety and give in to temptation? (978-1-63555-508-0)

The Inheritance by Ali Vali. Family ties bring Tucker Delacroix and Willow Vernon together, but they could also tear them, and any chance they have at love, apart. (978-1-63555-303-1)

Thief of the Heart by MJ Williamz. Kit Hanson makes a living seducing rich women in casinos and relieving them of the expensive jewelry most won't even miss. But her streak ends when she meets beautiful FBI agent Savannah Brown. (978-1-63555-572-1)

Date Night by Raven Sky. Quinn and Riley are celebrating their one-year anniversary. Such an important milestone is bound to result in some extraordinary sexual adventures, but precisely how extraordinary is up to you, dear reader. (978-1-63555-655-1)

Face Off by PJ Trebelhorn. Hockey player Savannah Wells rarely spends more than a night with any one woman, but when photographer Madison Scott buys the house next door, she's forced to rethink what she expects out of life. (978-1-63555-480-9)

Hot Ice by Aurora Rey, Elle Spencer, Erin Zak. Can falling in love melt the hearts of the iciest ice queens? Join Aurora Rey, Elle Spencer, and Erin Zak to find out! (978-1-63555-513-4)

Line of Duty by VK Powell. Dr. Dylan Carlyle's professional and personal life is turned upside down when a tragic event at Fairview Station pits her against ambitious, handsome police officer Finley Masters. (978-1-63555-486-1)

London Undone by Nan Higgins. London Craft reinvents her life after reading a childhood letter to her future self and in doing so finds the love she truly wants. (978-1-63555-562-2)

Lunar Eclipse by Gun Brooke. Moon De Cruz lives alone on an uninhabited planet after being shipwrecked in space. Her life changes forever when Captain Beaux Lestarion's arrival threatens the planet and Moon's freedom. (978-1-63555-460-1)

One Small Step by Michelle Binfield. Iris and Cam discover the meaning of taking chances and following your heart, even if it means getting hurt. (978-1-63555-596-7)

Shadows of a Dream by Nicole Disney. Rainn has the talent to take her rock band all the way, but falling in love is a powerful distraction, and her new girlfriend's meth addiction might just take them both down. (978-1-63555-598-1)

Someone to Love by Jenny Frame. When Davina Trent is given an unexpected family, can she let nanny Wendy Darling teach her to open her heart to the children and to Wendy? (978-1-63555-468-7)

Tinsel by Kris Bryant. Did a sweet kitten show up to help Jessica Raymond and Taylor Mitchell find each other? Or is the holiday spirit to blame for their special connection? (978-1-63555-641-4)

Uncharted by Robyn Nyx. As Rayne Marcellus and Chase Stinsen track the legendary Golden Trinity, they must learn to put their differences aside and depend on one another to survive. (978-1-63555-325-3)

Where We Are by Annie McDonald. Can two women discover a way to walk on the same path together and discover the gift of staying in one spot, in time, in space, and in love? (978-1-63555-581-3)

A Moment in Time by Lisa Moreau. A longstanding family feud separates two women who unexpectedly fall in love at an antique clock shop in a small Louisiana town. (978-1-63555-419-9)

Aspen in Moonlight by Kelly Wacker. When art historian Melissa Warren meets Sula Johansen, director of a local bear conservancy, she discovers that love can come in unexpected and unusual forms. (978-1-63555-470-0)

Back to September by Melissa Brayden. Small bookshop owner Hannah Shepard and famous romance novelist Parker Bristow maneuver the landscape of their two very different worlds to find out if love can win out in the end. (978-1-63555-576-9)

Changing Course by Brey Willows. When the woman of your dreams falls from the sky, you'd better be ready to catch her. (978-1-63555-335-2)

Cost of Honor by Radclyffe. First Daughter Blair Powell and Homeland Security Director Cameron Roberts face adversity when their enemies stop at nothing to prevent President Andrew Powell's reelection. (978-1-63555-582-0)

Fearless by Tina Michele. Determined to overcome her debilitating fear through exposure therapy, Laura Carter all but fails before she's even begun until dolphin trainer Jillian Marshall dedicates herself to helping Laura defeat the nightmares of her past. (978-1-63555-495-3)

Not Dead Enough by J.M. Redmann. A woman who may or may not be dead drags Micky Knight into a messy con game. (978-1-63555-543-1)

Not Since You by Fiona Riley. When Charlotte boards her honeymoon cruise single and comes face-to-face with Lexi, the high school love she left behind, she questions every decision she has ever made. (978-1-63555-474-8)

Not Your Average Love Spell by Barbara Ann Wright. Four women struggle with who to love and who to hate while fighting to rid a kingdom of an evil invading force. (978-1-63555-327-7)

Tennessee Whiskey by Donna K. Ford. Dane Foster wants to put her life on pause and ask for a redo, a chance for something that matters. Emma Reynolds is that chance. (978-1-63555-556-1)

Bold Strokes Books
Quality and Diversity in LGBTQ Literature